DH8

Not All Bid *Farewell*

Tracy M'Cwabeni

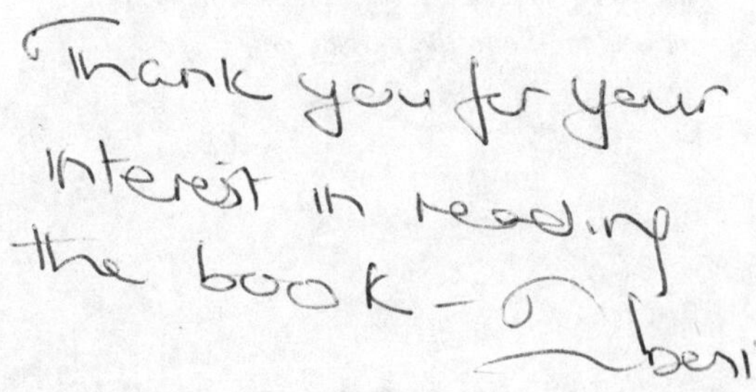

iUniverse LLC
Bloomington

NOT ALL BID FAREWELL

iUniverse books may be ordered through booksellers or by contacting:

iUniverse
1663 Liberty Drive
Bloomington, IN 47403
www.iuniverse.com
1-800-Authors (1-800-288-4677)

ISBN: 978-1-4759-9730-9 (sc)
ISBN: 978-1-4759-9737-8 (hc)
ISBN: 978-1-4759-9731-6 (e)

Library of Congress Control Number: 2013911813

Printed in the United States of America

iUniverse rev. date: 7/29/2013

Acknowledgement

I would like to extend special thanks to my family and friends for their encouragement and support that kept me motivated and on track. I also would like to express my profound gratitude to Allister Thompson for his professional editorial advice.

Chapter One

The Mbare Musika bus terminal was teeming with people from all walks of life. Some were would-be travellers to different parts of the country, some were entrepreneurs selling all sorts of wares and still others were there just to while away the time.

Ruva was feeling frustrated as she craned her neck high, hoping to catch a glimpse of a familiar face. She held a small parcel that contained a packet of sugar, a packet of tea leaves and two loaves of bread that she needed delivered to her only surviving uncle in the rural areas. But that frustration was instantly overtaken by a sudden spell of dizziness and pain. Ruva quickly squeezed herself into a gap on a full bench, guarding the parcel between her legs. She felt a slight pain in her abdomen, but it disappeared as quickly as it had come. When the dizziness was gone, she picked up her parcel and got on a bus back home.

In 1978, the white government in Rhodesia was holding on to power but was losing its grip on the war-torn countrywide, and Ruva Ganda was losing her own personal battle with another miscarriage. In the wee hours of the morning, she woke to the excruciating pain of abdominal cramps. She sat up and hunched forward in her bed, expecting the worst. She cautiously ran her hand under the covers, and as she pulled it out, it was smeared with blood. At that moment she knew it was the beginning of the end. With fear setting in, she slowly got out of bed and moved toward the light switch near the door, leaving the clear mark of her bloodstained fingers on the wall. Hopelessly, she glanced at the bed and saw a pool of blood where she had been sitting. She stood staring in disbelief, and the sight of her blood made her nauseous. Ruva had seen enough. She switched off the light and crawled to the other side of the bed, where she stayed, writhing in pain. At one point, she reached into a drawer for a bottle of painkillers. She shook it and could tell that it was empty. The pain of her past miscarriages was nothing in comparison to what she felt at that moment. She believed the pain was going to kill her. When it finally sank in that she was losing yet another baby, she sobbed.

She had a sad feeling of déjà vu as she recollected past miscarriages, and it seemed as though the world was crumbling under her feet. Death, amongst other things, was one of the fleeting thoughts that came to her mind. She also dreaded the depressing prospect of having to explain this over and over to those who cared to know. Although her mind was clouded with scary thoughts, she had the patience to wait until daybreak and ask Shungu, her neighbour and close friend, to call an ambulance. Holding her tummy and grimacing from the wrenching pain, she dragged herself out of bed and slowly walked to Shungu's house.

She knocked on the metal door, which bore an inviting sign that read "Welcome." Breathing heavily and staring at the sign as if she had never seen it before, she knocked again and stood for a little while before sitting down on the front step. Since it was early in the morning, Shungu was still sleeping, and by the time she finally opened the door, the wait had seemed like an eternity for Ruva.

Shungu observed her ill-looking friend. Her skin looked ashen. She kept licking her dry lips and looked years older.

"Ruva, what's wrong? What's wrong?" she repeated. "Come in." She led her friend to a chair.

"Let me open the windows." She almost tore up the sunburned curtains as she drew them back to let in light and fresh air. "Tell me, what's the matter?"

Ruva didn't want to give too much information, but just enough to let Shungu know that she needed help.

"I need your help. Please send for an ambulance. I need to go to Harare Hospital."

Ruva struggled to stand up. Shungu took her hand to help her but Ruva pulled it away. She leaned on the wall and took a deep breath.

Ruva looked down at her worn dress and noticed a bloodstain. "I'm going back home to get ready for the ambulance."

Shungu followed Ruva's movements and saw the big bloodstain on her dress. There was no need to ask any more questions, for the answer was right there in front of her.

"Okay, I'll send for an ambulance at the clinic. Billy will go, and that boy can fly like an eagle. Meanwhile, I'll come and stay with you in case you need help. Are the girls still sleeping?"

"Don't you worry, I'll manage. Yes, the girls are still sleeping. A hurricane can pass by, and they will sleep through it. At their age, I would be up bright and early and be in the fields before sunrise. They are lucky, for life is different in the city," said Ruva with her eyes closed as another severe cramp paralyzed her. The pain was so intense that she thought her belly was going to rip open. She cupped the lower part with both hands and turned around. She walked back with one hand holding on to the wire fence that divided their small properties. Sadly, the fence was falling apart and was sagging as she put extra weight on it.

This needs to be repaired, she thought. In her fragile condition, she had no choice but to desperately hang on to it until she got into her bathroom, which was outside the house.

Before the ambulance arrived, Ruva had cleaned herself up and put on a fresh and well-pressed dress. She sat on her veranda, waiting. Ruva had very little strength left, but when she saw the ambulance, she pulled herself up and steadied herself. Shungu carefully watched her as she held on to a pole that supported the flat roof of the veranda.

"Ruva, I'll help the girls!" Shungu waved to her as she was wheeled into the ambulance on a stretcher.

She was familiar with the process at the clinic. This was not her first time. The nurse took down a history of the problem and did a quick clinical assessment to ascertain her vital signs and condition. Ruva was feeling weaker and was experiencing fainting spells.

"We're going to transfer you to Harare General Hospital," the nurse said without explaining further. "Do you have anybody to accompany you?" She was already tidying up the examination room in readiness for the next patient.

"No. My husband left two days ago for Malawi, and I'm worried about him, but I've a friend who knows that I'm here. She is going to follow up with you later," Ruva said.

Harare General Hospital had been one of the two main referral centres for "blacks only" for as long as many could remember. It was a busy hub for the sick and it had overflowed with the dead and dying from the battlefields during the war.

Upon arriving at Harare Hospital, Ruva was seen by a young doctor who diagnosed an ectopic pregnancy. He explained what was happening, and dejectedly she realized the hopelessness of the situation. She recalled another doctor telling her that one of her Fallopian tubes was blocked, and she would never be able to conceive through that diseased tube.

"Please, do whatever you can to save my life for the sake of my two girls," she begged him. Because her voice was so faint, the doctor had to place his hand behind his ear and cup it to make out what she was saying.

"I'll do my best, ma'am," the doctor reassured her with a nod.

She did not answer, since she was getting weaker and more lethargic. Her condition was deteriorating, and she was rushed into the operating room for emergency surgery. The last thing Ruva remembered was the anaesthetist telling her that he was going to give her an injection to put her to sleep. The surgery went well, and she was taken to a gynecological ward for recovery. Ruva had a high pain threshold, and a day after surgery she was up and moving around to facilitate a speedy recovery. She talked with fellow patients regarding different ailments, and from those discussions, she discovered that ectopic pregnancy was a common occurrence and was one of the main causes of infertility in women. Not that it was comforting, but she became aware that there were many women in the same predicament as her who were also looking for real answers.

Ruva had been in the hospital for three days when her sixteen-year-old twins visited with Shungu.

Ruva was in a big, open ward and was in bed number 12. As she sat in her bed, she watched visitors coming in and out. She unexpectedly saw the twins and Shungu as she was carefully looking from side to side. She waved to draw their attention. The girls could not miss that enthusiastic wave and hurriedly moved towards her. The twins both hugged her at the same time. For a while, they didn't seem to know what to say, but they were obviously relieved to see their mother in good spirits and feeling better.

The twins relaxed and looked around at the various activities going on in the ward. Most of the doctors in the ward were white but serving a black patient pool.

"Are there any black doctors in this hospital?" asked Matie.

"They are not many, but I have seen one or two," said her mother.

"Matie, it's a good question. We should have black doctors stepping on each other's toes. Something is not right. I hope your generation is going to change that. Do you understand now why our children are in the bush, fighting?" Shungu sounded displeased, like many others who believed that inequality had no place in society. The girls looked fascinated by what Shungu was saying.

"Hospitals have a certain smell that I don't like," Hilda said, rubbing her nose up and down.

"Anyway, Mama, why didn't you tell us that you were going to hospital?" Matie said in an accusing tone.

"I was in bad shape, and I didn't want you to think the worst and worry unnecessarily."

"Now that you're in good shape, when are you coming home?" Matie asked, giggling with her hand covering her mouth.

"You're being silly, girl. I'm far from being in good shape." Ruva took Matie's hand and squeezed it. She cleared her throat. "Nevertheless, I'm feeling much better. It won't be long. I'll ask the doctor tomorrow when he comes in to see me. He usually does his rounds around seven in the morning. I'm missing you too, girls. This place can be depressing."

Shungu was compelled to quickly warn her friend. "Don't

rush things. You have to be fully recovered before you can think of being discharged." She straightened Ruva's top blanket. "Everything is under control at home, and the girls are okay. Do you know when Mukai will be back from his trip?"

"I never know half the time." Ruva thought about it for a second. "My guess is it will be another two weeks before he is home. He was going to the northern part of Malawi. I've no clue where that is." She paused, anticipating one of the girls would help her out, but there was silence. "Each time he leaves home, I worry and always wonder if he'll come back home safely because of the war. He does not talk about it, but it's worrisome for me."

"Ruva, are these your twins?" A nurse placed her hands around their shoulders and shifting her eyes from one girl to the other, said, "Girls, you're so beautiful." Both girls smiled to acknowledge the compliment. The nurse moved on to another patient.

"Mama, have you been telling them about us?" Hilda asked.

"When one comes into the hospital, they take your family history, and that's when I told them that I have twin girls, and I also gave them your names. You're good girls, and I'm proud of you. I'm not ashamed to talk about you to anyone who can listen," she reassured them.

The girls left the hospital knowing that it would be a matter of days before their mother was home.

Ruva's recovery went smoothly, and after a week she was discharged. Gathering her belongings, she left hospital and started the long journey back home on foot, since she didn't have money for the bus. She arrived home tired and sweaty due to the blazing sun. She passed through Shungu's house to notify her of her return. She sat down on the little veranda, which mirrored hers, and asked for some water. Shungu brought the water in a big enamel jug, and Ruva gulped it down. After quenching her thirst, she got comfortable and dozed off.

Shungu let her be and went inside to continue with her sewing. She made children's clothes and sold them in the countryside to make ends meet. Her small business was not doing well, since it was affected by the war. Over time, she had built a clientele that paid her in small amounts on a monthly basis, but debt collection was difficult. At times, she was forced to confiscate something and in turn would go and sell it at the market. Her husband had died young of an unknown cause, and she worked hard to support her two boys, who did not have any recollection of him.

Ruva woke up rested, and she quietly left and walked to her house. She opened her door and the stuffiness prompted her to open all the windows to allow fresh air in. The walk from the hospital had aggravated the pain in her abdomen, and she went straight to bed to lie down.

The girls quietly opened the door to the house and peeped into their mother's bedroom. She heard their light and quick footsteps and said, "Come in, girls. I know you're there."

Matie was the first to come in, and with a wide, beaming smile, she said, "Welcome back, Mama. Finally, you are home. Are you okay now?"

Before Ruva could answer, Hilda enthusiastically added, "Hello, Mama, we missed you."

"I'm much better. I'll have to take it easy," Ruva said.

"What was wrong with you? I didn't want to ask you too many questions when you were in hospital," asked Matie, moving closer to her mother.

Ruva was caught by surprise but thought about it for a

second and then decided there was nothing to hide. "I was bleeding," she said.

Matie rolled her eyes and said, "We also have our monthly woman's thing, but we don't get admitted into hospitals." They knew she was not being forthcoming. "We are old enough to understand." The girls knew what was wrong with her. They had overheard Shungu telling another lady from church about their mother's miscarriage.

"I know, I know, but I was bleeding profusely, for I had lost a baby, and they needed to do a small operation to stop the bleeding."

"It would have been good to have a little brother," said Hilda.

"Enough talk. Why don't you girls prepare something to eat? I'm tired and not feeling well enough to help. There isn't much around, but make the best of what we have."

When they left the room, Ruva reminded herself to count her blessings, for she had two healthy girls. But she could not help brooding over her loss.

Hilda went into their bedroom, straightened the covers, and picked things up from the floor. She was hoping that their mother had not seen their messy room. The girls shared a bed in a small, plain room, and the white paint that needed retouching made it look bigger than it actually was. Hanging on the wall opposite the window was an eight-by-five picture in an old frame taken on their baptism day. Below was an old dresser with drawers that could hardly close due to wear and tear. Next to their bed on Matie's side was an old trunk, which functioned as a bedside table. Ruva had borrowed Shungu's old machine and made green floral curtains to match the green-painted cement floor. She crocheted a green-and-white blanket, which they used as a bed cover, and it kept up with the colour scheme. Emerald green was the twins' favourite colour. The room was plain and simple but functional.

"Hilda, what are you doing there? We have to make dinner," shouted Matie, who was already looking in the cupboards for something to cook. There was some maize mealie meal for cooking sadza. They went out into the garden and pulled a few leaves of muriwo, which they fried. They made gravy with freshly picked tomatoes, onions, a bit of oil and a pinch of salt. They took dinner to their mother's room, but she asked if it was all right to eat in the living room where they always had dinner.

"There is no school tomorrow."

"It's only mid-week. What's happening?"

"There was bombing somewhere in the outskirts of the city and it's for precautionary measures," said Matie, who liked to listen to the news.

"We can sleep in," Hilda added.

"I hope they won't start bombing here in the townships," said Matie.

The war had been ferociously fought in the rural areas for a number of years. In 1978, those living in the cities were gripped with fear as the momentum gathered and threatened their very own backyards.

Ruva went to bed early. As she lay there thinking of her loss she felt sad and forlorn. She yearned for a son and could not imagine a life without the only assurance that would cement her marriage. Culturally, it was very important for her to have at least one son. It was more a cultural obligation than a personal desire. The doctor had confirmed that she could not have any more children because of the complications caused by the latest miscarriage.

As her gaze focused on the water stain that was clearly visible on the once-leaky ceiling, her eyes filled with tears that slowly trickled down her cheeks. She didn't feel the need to wipe them away since they truly represented how she was feeling. The sadness was accompanied by a sense of guilt and failure. Ruva was lonely, with nobody to share her grief. It was not the best time to tell the girls how she felt about losing the baby. This was one of the few times she longed to see her husband, Mukai. Ruva never knew when he would come home. He could be gone for a month at a time, and there would be no word from him. She wanted to share their loss, but she was not sure how he was going to react. All she knew was that he wanted a house full of children. With the previous four miscarriages, he never showed any emotion, sympathy or openly expressed his feelings. Probably he felt there would be a next time. His detached attitude annoyed Ruva, but she suppressed her frustrations, or if she showed them, it was short-lived. She always wanted to make the best of the time they had together since his work was stressful and challenging, especially because of the war raging in the countryside.

She cried herself to sleep but she woke up startled by a dream in which she was holding a small boy in her arms and breast-feeding him. After the dream, she could not get back to sleep. The bed itself was not conducive to a restful sleep, for it was sagging in the middle, and she could feel broken springs probing her flesh. There was also a pool of blood that had dried up and hardened on the mattress, leaving a pungent smell.

As she lay there thinking about how she could get a new bed, vivid memories of her uncle delivering the bed after her mother died rushed through her mind. That piece of furniture was the only item she inherited from her mother, whom she hardly knew. Her maternal grandmother had raised her. The memory clouded the initial thought that had woken her up. She was aware that if she remained in the room, she would begin to count her numerous misfortunes, which would ruin her day. She forced herself out of bed, and on her way out, she noticed the bloodstain that her hand had made near the light switch. She wondered if the girls had noticed it. If they saw, they didn't comment. Quickly, she left the room and resumed her daily routine of helping the girls get ready for school in the morning.

When the girls were gone, she cleaned the bloodstain from the wall and stripped off her bed to see if she could wash the mattress. She turned it and saw that the blood had seeped through. Cleaning it was not going to get rid of the smell. She remembered there was a store at the nearby market that sold old beds and mattresses. She slowly walked to the market and found an old mattress that she could afford. Money was always scarce, but this time she barely had enough.

Hilda and Matie noticed a change in their mother's demeanour and could see the pain oozing out of her. She did not have any life in her. She looked sad and appeared to be in deep thought all the time. Unfortunately, there was very little they could do to ease her pain. Ruva continued to love, protect and provide guidance for her girls, despite the depression that was dragging her down. The girls looked up to her and were not that close to their father, who was away most of the time. When he was home, Mukai didn't spend time with them or have much to say to them. The girls were courteous, but their relationship with him was aloof.

Matilda had affectionately been called Matie right from birth, since it was easier, especially for Hilda when she was learning to talk. The girls bore a strong resemblance to their mother in their gait that brought attention to their swaying hips, beautiful facial features that were accentuated by neatly combed short hair, and the height they had inherited from their father that gave them a statuesque appearance. As teenagers, the girls began to bloom, and their beauty grew more striking by the day. At school, they towered over most of their classmates, which made them somewhat uncomfortable. They were identical twins, and their classmates mixed them up all the time, but the girls played along by answering to both names.

It also took their father a long time to tell them apart. Yet Ruva looked for obvious differences that helped her do so right from their birth. She recognized them by their different voices when they cried. Matie made a loud shriek and Hilda whimpered. Matie had a small birthmark on her right ear, was left-handed and used wild gestures to make a point. She had a good sense of humour. On the other hand, Hilda as a baby had sensitive skin and as a result always had some kind of rash. When Hilda was young, she sucked her left thumb, and as she grew older, she always hid the thumb under her fingers. She deliberately spoke slowly. When they sang, which they loved to do, they held a tune together with similar angelic voices. Once in a while they played tricks on their mother, but she could always beat them at their own game.

Although Ruva had little education, she was a smart and tough woman who understood the importance of higher education. She was a disciplinarian who did it with lots of love. She wanted the girls to do better than her and break the cycle of illiteracy and poverty. Ruva was never able to help the girls with schoolwork, but she encouraged them to be the best they could be. The girls made an effort to learn and speak proper English with their schoolmates. At home Ruva insisted that they speak Shona, her mother tongue. After every test, she demanded to see their grades, and she followed their progress with great enthusiasm. Matie was always top of her class. She was very good in mathematics and science. Hilda had nothing to be ashamed of either, because she was always in the top ten, but she could never compete with her sister. She found mathematics truly challenging, although giving up was out of the question. Matie was there to help her out with mathematical problems and concepts to ensure that she made the honour roll.

With a test looming, Hilda asked Matie despondently, "Matie, can you please help me with tomorrow's math test? I don't understand why you just whiz through this and I have to work so hard."

Matie massaged her sister's shoulder and gently lowered her head onto it. "Does that feel good, sis? Your math grades are good. You put too much stress on yourself and that somehow distracts your problem-solving process. Surely, there are so many other things that you do better than me."

"What's that supposed to mean, Matie?"

"Mama believes that you're a better cook than I am."

"Oh, I didn't know that you and Mama want me to go out there, get married and stand in the kitchen all day long to prove my cooking skills."

"Hilda, you're getting it all wrong. That was meant to be a compliment."

"Okay, okay, I get it. I have no intention of being a chef any time soon."

Matie, already knowing the importance and power of money, encouraged her sister further. "Do you know that you can go and work in a big hotel and earn a lot of money? One of us has to make it so that we can give our parents a better life. Wouldn't you like to see them living comfortably like those white people in the suburbs whose lives are perfect? Money is the least of their worries."

"Enough, Matie. I want to see them financially stable, but I'm not interested in becoming a chef and being closed up in a hot kitchen day in and day out. I can see you buying them a house in the suburbs, since you're the one who is going to be a doctor. Doctors make a lot of money, they say. I don't know about you, but I'll not be making money any time soon. Instead, let's do this math and go to bed early today. I'm exhausted."

"Hilda, you're always tired, you should let Mama know. I'm sure she'll do something about it. If you don't, I'll tell her. Let's go back to the subject of making money. We might be young, but this is the right time to start planning ahead. Whatever we start doing now will pay off later. Let's make it our own goal, and hopefully we'll fulfill those dreams. Anyway, making money is a big dream of mine." This forward and philosophical thinking was not surprising, coming from Matie.

"I totally agree with you. That's why I'm trying so hard to get this math right. I want to prepare myself to be a good mathematics teacher," Hilda answered cynically.

"We're on the same page of prosperity. Now, let's focus on the math."

Chapter Two

School started in January, and in August the girls were in the process of making applications for places in high school, with the assistance of their teachers. It was imperative to do so as early as possible to ensure places in their preferred choice of schools. Ruva trusted the teachers to help in the search for good boarding schools that would meet the girls' needs. She wanted them to be in institutions that would better prepare them for university education, since she saw her daughters as her biggest investment.

Ruva called Hilda first to the privacy of her bedroom and asked her to lock the door. She invited her to sit on the bed. Hilda was apprehensive, for her mother had never done that before. Ruva threw a small brown blanket frayed on the edges over their legs, and then she put her arm around Hilda's shoulders and squeezed her. Ruva took out her small notebook and gave it to Hilda to write down the things she thought important.

"Mama, what is all this about?" Ruva did not show much outward affection, but the girls knew how much she loved them.

As they got settled on the bed, Ruva asked, "Where have you decided to go for your lower sixth?"

"My first choice is St. Theresa's Secondary School. The

school has a good reputation and high standards. A lot of girls from there have done well. Actually, one of my best teachers studied at St. Theresa's. Also, I hear that the Eastern Highlands are beautiful."

"Can you give me another reason? Because the beauty of the Eastern Highlands is not of any importance to your education?"

"It's an Anglican girls' school in Mutare."

"Glad that you are sticking to our religion." Ruva cupped her daughter's face in both hands and looked her straight in the eye. "I want you to go to a good school which prepares you for the world out there. I'll do whatever it takes to help out with school fees. I might have to look for a job cleaning white people's houses."

"I want to give you my word that I'll not let you down."

"Hilda my dear, you have my blessings. That's all I wanted to know. Can you write the name of the school in the notebook, please, so that I don't have to keep asking you for it? Do you know when you're likely to hear from them?"

"No idea, but it should be soon."

When the conversation was over, Hilda stood up and turned the handle to open the door. Matie, who had her ear pinned against the door trying to catch the drift of the secret conversation, staggered in like a drunken sailor and fell at Hilda's feet.

"Matilda, what are you doing?" shouted Hilda, annoyed. She had showed her disgust by calling her sister by her full name. "Matie, I can't even have bonding moments with Mama without you wanting a piece of the action? You should be ashamed of yourself!"

Matie stood up and straightened herself. "I'm sorry, Hilda, the door drew me in. Mama, is it my turn?"

Ruva chuckled and said, "Matie, that was not fair." She decided to take the meeting outside to create a different ambience. "Matie, let's go outside. Hilda, you can come too."

"No. She told you it's her turn. I'll go to our room and read. I know the school on top of her list. Anything else you want to know?"

"Don't be angry. You know your sister, she never wants anything to pass her by." Ruva turned to Matie. "You should apologize to your sister. It's the right thing to do."

Matie turned to her sister. "I said I'm sorry. I can't believe that you're upset over this."

"That wasn't an apology," Hilda said.

Ruva directed Matie to the only tree that provided shade. It was burdened with mangoes, some ripe, more still green. Some had fallen off and were rotting on the ground. She swept and piled them into the small compost pit that Mukai had dug out in the garden. A few had germinated into seedlings. Ruva spread a reed mat on the ground for them to sit on. Matie gently put her head on her mother's lap.

"Since you were eavesdropping, you should know the first question."

"I missed that one," Matie laughed.

"Where have you decided to go for high school?"

"I'll not be going too far from home. It's a mixed high school, with boys and girls. By the way, it's not run by Anglicans." Matie waited for her mother's response.

"Then it must be Catholic," Ruva said.

"Wrong. It's a government-run school called Lord Armstrong Secondary School. I'm sure I'm going to get a bursary because of my high grades. You won't have to worry about paying for my school fees," she said reassuringly. "I want to go to a school where I'll compete with the best, whether it's girls or boys. My dream is to be a medical doctor. Did I answer all the questions fully?"

"You did, and that's the best news I have heard in a while." After saying that, Ruva looked around to see if Hilda was nearby listening. She didn't want Hilda to interpret it negatively. Believing the coast was clear, she continued. "I know you can do it. I can't wait for the day when you will graduate." She closed her eyes for a moment and got lost in her imagination, and then she thought aloud. "Dr. Matilda Ganda."

"We have to wait a few more years before you can call me that." Matie was being modest, but she always dreamed big. It was reflected in her choices. She wrote down the name of the school for her mother. Both girls were determined to do what their parents had not had the chance to do.

Ruva had listened patiently to the girls and approached things with an open mind. This was a turning point for them as they prepared to leave home for the first time at the tender age of seventeen. The girls showed maturity beyond their age. She was beginning to give them their due respect.

Mukai, their father, was of average intelligence but could not go further in his education due to lack of resources. He obtained a truck-driving license, which was a great achievement for him, and he got a job with a cigarette manufacturing company. Although it was not a high-paying job, Mukai was glad that he had one, and he was able to put food on the table for his young family and send the children to school. The downside was being away from his family from time to time.

It was a lonely job as he travelled alone for hours on end. His company gave him a small allowance for hotels and food, which he never used as intended. Instead, he would sleep in the back of the truck on a thin sponge mattress. It was so thin that after using it he would roll it and tuck it in between boxes of merchandise. His bundle of clothes was his pillow.

When he was tired of driving, he preferred to park his truck close to a river or stream and enjoy the sound of water flowing, rushing down or slapping hard on rocks. He liked listening to birds singing and watching animals come to the banks of the river to drink. At times he would perch on a large boulder and marvel at all nature had to offer. He would admire the beauty of the sun going down in the evening or rising in the morning. He loved the feeling of wading in the river on a hot day or dunking to bathe. He hung his clothes on twigs to dry, which always provoked memories of his boyhood, when he tended to a small herd of cattle from his homestead.

However, he made a lot of friends along the way. At times they invited him into their humble homes. He loved those invitations, since he was treated just like family. Mukai loved to laugh and joke around with friends, and yet he could never warm up to his daughters. He drank with his buddies and was a chain smoker. He maintained secrecy about his family — that was sacred to his values, and he chose to remain an enigma.

One November day, the sky was dark with clouds impregnated with heavy rain. Amid flashing lightning and deafening thunder, Mukai emerged from the rain thoroughly soaked. He walked into the house dripping wet, chattering his teeth and exaggerating the shivers to attract attention.

"What a miserable day! I'm chilled to the bone," Mukai said loudly. In one hand he was holding a small black bag with all his personal belongings, which he hung behind the door, and in the other hand was a plastic bag full of groceries, which he placed on the floor. Ruva saw him and quickly welcomed him home with a firm handshake and a glowing face. The girls had seen him through the window, since they were watching the rain pounding hard on the asbestos roof, making a deafening sound.

Ruva picked up the bag of groceries and joyfully called, "Hilda, please bring your father the blue bedsheet on the chair in my bedroom. Hurry up, he is wet." Mukai enjoyed those moments when Ruva fussed over him.

The requested sheet was old and tattered and had served its purpose. In the Ganda household, nothing was thrown away unless there was absolutely no other use for it. This sheet would eventually be a cleaning rag or would be stuffed into a pillow.

"How are you, Baba?" Hilda politely asked while handing him the sheet.

He did not look at his daughter, but he smiled in acknowledgement. Matie followed her sister, and together they patiently watched their father taking his time wiping himself dry. When done he handed the sheet to Matie. He missed the girls but would never say anything to show that he cared. Without much to say, the girls exited the room.

After changing into dry clothes, Mukai sat down in the small living room on the bright floral-printed sofa and dozed off. An hour later, Ruva woke him up. He struggled to sit up, for he was exhausted and was ready to crash for the night. Ruva said a short prayer before they shared dinner, a regular practice.

After dinner the girls disappeared into their room. Ruva cuddled next to Mukai on the couch. She anxiously started telling him about how well the girls were doing, especially at school, and how they were looking forward to going to boarding schools. She liked to keep him up to date on extended family matters and happenings at church, although he didn't go to church himself, and the latest gossip running rampant in the neighbourhood. They decided to move into their bedroom, since Mukai continued to show signs of weariness.

Ruva was closing the curtains when Mukai moved to his side of the bed and carefully asked, "Is it my imagination, or have you lost some weight?" Mukai loved his wife, for her beauty oozed from inside to outside. He loved the softness of her skin, which she scrubbed daily with Lifebuoy soap. She had a permanent scent from Pond's Vanishing Cream that aroused his senses. Ruva had tremendous patience, was affectionate, and met all his needs.

As she was undressing and getting ready to climb into bed, her response was rather slow, and she didn't answer his question directly. "I'm glad to see you looking so good. Actually, you have put on some weight yourself. Am I correct?"

He nodded. They both sat upright with their backs against the wall. Their hands were clasped tightly together under the covers, and their bodies were already beginning to feel each other's heat.

"I had a miscarriage a few days after you left, and they had to operate on me." She exposed her tummy and showed him the suture line that had completely healed. "It was rough for a while, but I'm fine now. The doctor took time to explain clearly what happened. He said I had an ectopic pregnancy."

"What's that?"

"It's a condition whereby the baby starts to grow in the tube, not the right place for a baby to survive. The unfortunate thing is I'll not be able to conceive again."

Mukai listened carefully and then began to rant. "You had a miscarriage again? Is this not the fifth time this has happened? Are you doing something to cause these miscarriages?" Anger quickly clouded his judgment, and he released his grip on her hand.

"I can't believe that you are accusing me of deliberately bringing on these miscarriages. Why would I do that? Do you think I enjoy going through such intense pain? If I didn't want children, I would go to the clinic and get contraceptive pills," said Ruva.

"Well, can't you find a doctor who can do something? This country has excellent British-trained doctors who are capable of doing wonders. The government is controlling the number of kids we can have. It's not right, but it's the truth. They are determined to see our population dwindle to nothing, for they think that every child being born is a damn terrorist. I didn't choose to be poor. Do you think I wanted to be in this rut? I'm entitled to as many kids as I want." Mukai was gnashing his teeth in rage with deep resentment for the white government.

Ruva quickly interjected. "Let's not put blame where it's not warranted. Yes, I'm alive and here today because we have well-trained doctors. But to answer your question, it would be an upward battle to correct it. In fact, they removed the one tube in which the baby was trapped, and the other one is not healthy either. We have two beautiful daughters. Let's be content with what we have been blessed with."

There was silence, and Mukai's face said a thousand words. He folded his hands across his chest, contemplating his next question.

"Wait a minute, why do you keep on telling me about tubes? Isn't it the womb that's important? The bottom line is that they can say and do whatever they want because they know that you cannot do anything since you don't have any money. Money talks volumes."

Ruva explained it as well as she had understood the biological process. "Of course, the womb is important, but tubes carry sperm into the womb from the point of entry. If the tubes are not working, that process of transporting the sperm to the womb is disturbed."

Mukai looked intensely at his wife, trying to make sense of this recurring misfortune. Ruva clicked her tongue, slid down the bed, turned away from her husband, and pulled the blanket over her head. Mukai was enraged. He took this as rejection, since he had been looking forward to a night of intimacy. Ruva had also been expecting a pleasurable night after his long absence. Sadly enough, their first conversation had not created a romantic ambience. Furiously, he turned towards Ruva and angrily stripped the blanket off her face. He raised his voice louder. "I'm still talking to you. Do you hear me?"

"Mukai, I cannot give you any more answers. Maybe we should go and see the doctor together on my next check-up date. Will that be helpful? We are both tired and losing focus. You have blown off a lot of steam. I'm sure a good night's sleep would do you wonders. Can we continue this discussion tomorrow with clear heads?"

"Don't tell me what to do," he said defiantly. Mukai had never displayed such deep anger in their marriage.

"Look here, I'm not telling you what to do, but it's not right to blame the government for everything besides yourself. This government didn't do anything to my tubes. Think about it for a moment. I don't know about you, but I'd like to have my beauty sleep, if I may." Ruva was not accepting the victim mentality any more. Strength was going to be her new weapon. She turned away again.

Mukai understood what Ruva had said. What surprised him was how well Ruva knew the problem and that she had accepted the misfortune. He stormed out of the room and went to sleep on the sofa in the living room.

The following morning, Mukai woke early and went out to

look for *The Herald*, a national newspaper. While he was out, he bought a carton of milk and a fresh loaf of bread. He came back and stepped into the kitchen. He put cold water in a bowl and placed the carton of milk in it to keep it cool. He took out the small and old piece of stale bread from the wooden bread bin and replaced it with the fresh loaf. He went back outside and stopped on the veranda, looking for a comfortable place to sit and read his paper. He pulled the old rattan wicker chair from the shade to a sunny spot. Some of the twigs on the chair were hanging loose. The cushion was in need of re-upholstering. In fact, it was the only piece of furniture that dressed up the veranda. Mukai had bought it in Malawi a few years back. When he bought it, it was part of the living room furniture, but as it began to fall apart, it found a permanent place on the veranda. He lifted the cushion and vigorously shook it to get rid of the dust. He knew it was no longer steady, but he sat down and tested it by moving from side to side to make sure that the chair would hold his weight.

As he got comfortable, he lit a cigarette, took in a few drags, and then balanced it at the corner of his lips. He pulled his newspaper from the plastic bag and went directly to the sports page to check on his favourite soccer team, the Highlanders, before perusing the rest of the paper.

Ruva went to the veranda, acting as if all was well. "Would you like some porridge? I made enough for everybody." She remained that stoic wife.

"Yes, please, I'd love that," replied Mukai.

Mukai waited for the girls to leave for school before he attempted to apologize. He also suspected that they had heard all the argument during the night, for they ran through their morning routine quietly. They were not the usual happy and chatty duo.

"Good morning, girls," said Mukai to break the silence and repair the damage.

"Good morning," they replied in unison and both looked at him with sad faces that were deprived of sleep. Mukai realized that the problem he had created was bigger than he had envisioned. Now he had to make peace with the girls and apologize to Ruva.

Ruva went into her room, climbed into bed, and as soon as her head hit the pillow, she was fast asleep.

It seemed as if Mukai's shadow woke her up, because when she opened her eyes, he was standing there with his arms folded. He sat down and reached for her hand, but she withdrew it. He hesitated for a minute and said, "I'd like to apologize for what happened last night. With all those miscarriages, I didn't show you any compassion, as a loving husband should do. I guess I kept on hoping that we would have more children and at least one of them would be a boy. It was never meant to be, but I love you, Matie and Hilda with all my heart. The girls are a blessing to us. I strongly believe that these girls are going to help us transform our lives one way or another. Ruva, you're the glue that keeps everything together here. Don't ever think that I don't appreciate your efforts. I love you, and please forgive me for being so foolish. Whatever happened, I had no intention of hurting you. It's unfortunate that I overlooked your pain, because I focused on my selfish reasons."

"Are you done?"

"Yes, I said things I shouldn't have said last night."

"I'm glad that you have put this into proper perspective. Thank you for being forthright and candid about your feelings. I also had plans for a bigger family but will always be grateful for what I was given. Nothing can take the place of those girls in my heart."

Ruva took a deep breath and looked at him. "I need to go away for a few days to visit my uncle. The countryside and fresh air might give me my energy back, and I'm losing touch with people from my past. I need to reconnect with them. At the same time, it will give you a chance to build a relationship with the girls." She sat up, tapping her feet on the floor.

"I don't think you should go. It's not safe out there."

"Nothing is going to stop me. When are you going back to work?"

"In two weeks' time."

Ruva went searching for her calendar that she kept under a pile of old clothes, and she counted the days then said, "I'll be back a day before you leave. According to the calendar, it will be a Sunday."

"Do you have to go for that long?"

Ruva just stared at him, offering no response.

Mukai wanted to negotiate, but he decided to leave it at that.

The girls came back from school and went straight to their room. Ruva knocked on the door, and they did not answer, but she opened the door anyway and went in. Hilda was perched up on the trunk, and Matie had stretched her legs out on the bed. Both were doing their homework.

"I won't take much of your time, since you both look rather busy," Ruva said.

"What is it now?" Matie asked, suspecting bad news.

"I'll be going to the rural areas tomorrow for almost two weeks, and your father will be here with you."

"Is it because of what happened yesterday?" asked Hilda.

"Partly, yes," Ruva answered vaguely, but she left them hanging. "You can get back to work." She closed the door behind her.

Matie looked at Hilda and said, "This is it as far as their marriage is concerned, don't you think? I don't remember Mama going to visit that uncle. She has always said she can't go because of the war, which is still going on today. She must be desperate to talk to her uncle about divorce. What are we going to do?" She was imagining all sorts of scenarios.

"I'll go and live with Mama," said Hilda.

"Who said she is moving away? It would make sense for her to stay here. Where can she go? You are already taking sides."

The following morning, Ruva got up early and left before the girls went to school. Mukai didn't expect her to say goodbye because of the mounting tension between them.

"Please come back. The girls are going to be lost without you."

"If you show them that you care, they will respond positively," Ruva said as she picked up her tattered old suitcase and walked out the door.

On her trip, Ruva visited with her uncle and family members she hadn't seen for years. She took time to visit her mother's grave, for she had not yet been there. By the time she heard of her mother's death, they had already buried her. She visited the site with one of her old aunties. The grave was hidden away in tall weeds, but the little wooden cross with her mother's name had survived the elements.

Life was tough and people had sacrificed with their lives. Signs of war were evident everywhere. The landscape was full of burned houses, deserted businesses, and destroyed army vehicles that marked battlegrounds. Ruva was forced to extend her visit for five more days since there was heavy fighting not far away. Her uncle used his networking system to help her out, and she walked at night to a safer place where she could catch a bus back into the city.

When she finally got home the girls were delighted to see her. They reported that they had not spent much time with their father since they were busy preparing for exams, but he had taken care of things. Mukai had left on another trip. Before he left, he asked Shungu to check on the girls. Shungu took pride in knowing that she could be counted on when friends were in need.

On this particular trip, Mukai was not gone for long. He surprised Ruva when he got home early in the morning only a couple of days after she herself got home.

"Glad to see you back. When you didn't come on Sunday, I was worried about you. I heard on the radio that there was a ferocious battle close to where you were visiting."

She caught a whiff of cigarette smoke and sneezed into her hands. "I was okay and I was having a fabulous time with my relatives." She did not tell him about the overnight walk through the bush and the fighting that left her shaking in her shoes.

Mukai noticed a calmness in her, and he took advantage and moved closer. "Am I forgiven?"

Ruva took his hand, and looking him directly in the eyes she said, "Of course, you are forgiven, but you owed me an apology. I have the last word. We can now declare case closed." They were both thankful that the fight was over.

Mukai was excited that all was forgiven, and he started kissing and massaging his wife passionately. He unbuttoned her long, old flannel nightdress. It was beginning to show some loose threads here and there. The floral design was fading, but cleanliness was not compromised, despite being worn daily, either summer or winter. It was like a security blanket for her. Mukai quickly slipped off his pants. Desire was mounting and they were both ready and anxious. In no time they were both panting as if they had run a marathon. They lay there quietly, listening to each other's heavy breathing. They fell asleep with their bodies glued together by sweat. Mukai woke up first, while Ruva was still sound asleep. He slightly opened the curtains they had drawn to darken the room. That slight movement woke Ruva, who was a light sleeper.

"I'll leave you to sleep, because I want to tend to the vegetable garden. It needs weeding. I need to keep up with my garden boy duties."

"That makes me the house girl. What time is it?"

He glanced at his Timex. "It's 12:05 p.m. already."

"Time to get up. Sweet potatoes okay for lunch?" Ruva offered while running outside to the bathroom.

Matie was advised by her principal to apply for a government scholarship. Her application was approved with no problem, since she had outstanding results during her four years at the school. She was awarded a generous scholarship, which included school fees, books, uniforms and pocket money. Mukai was relieved because it meant he only had to worry about Hilda's fees. He had managed to open a savings account at the post office a few years before. He saved a bit of money from his overtime pay and hotel allowance. The twins were excelling at school and Mukai realized early on that the only way they could further their education was if he had some money stashed away. He kept Ruva in the dark, and they lived frugally. He wanted to surprise her when the time was right. When Mukai revealed his secret, she was overjoyed.

"How did you manage to save the money?"

"By working hard. That's all you have to know."

"This is a welcome surprise. We have the money for school fees, and if the girls don't succeed, it won't be for lack of money but their own doing."

In January 1978, the girls were ready to start a new chapter of their lives. Because of the extra cash at their disposal, Ruva managed to buy the girls some nice clothes and a few extra girly things they needed. Mukai promised to take them to their separate boarding schools. The girls were taken aback, because he never did much with them. It was going to work perfectly for him since he had learned that the schools were on his the way to Mozambique, where his next trip would be. Nonetheless, he had to deviate a few kilometres from the main highway to reach the schools. Although the girls preferred to travel with other students, Mukai left no room for negotiation.

Chapter Three

On the day they were leaving, Mukai woke up at dawn and went to work. The truck came roaring along with their father at the wheel, something he had never done before. Driving on the streets of the township was a challenge, since the roads were far too narrow. But Mukai was determined to make this a memorable occasion.

Hilda looked through the window to see what was happening. She beckoned to her sister. "Matie, the truck is here. It's embarrassing to be seen riding in that big thing."

"Let's enjoy the ride and stop worrying about what the world thinks," Matie said.

Mukai loaded their new suitcases into the truck and when done, he calmly said, "This is it, girls, the time we have all been waiting for. You should say goodbye to your mother, and we can hit the road." Ruva was not taking this very well. Her life revolved around the girls, but she knew this day would come. She had been crying, and she wiped her tears before saying goodbye to her husband and the twins.

Matie, the observant one, noticed the sadness in her mother's eyes and reassured her. "Don't be so sad, Mama. We'll be all right. We'll write you as soon as we get settled."

Ruva finally cracked a smile and said, "Goodbye, girls."

They climbed onto the truck, where they felt as if they were sitting on top of the world. Mukai was negotiating the road slowly as the girls waved furiously at their mother, who stood motionless.

Ruva envied them, for Mukai had never taken her on a ride. "Let this be their day with their father. My turn will come someday. And it will be just Mukai and I." Ruva was talking to herself, not aware that Shungu was standing behind her and waving too.

"They aren't going to the slaughterhouse, my friend. They'll be back before you even miss them."

"Shungu, how long have you been standing there watching my back?"

"Long enough to see you feeling sorry for yourself."

"Can't you be nice?"

"If coming to say my goodbyes to the girls isn't being nice, I don't know what you want me to do. I'll go back and get busy with my sewing. I have a few orders to fill." Shungu stuck out her tongue and left.

Ruva went back into the house. "Life is not going to be the same. I'll have to find something to do to fill the void," she muttered quietly. "This is not the time to whine about the girls leaving their nest. I believe that they are destined for bigger things. I'll have to discover myself again, who I am, and where I go from here." She left herself with unanswered questions.

Matie was the first one to be dropped off at her school. The twins stared at each other, and without saying a word, they hugged. The embrace seemed to last forever, until Mukai opened the door of the truck and said, "Girls, we have to move on, the journey is long." He helped Matie jump off the truck.

When she was off, she turned to her father and said, "Can Hilda just come down and feel the air at this school?"

"Matie, you're talking as if this is some sacred and holy place. I understand it's hard for you girls to say goodbye to each other. Hilda, you can come down."

Hilda took her father's hand and jumped down, but she asked one more favour. "Can I go and see where she'll be staying?" Separation was proving to be difficult for the girls, since they couldn't remember ever being away from each other before. He decided it would be best to give them extra time together. "How much time do you need, girls?"

They spoke simultaneously. Hilda said, "Thirty minutes maximum." Matie said, "Thirty minutes is enough." Mukai was always fascinated when they came up with the same answers, as if their brains were somehow connected.

"Surely you can go and spend a few more minutes together. I'll be here waiting." Mukai welcomed the break, because he also wanted to take a few puffs. He'd tried to quit smoking a number of times, but it was proving difficult.

Matie turned around, and standing there was a school prefect welcoming new students. "Hello, I'm Hama. You don't want to know my full name, but what are yours?"

"I'm Matilda Ganda, but I prefer to be called by my pet name, Matie. This is my twin sister Hilda. She is on her way to St. Theresa's. She wants to see my dormitory. Will that be a problem?"

"Not at all. If Hilda was coming here, I don't think I'd ever tell you apart, you look so much alike. Matie, which subjects will you be taking?" Hama asked while leafing through his list of names of new students.

"Science and mathematics," Matie replied.

"Oh, that's fantastic. Anyway, you're in dormitory number 3."

"Thank you," said Matie politely.

Considering Hama was pushing Matie's suitcase and a bag with her provisions in a wheelbarrow, he was walking fast, as if he were in a race. The girls were trotting behind him. They found themselves walking two strides behind and could not even hear what he was saying since he was huffing and puffing. He let one hand go from the wheelbarrow handle and pointed to the right.

"Matie, he's showing you something. Oh, it's the dining room."

They got to the dormitory, where Hama introduced them to Bernadette, the dormitory head.

"Here are Hilda and Matie, but please don't ask me to identify them by name. Hilda is here visiting. Good luck Matie, see you around." Hama lifted the handles of the wheelbarrow and ran, pushing it toward the gate to meet more students.

"I don't have anyone by the name of Matie on my list," Bernadette said.

Matie placed her left hand on her chest and introduced herself properly. "I'm Matilda but I have always been called Matie. This is my sister Hilda, who is on a brief visit and is on her way to St. Theresa's."

"Hello, Hilda, why didn't you come to our school?"

"It's good to give each other space."

"Matie, go ahead and choose your bed. You're the first girl to arrive."

Matie glanced around and noticed that it was a big open room with small windows on one side. The single beds were close together. She took a quick count of the beds. There were ten on each side.

Matie whispered into her sister's ear, "This is where I'll be for the next two years, unless something drastic happens.

"Where's your bed?" she asked Bernadette.

"I share the next room with another dormitory head. I'll show you in a minute. The positive thing is that we have some privacy, and the negative aspect is its size."

Hilda looked at the clock on the dormitory wall. It was well past the thirty minutes they had asked for. "Matie, I have to go now. You're going to have a fabulous time with the boys. I wish I had come here, too. You keep everything in perspective and remember Mama's favourite motto, 'Too much fun can backfire'."

"I'll live by it. You get going. Do you know your way back to the truck?"

"I'll find my way."

They hugged again, and as Hilda was walking away, they blew kisses at each other.

"Have a safe journey, sis. Who knew that one day we would go in separate directions to meet our own goals," Matie said, fighting back tears and already beginning to feel separation anxiety.

Once Hilda was gone, Bernadette invited Matie to her room, and they sat on her bed. There were two single beds and a shared bedside table between the beds, and on it was an old lamp. Their suitcases were at the foot of their beds, which made the room rather crowded. The window let in minimal lighting. It looked like a jail cell.

While waiting for other girls to arrive, they talked about a lot of things, including what they wanted to do after high school.

An hour later, Hama came back, calling for Bernadette. She stepped outside to meet two more girls.

"I have another set of twins but these ones are easier to tell apart. They will introduce themselves. I have to go back." He quickly left.

Bernadette, who had studied her list, asked, "Which one is Wilma?" One girl raised her hand. "I guess you're Winnie," Bernadette said, pointing at her with her pencil. "You're the second set of twins I have met today. How often does this happen? Must be a good omen."

When Matie heard her say something about twins, she hurriedly ran out of Bernadette's room to meet them. They were a classic example of fraternal twins. She had read a book about different types of twins and was always looking for more information. Wilma was two inches taller than Winnie, and they looked very different in all aspects. Right from the beginning, Matie took a liking to Wilma, whose outgoing character well suited hers.

"Matie, where do you come from?" Wilma asked.

"We live in Highfield. My sister and I attended Highfield Secondary School. We had fun there. Which school did you go to?"

"We went to Harare Secondary School. I'm glad to be out of there. My mother is one of the teachers. Can you imagine being with your mother at school and at home all the time? I never thought she would let us come to a boarding school because she likes to keep us under her watchful eye."

"Did she show you the final exam papers prior to sitting for the actual exam? I'm kidding, Wilma."

"I wish she did, and then I'd never have studied so much, to the point of hating school. At times I felt as if my brain was going to explode when I was cramming those lousy scientific formulas for exams. Did you ever feel that way?"

"There was no other way of doing it," Matie confirmed.

At lunchtime, Matie and Wilma walked together to the dining room and continued their discussion. Bernadette saw Winnie walking alone and went to speak to her. The four girls ended up sitting together in the dining room for the whole year. The first lunch was simple, bean soup and bread. Matie and some of the girls couldn't find reason to complain, since the menus were much better than what they had at home.

When Hilda got back, her father was snoozing. She threw a small stone through the open window to wake him up. He looked at his watch and shook his head because she was late, but he helped her back into the truck.

Hilda enjoyed the scenery and the small towns they passed along the way. She also marvelled at how at ease her father looked behind the wheel. At times the big truck drivers used their horns, especially when passing from opposite directions, to warn each other of trouble on the road, which could be roadblocks by either the Rhodesian forces or the freedom fighters.

For a while they were quiet, not knowing what to say, but they glanced at each other now and again. Mukai occasionally lit a cigarette and blew smoke out of the side of his mouth. He watched the smoke swirling upwards. He did it with style.

They had been going for almost two hours when Mukai noticed that Hilda was licking her lips.

"Are you hungry?" he asked.

"I'm more thirsty than hungry. Mama prepared some sandwiches for us."

"Do you think you can wait until we find a nice place to eat?"

Mukai had travelled that road many times and had seen the restaurant called Half Way House, but he had never dined there.

"I guess so," Hilda replied.

Mukai exited onto a small road that led to the restaurant. It was frequented by busloads of people because of its food and beautiful local crafts for sale. It was apparently a very popular restaurant because of the quality of service. There was a tea room for those who were not interested in a big meal, a full-service bar for those in need of something to quench their thirst, a restaurant that served big, tasty meals to fill the hungry, and a playground for children to release their energy after sitting in the car or bus for long periods.

"Let's go and see what's in there," Mukai said. "It happens to be my birthday and I would like to make this a memorable day for the two of us."

"It's your birthday today? What a surprise! Do you remember my birthday, which happens to be Matie's too?" she teased.

Mukai smiled. "How can I forget that? You were born when my father was in the hospital. He died a week later. He never had a chance to see you girls, but he knew of your birth. That was in July but the actual date has just escaped my mind. Can you help me out?"

"You're on the right track. It was July 28, 1962." Hilda tore a piece of paper from her journal and wrote it down. He carefully folded it before putting it in his torn old wallet. In their household, there was no importance placed on birthdays, so they came and went without any mention. Even the girls never fussed, for they associated celebrations with money, which was scarce.

"This is the first time I have heard you say something about your father," Hilda said with genuine interest.

"My father was an ordinary man who didn't have much in terms of material things, and life was a struggle for us. We lived in abject poverty. There's nothing much more to say about him. I'm trying to change that cycle for you and Matie, but the political situation does not make it easy for me. I can't wait for our independence because we should see some big changes, which would benefit us." He pulled out his handkerchief and dabbed at his sweaty forehead.

The sudden dismissal of her grandfather made Hilda curious. "Can we talk about it some other time? I'd like to know more about my grandfather, especially how you two related to each other."

"I'd happily tell you more about my family, our family rather, but today is not the day." Mukai regretted opening a can of worms. His father was an alcoholic who was abusive to him, his siblings and to his mother. To go down memory lane would only be painful, and he was not ready to share the horrors.

They walked into the restaurant and sat at a table for two, in a corner that looked cozy. They went past the "wait to be seated" sign. A white middle-aged woman came over and introduced herself. "I'm Sara, and I'll be your waitress this afternoon. Here are your menus." She threw them, and one of the menus flew across the table and landed on the floor. She did not pick it up and moved on to another table.

It was a while before she came back. "Anything to drink?"

"I'll have a Castle beer," said Mukai. "Cold one."

"And you, missy?" the waitress asked Hilda, who seemed unsure. "Hurry up! Didn't I give you enough time?"

"I'll have a cold one too." Hilda was distracted by the anxiety of being in an unfamiliar place and being served by a white woman whose tone was forceful. Hilda realized the gaffe and said, “Oops! Coca-Cola, please.” She covered her mouth with embarrassment.

They both looked at the menu. “What are you going to eat?”

“I’m going to have a steak, vegetables and potatoes.” Mukai pointed at the picture of a full meal.

Hilda was following her father’s eyes. “That looks good, but I’m going to have chicken, salad and rice. Is this how much it costs? It’s expensive.”

“Remember, it’s my birthday, we’re here to celebrate.”

The waitress brought both plates balanced on her arm, and she placed them down in front of Mukai and Hilda.

“*Bon appétit!*” she said and quickly moved away.

“What did she say?” asked Mukai.

“Enjoy your meal. It’s French.”

“I didn’t know you speak French.”

“I get by with a few words here and there,” said Hilda, who had taken one basic French class. “I’ve never seen so much food!” She shifted and straightened, ready to dig in.

Mukai polished off his plate but Hilda could not finish her lunch, since the portions were too generous. A black waiter overheard bits and pieces of their birthday conversation, and he said to Mukai, “You should order a dessert. It can’t be a birthday without a cake.”

“Why not?” asked Mukai.

At the back, while the black waiter was waiting for the cake order, he asked Sara to go sing happy birthday with him, but she refused.

“What’s in it for me? These people never give even a penny for a tip. They are your people. You do it. I didn’t want to serve them in the first place.”

The black waiter placed on top of the cake a used little

yellow candle that had dripped wax onto its sides. To Hilda and Mukai's astonishment, he began to sing "Happy Birthday." Hilda joined in, adding her soft, angelic voice to the mix. Mukai grinned from ear to ear and kept his gaze on his daughter.

All the fuss was too much for Mukai, and he became emotional. Tears welled up in his eyes, and wiping them was not an option, for they were tears of joy.

The waiter then said, "We aren't through yet. You have to blow out the candle, brother."

"Can you do it for me, my child?" Mukai asked Hilda, who pulled in a big breath and blew out the candle with all the energy she had.

Mukai pushed the cake towards his daughter and before he could say anything, the waiter had placed a clean fork in Mukai's hand. "You can share the cake, since it's a big helping." They'd never had such a good piece of cake that melted in their mouths.

"Take the candle as a souvenir," the waiter said. "This celebration will not be complete without a picture. Look at me and smile."

He clicked twice with his Polaroid. Within a few minutes the picture rolled out, and the waiter fanned it before handing it to Mukai, who looked at it and covered it with both hands as it rested on his chest.

"Careful, it might smudge," warned the waiter.

Hilda waited a few minutes before asking to see the picture. She glanced at it with admiration. That was the first picture of her and her father that she had seen.

Mukai and Hilda got back into the truck and resumed their journey. Hilda took out her little journal that she got from Aunt Emily, her godmother, as a going-away gift, and she tucked the picture away in it. She jotted down her father's birth date and all the details of what had happened in the restaurant. She promised herself never to forget his birthday again. When she was done writing, she put the journal on the dashboard in case she remembered something else.

By then, Hilda was struggling to keep awake. She dozed off, and when she woke up, she could not believe that they were at the school. Mukai parked the truck outside, since it was too big to pass through the gate. The name of the school was written in big bold letters on a huge pillar: "St. Theresa's Secondary School." Hilda noticed words written underneath that were very obvious to the naked eye: "St. Theresa's Girls Jail."

She drew her father's attention to it, and he said, "Whoever wrote that should be suspended before they even walk into the classroom. It's a cheap joke. I'm going to report it to the superiors in case they have not seen it yet. This gives a bad impression of this school."

"Baba, let it pass, I'm sure the nuns know it already."

"If we all pass through here and have that kind of attitude, it would never be corrected."

They kept going till they finally saw a sign clearly posted. "Please Report at the Principal's Office."

They went into the office where a nun was sitting. She stood up, pulled down and adjusted her habit, tightened her rope belt and touched her black veil to ensure that it was flowing down below her shoulders. She ran her fingers across the forehead, feeling for stray hairs, then finally she straightened her glasses and said, "Welcome to St. Theresa's Secondary School."

Mukai put on a mischievous smile. "I'm glad we are at the right place. We were beginning to wonder if we had walked into a jail." Hilda was surprised by her father's sarcastic comment, because he was always coy about those kinds of things.

The nun didn't seem to find the comment amusing. "I know what you mean, sir. That'll be straightened out as soon as possible. And what is your name, young lady?"

"Hilda Ganda."

The nun flipped through the files then handed Hilda a three-page document of rules. "Welcome. There is a bench outside on the veranda. You should sit down and read this document carefully. After reading it, please put your signature on the last page to show that you understood everything in it. Take your time, because it's very important. Do I make myself clear?"

"Yes," Hilda said.

"Yes, Sister. A bit of respect will take you far," the nun said sternly.

When they were seated on the bench, Mukai looked back to check where the nun was before whispering, "She must have joined a good military school before becoming a nun."

"Baba, she can hear you." Hilda was surprised by her father's attitude, for she thought he believed in that kind of strictness.

Mukai laughed and said, "I'm not going to give you a three-page speech, for you know why you're here. I have to leave now. I'm running late." He was proud that he had played his role as a father and was beginning to build a relationship with his daughters.

On the way back to his truck, Mukai saw two men standing at the gate, cleaning the unwanted inscription. "Who could have written such an awful joke?" he asked.

"We see some really weird things here. This is nothing," one of the men replied. "Some of the girls take things too far."

That threw Mukai off. "Like what? It sounds serious."

"What you don't know will never hurt you, sir," the other man answered.

"It might not hurt me, but surely it'll hurt my daughter."

"Your daughter will be okay. You appear to be a good father who raised his daughter to know what is right and wrong."

"What I'm reading from you is that this place has its own problems."

"Only a few bad apples are dropped here from time to time. Despite all that, girls here receive good education. Many have gone on to become teachers and nurses, and some went to university to become lawyers and doctors."

"Have to go now and hope for the best." Mukai left with doubts about whether this was the right place for his daughter's education.

Chapter Four

After the girls and Mukai had left, Ruva's life seemed empty already. She retreated to her small living room and sat at the edge of the sofa with her head down. Memories of the girls growing up, the miscarriages and her husband began to flash back and forth. She had been thinking about what she was going to do even before the girls left. She wasted no time in designing and formulating a plan.

Her first big decision was not to live in self-pity. She needed to change her mindset, believe in herself and accept the things she could never change. Willpower was her strong suit.

Second, she wanted to go back to school. She wanted to be proficient in writing and enjoy reading those promised letters from Matie and Hilda. She was a hardworking and intelligent woman patiently waiting for a few doors to open.

Third, she had to look for a job. She was going to take whatever came her way, for she knew her limitations. When she and Mukai were discussing the girls' education, she mentioned that she wanted to work, since money was tight. Mukai didn't agree, because he was rather old-fashioned. He believed that it was the man's duty to take care of his family. She begged, and he reluctantly gave in.

Ruva wasted no time in following her ambitions. She knew of a friend who got her job through a certain employment agency. After church on Sunday, she asked for information on how to go about it.

Monday morning, she woke up and put on her best clothes. She kept her long hair in braids, but that day her hair was nicely coifed in a bun. She took the bus to the employment agency. In the part of the city where the office was located, the streets were lined with jacaranda trees, which gave off a sweet aroma and had pretty purple flowers. She went into the office, where she noticed people sitting looking hungry and dejected. Some were reading newspapers and others were filling in forms. She walked straight to a clerk's desk.

"It's my first time here. Where do I go?" Ruva was intimidated by the whole experience.

"You should register your name here. What kind of job are you looking for, ma'am?" the clerk asked.

"Domestic worker."

"Please go there and join that queue. Someone will come and get you for an interview."

She sat there until about noon, but nothing happened and she left. She went back to the employment office daily for a week, following the same procedure. She was beginning to wonder if there was something wrong with her, because she was not getting any interviews. Nonetheless, Ruva had some reservations about working as a house servant, because this was not the type of job that would elevate her to a role model for her two girls. Her aim was to live by example. She had no intention of being a *bona fide* domestic worker waiting on white women hand and foot for the rest of her life. In the short term, she knew that if she needed to fulfill her dreams, which would not be achieved overnight, she had to do something that would help her to get to her destination. Those were tough times for her, financially and politically, and thus far she was prepared to work as a house servant with a positive attitude, as hard as it seemed.

❧

On her lucky day, the queue was moving slowly when a regal-looking white woman came out and scrutinized each job seeker as if she were performing an inspection of the guard. When she got to Ruva, who was almost at the end of the line, she beckoned her for an interview.

Ruva was nervous but was determined to get over her fears. She sat up straight and looked polite with a smile that screamed, "Hire me."

She was up-front about her lack of qualifications, but to Beth Sanderson, that was not the deciding factor.

They discussed many things, including the salary. She was offered more than she was expecting. Even though it was not much, she was already looking forward to some degree of financial independence.

Beth liked Ruva's warm smile that drew her in. She appeared trustworthy and was well groomed. Before interviewing Ruva she had seen two other women, but Ruva fitted the bill.

Ruva had a feeling that Mrs. Beth Sanderson was different and looked beyond colour. She saw a respectful and refined woman stylishly and gracefully dressed in a beautiful dark coral two-piece silk suit. She wore black patent high-heeled shoes with a matching leather handbag. Her nylon stockings had seams at the back that looked as if they were glued on because they were so straight. Her hair was long and straight, with bangs covering her sunburnt forehead. She had a fair complexion. The scent of her perfume was fruity and not overpowering.

"I live in Highlands. Would you come with me today? If

it's all right, I'd like to show you some of the work you will be doing and where exactly I live with my husband and three children. Where are you staying right now?"

"In Highfield, madam."

"Please, just call me Beth." Beth put her hand on Ruva's back and said, "Excuse me, you go first. Let's go across the road, for I left my car near the bank."

She took keys from her purse and opened the driver's door of a black Mercedes-Benz 280 CE. She then opened the passenger door to let Ruva in. She lowered the windows to let in fresh air, adjusted the rear view mirror and pulled her sunglasses from her leather handbag. She put on her seatbelt and also helped Ruva with hers before driving off. Ruva noticed that the interior had white leather seats and there was not even a speck of dirt in the car. She enjoyed the car's smooth performance; it didn't compare to any of the cars she had ridden in that left a trail of smoke from the exhaust, smelled of petrol inside and had sounds of rattling parts from everywhere.

They arrived at Beth's ranch-style house. It was painted white and had a black roof. It took Ruva a minute or two to step out of the car, for the beauty of the garden charmed her. She admired the neatly manicured lawn and the painstakingly tended flowers, shrubs and hedges. The driveway was paved with interlocking bricks. Ruva got out of the car and Beth invited her into the house through the intricately hand-carved and stained wooden front door. She wiped her feet on a doormat that said "Welcome to Our Home." This reminded Ruva of Shungu's welcome sign, although there was no comparison.

"Please come in." Beth led her directly to the kitchen, and as she sat at the kitchen table, Beth offered her a drink.

"Is Orange Crush okay?"

"Yes, madam." Ruva quickly remembered that Beth

preferred to be called by her first name and corrected herself shyly. She drank the juice quickly, for she was thirsty. Beth disappeared for a little while, and when she came back, she had changed into a pair of blue shorts and a white golf shirt, since it was scorching hot outside. She took a jug of cold water from the fridge and poured herself a glass, which she sipped slowly.

"Can I show you around the house?" They started with the living room that had well-polished and beautiful antique furniture. Ruva had never seen the like before. The navy blue velvet sofas and matching chairs gave the room a splendidly regal atmosphere. Above the fireplace was an enlarged wedding portrait of Beth and her husband Larry, a geologist in the gold mining industry. On the mantelpiece were family portraits of the children. Accessories of African art comprised of sculptures and beautiful paintings, complementing the design of the room. On the centre coffee table were freshly cut flowers arranged in a crystal vase. The Persian rug partly covering the parquet floor bore a rich and intricately woven pattern. Valuable artifacts were strategically placed all over the room.

They went into the dining room, where there was a huge table that could easily seat twelve people. The chairs had comfortable high backs and were upholstered in deep brown leather. On one wall was a big picture of the Last Supper. Ruva deduced that this must be a Christian home. On the table was a big wooden bowl full of fruit, some of which Ruva had never seen. The silverware and crystal was displayed in the hutch, and it looked spotless. A chandelier was hanging directly above the dining table.

In all the bedrooms, the curtains matched the bedspreads. The children's bedrooms had all-white furniture. All the toys were tidily arranged in the playroom, which was brightly painted egg yellow and accentuated with reds. There were colourful alphabets and character cartoons adorning the walls.

The master bedroom's centre of focus was an imposingly huge four-poster bed made of solid oak. It was flanked on each side by a small table. There were two his-and-hers wardrobes, neatly organized and divided into sections. The windows were draped with gold taffeta curtains that matched the bedspread. There was a refreshing whiff of lavender coming from the adjoining *en suite* bathroom.

They moved back to the kitchen and sat at the kitchen table. The kitchen had oak cupboards and a brown-tiled countertop, which matched the floor ceramic tiles. Off the kitchen was a big, well-stocked pantry. On the other side of the kitchen was a scullery with two deep sinks, a stainless steel countertop for dishes and a laundry sink. There was an ironing nook and a built-in rack for ironed clothes. They stepped outside into the backyard. There was a fairly big swimming pool and behind the trimmed hedge was the servants' house.

They went back into the house. Directly adjoining the kitchen was a television lounge with a fireplace. This room was decorated in a contemporary style and looked lived in. There was a desk in one corner where the children could do their homework. The sofas were big, puffy and comfortable.

"Let's sit in here. You can stay in the servants' quarters over there if you like. There is room for two people. Harry, the garden boy, lives there too."

"I have a family and would like to go back home after work."

Beth had assumed Ruva would be staying, because she needed her to mind the children at night from time to time when she went out with her husband. It was a regular occurrence because of her husband's position in his company.

"How many children do you have?"

"I have two twin girls attending boarding schools, and my husband travels most of the time with his job."

"Oh, that's wonderful. I hope to meet them sometime when they are home on holidays."

They agreed that Ruva would stay over whenever Beth needed her to mind the children in the evenings. That arrangement worked out well for Ruva since she was home by herself most of the time anyway.

Back in the kitchen, Beth said, "You should not be afraid to touch and clean anything in this house, but you need to be extra cautious. These things are impossible to replace if they are broken. Do you have any questions?"

"No. You have a beautiful house, and I'm ready to start."

"My Shona is limited. I'm even ashamed because I was born here and made no effort to learn the language. At least I know that Ruva means flower, doesn't it? Correct me if I'm wrong."

"Yes." Ruva nodded.

"Back to important things. I'm going to leave a notepad in this drawer for you to jot some reminders for yourself and messages for me when I'm not around. Can you start tomorrow?"

Ruva nodded.

"Do you think you can be here at eight in the morning and be done by five in the evening?"

Ruva nodded again.

As Beth and Ruva were finalizing their discussion, Harry, the garden boy, came in and said, "Excuse me, Beth. There is a policeman outside who wants to talk to you."

"I'll be out there in a minute. Can you go and show Ruva where she catches the bus into town? Please write down our address for her on a piece of paper. One person got lost and never found this place again. A month later, she saw me in the grocery store and came and told me what had happened. See you tomorrow, Ruva. Here is your bus fare for the week. I have to attend to this policeman."

The policeman had come in. "Good afternoon, madam. I'm here to let you know that your stolen property has been recovered. You'll have to go to the main police station and identify the goods. Here is the letter with the identification number of the case."

"This thief should be incarcerated for life," said Beth as she was examining the document.

"It's not a murder case, madam."

"I know, but they keep on doing it. They are heavily armed and could end up hurting innocent people."

"I agree with you, but we have to follow the law."

"The laws could be made more stringent."

"You're talking to the wrong person." He got on his bicycle and pedalled away.

Ruva observed that there was a difference in lifestyle between blacks and whites. Even Ruva, although not overly political, wanted to see some changes towards equality. Despite those differences she felt powerless but was determined to work hard for her family.

The racial segregation policy ensured that blacks lived in their own enclosed, deprived world, full of daily challenges with no real opportunities. On the other side, the whites enjoyed all of the privileges bestowed on them by the colour of their skin. They governed the country with an oppressive, divide-and-rule ideology, owned most of the corporate businesses and farmed some of the most productive land. Economic power gave them the upper hand. For their own benefit, they had designed an exceptional educational system that paralleled any in the Western world, and enjoyed a solid health care system.

Racial discrimination was the order of the day, and the inequalities were like day and night. Blacks used to joke that the only thing distributed equally in the country was the weather, and if white people had their way, they would change that too. The war of liberation had peaked in Rhodesia in the late 1970s. Most of Ruva's family and many other people living in the countryside were caught in the fighting, and there were high numbers of deaths. Those living in cities were gripped by fear as well, since the war was building momentum in their backyards.

On her way home, Ruva decided to pass through one of the schools in the city and enquire about evening classes. She had no reason to rush home, since she was going to an empty house. She was now more determined than ever to continue with her education. She went into the office and asked for some information.

"Can you advise me on what path I need to take to finish my secondary education?"

The clerk replied, "You should take a test to determine the level you are at now. Then I suggest you take one class for now. When you're done with this course, you can decide if you can cope with more than one class. What would you like to do?"

Ruva thought carefully about what he had said and concluded that it was a good idea to take the test and go from there. She went back a few days later, wrote an aptitude test and passed. She took English as her first course.

On the first day of school, there were twenty-nine students in the class. Most of them were adult students. The teacher welcomed them and said, "I'd like you to introduce yourselves. Tell us your name, why you're in this class and your long-term goals. You have to think of a career, and that will determine what courses to take. Put your long-term plans into action early and that way you can have a career path to follow."

Some of the students had no clue of their long-term goals, but they were there to take it day-by-day. The teacher explained what he expected from them. The classes were going to be twice a week, Mondays and Thursdays. Those days worked well for Ruva, because she had a half-day off on Thursdays.

"Please listen very carefully. I'd like you to write a one-page essay on why education should be free. You'll hand it in on Thursday," he said. "Don't let other people write it for you because you will do a big disservice to yourself."

After school, Ruva went back to her empty house and rested for a while before she picked up her books, intending to start her essay, but she had no energy left. She put the books away and went straight to bed.

The following morning, she was beginning to have some doubts about whether she would be able to cope with all the homework and working at Beth's. Besides that, she still treasured the quality time she spent with her husband during his off days. She was also concerned about the lack of supervision of the girls during holidays.

Ruva got to work fifteen minutes before her starting time because she had left early.

"I'm glad you're here. I'll introduce you to my children before they go to school." Beth tapped each of the children on the head as she introduced them. "Kyle is ten, Keith is eight and Keira is six."

On her way out, Beth noticed that Larry had left his lunch box in the scullery. "I might take a bit longer because I have to take my husband's lunch to his office. He usually ticks off all the boxes before he leaves. I guess he didn't do that today."

The children stood there looking at their new housekeeper, trying to figure her out. Little Keira asked, "Mum, did she come by bus?"

"Yes, darling. She will be okay. Let's go."

Ruva thought they looked cute in their school uniforms. The boys had khaki shorts, white short-sleeved shirts, maroon blazers, matching bucket caps and knee-high socks with black shoes. Keira wore a skirt and the other part of her uniform was the same as the boys'. They sheepishly waved goodbye to Ruva, who looked on nervously.

She looked around the kitchen to see where she could begin. In the scullery, the sink was full of dishes. There was a pile of shoes for cleaning and polishing and dirty clothes filling up two laundry bags.

One of Ruva's positive attributes was that she was very organized. She wasted no time washing the dishes and tidying up the kitchen. She cleaned and polished the shoes until they were shining then took them outside for airing. There was so much laundry, because Beth hadn't had help for three weeks.

When Beth came back, Ruva was sorting the laundry according to colours. "You're already at it, are you? I see you have put the shoes outside? After cleaning them, you can put them back in our bedrooms."

"I'm airing them out so that when you put them on, they are nice and fresh. I'll bring them in if that bothers you."

"No, it's a good idea. I had never thought about it. I bought you two sets of uniforms yesterday. They might be slightly big. Without thinking, I picked up Anna's size. You won't mind, will you?"

"No, thank you. You must have loved her, if she lingers in your mind."

Beth nodded and pressed her lips together, and seemed to

blink furiously as if to fight off tears. "Did Harry tell you what happened to Anna?"

"He told me a little about it on our way to the bus. I could tell he was having a hard time himself."

"Let's sit down and chat a bit," said Beth.

Before they even sat down, Beth started. "I'm sure that Anna's death affected Harry too. He asked if he could take time to go to the village for her funeral. I hope that gave him a sense of closure. I strongly suspected that there was something more than friendship between those two. I noticed that they had become very close, but I never had the nerve to ask if there was a love bond. It was not my place to ask. Now that I think about it, Anna had put on more weight. Whether she was pregnant, I'll never know. But I'm certain that I shall miss her. I have pictures of Anna in my album. I'll show you tomorrow. Let's get back on track."

Beth pulled two tissues from a box. She used one to wipe her eyes and the other for blowing her nose. She was a very sensitive, good-hearted person who had a tendency to inherit other people's problems and make them her own.

Ruva was not sure how to respond, but she managed to say, "I feel sorry for her children, for they will grow up without a mother."

"So Harry told you about the boys? The father or fathers were never in the picture. Anna never said anything about them."

By the end of the day, Ruva was exhausted, and there was a lot of information to absorb. She learned a lot of things on her first day, but she was left wondering if she would be as good a worker as Anna and earn Beth's trust.

"I'll ask Harry to clean Anna's room for your own use when you're staying over."

Anna had worked for Beth for nearly eight years, and she was a single parent. She had started working for the Sandersons just after Keith was born. She was a hard worker who was thorough and truly enjoyed her labour. She always took time off around national holidays to go to her rural village to see her two sons who lived with their grandmother. She always came back Sundays around eight in the evening and reported to Beth. That particular Sunday, Beth hadn't thought much of it. The next morning, Anna didn't show up, which was odd, since she always prepared breakfast. Beth thought she had overslept. She saw Harry in the garden and asked him, "Is Anna still sleeping?"

"I was coming to tell you that she didn't come back yesterday."

Beth could see that Harry was concerned.

"Oh, she will be here. She must have missed the bus, but that's not like her."

When Larry came home, Beth told him that Anna hadn't come back. Larry said, "I heard on the radio as I was driving home that a bus plunged about thirty feet down a gorge in the Kariba area, and fifty-eight people died. Let's hope she was not on that bus."

"Did you hear what time the accident occurred?"

"They said it was raining heavily around 5:00 p.m. yesterday."

"She must have been on that bus. There is a tight bend on that gorge, and if one does not negotiate it carefully, it's easy to go down. Remember I took her to the village when one of her sons was ill. It was a journey I vowed never to repeat again."

Larry could tell that Beth was disturbed, and he was sensing the worst. "How are we going to know if she was on the bus? I'm going to the police station. They might have some information."

"Larry, please go. I'd like to know for the sake of those two boys. Wait, Anna has a cousin who works here in Highlands near the shopping centre. I have her address. Do you think we should go and ask if she has heard anything? Actually, let me go, because I have met her before."

Since it was raining, Beth grabbed her umbrella and left. She met Anna's cousin, Stella, at her employer's gate as she was on her way to the shops. The woman's face said it all. "Hello, I'm Beth. Do you remember me? Anna gave me your address when I asked her for contact in case of an emergency. She didn't come back to work. Do you know anything?"

"The police contacted me and told me that Anna was in a bus accident, and she was amongst those who died. I'm going home tomorrow to help with the funeral arrangements," said Stella, sobbing.

"I'd like to help in any way I can. I'll bring you some money in the morning." Beth offered to cover most of the funeral costs.

The following morning she picked up Stella and on the way to the funeral home they were both quiet, reflecting on what Anna meant to them. Beth bought Anna a simple pine coffin.

There was one more thing she had to do, and that was to see Anna for the last time.

When the funeral attendant called her in, Beth looked at Anna's face for a moment. There was a deep gash on the forehead, and her skin had turned black. The body was covered with a blanket, which Beth lifted slightly and was horrified at what she saw. Part of the gut was hanging outside the body. The stench in the mortuary did not help. Beth felt sick to her stomach, and she ran outside, leaving a trail of her own vomit.

Stella did not see her outside and followed her to the car. "Are you okay, Beth?"

"Yes, but what I saw today is not how I'd like to remember Anna. I hope that sight will fade out of my memory, and I'll remember the person she was to my family and me. I'll miss her. Here is some money, and please tell Anna's mother that I'll continue to pay for the boys' school fees. When the dust settles down, ask her to come and see me. Here is my address and phone number."

The day after hearing this story, Ruva got to work earlier and was going to enter the house from the back, for she had her own house key. Beth saw her from the kitchen window while making breakfast. She opened the door and said, "Good morning, Ruva. You're here bright and early. There is an album with some family pictures on the kitchen table. You will find Anna's pictures in there. Why don't you sit down, relax and thumb through it before you start work? There are some amazing pictures of Anna in there."

"I'll look at them later. First, can I watch how you prepare breakfast?"

"Wonderful! My husband prefers a poached egg. The children are into scrambled eggs. I'm not crazy about eggs but occasionally I have a soft-boiled egg."

Ruva was used to throwing her eggs into a frying pan full of oil and turning it over and over until the egg yolk tasted rubbery and the white was burnt. She hated an egg with a runny yolk or sunny-side-up.

"The bacon tastes better when it's slightly crispy. At times we have baked beans warmed up. The children normally have a little bit of hot oatmeal. If we are having dry cereal, the milk should be warmed up. My husband and I take black coffee in the morning, without sugar. I encourage the children to take a glass of milk before they go to school. I set the toaster at three so that there are no complaints about burnt toast. That's breakfast in our household. It sounds complicated, but you will get it."

"That's a lot of food," Ruva commented.

"The portions are small."

Ruva was struggling to remember and figure out the key words: poached egg, scrambled eggs, boiled egg and her own specialty, fried egg. She was happy that she had learned something new. She quickly pulled out a notebook that Beth had given her from one of the drawers and scribbled some notes on how each member of the family liked their eggs done.

"I hope I'll be able to make them as well as you do," she told Beth.

"You're going to do it better than me once you've done it a few more times."

"Can I do it tomorrow? I need to practice more."

"Don't stress yourself, I'll be here to help." Beth called her husband and the children to the table. After finishing breakfast, they all left.

When everybody was gone, Ruva sat at the table and started looking through the pictures. She noticed that Anna accompanied the Sandersons on holidays to help with the children. That led her to believe that she might also be asked to accompany them overseas one day. That alone was beyond her imagination. She could see from the series of pictures taken in South Africa when they were on a safari at Kruger National

Park, Anna's smile was infectious. Her energy was evident through the lens of the camera, especially when she was playing with the children. Her happy-go-lucky attitude truly seemed to allow her to enjoy the good times. Ruva focused on one picture in which Anna was at the beach playing with the children, and she felt as if she knew her. She admired the characteristics she imagined. She thought Anna was someone she would have easily befriended.

After dropping off the children, Beth came back and asked, "Have you had a chance to look at the pictures?"

"Yes! She had lots of energy."

"Oh, that's an interesting and true observation," agreed Beth. "Now back to work."

Beth showed her as much as she could, from polishing the silver, oiling the sculptures and furniture, dusting the chandeliers to operating the appliances. Ruva was eager to do the right thing. If she was in doubt, she always asked. At the end of her day, she went into the playroom to see what the children were doing. She took some time to play with them and get to know them.

"Can I help you?" she asked as she knelt down beside Keira, who was putting together a jigsaw puzzle.

"I know how to do it. Anna showed me how to put this one together."

"Do you have one that you haven't tried yet?"

"I have a grizzly bear puzzle that my dad brought for me from … I can't remember." Keira ran to her room and ripped the paper covering from the puzzle's box.

They started working on the puzzle together, and Ruva quickly got the hang of it. As Ruva was concentrating on the pieces, Keith asked, "Do you have children?"

"Yes, I have twin girls."

"What are their names?"

"Hilda and Matie, and they are away at boarding schools." She always wanted people to know that her children were getting a quality education.

"Do you miss them?"

"Yes, I do. I can't wait to see them back for the holidays."

Kyle, not wanting to be left out, joined the conversation. "Anna used to live here. Why don't you stay in her room?"

"I have my own house, but we should have time to do things together when I'm here."

Beth walked in and watched the children interacting with Ruva. "Ruva, it's time for you to wind up for the day. You don't want to miss the last bus." She seemed glad to see that Ruva was showing interest in the children.

"You're right. I should be going."

"Can you wait?" Keira was beginning to warm up to Ruva, and she dashed to her bedroom and got a chocolate bar from her satchel. "This is for you."

"No, please don't. That's your snack at school tomorrow."

"Ruva, please accept it. She wants you to have it," Beth interrupted.

"Thank you very much, Keira, but now you won't have a chocolate bar for a snack tomorrow." Ruva shyly accepted it and put it in her apron pocket.

"I have another one. That one is yours."

When she was leaving, there were joyous goodbyes from the children, which gave her a good feeling.

As she got home and was opening her door, Shungu was there behind her. "Where have you been going so early in the last few days?" she asked with her arm raised up high and resting on the wall, showing a fuzzy ball of thick hair under her armpit.

"I'm a working woman. It's good to earn my own money."

"My goodness! Where?"

"I was going to pop in one of these evenings and tell you about my new job, but you know how it is. I'm a housekeeper and a nanny and loving it. Those are the only jobs for us the uneducated, but I have to work with the skills I have."

"Is your boss a white woman?"

"Yes, but that is irrelevant. What is important is I'm honestly earning my living."

"I suspected it anyway. Wait until she starts accusing you of this and that when she wants to get rid of you."

"Shungu, if that day comes, let it be. Otherwise, she's a wonderful person."

"Look at you, you are about to crash. Be careful, they can make you work like a horse."

"I will let you know how it's going." Ruva didn't invite her in, and Shungu got the message and left.

Chapter Five

On a Saturday morning, a month after the girls left for school, Mukai came back from his Mozambique trip. Ruva was home busy cleaning her own house. She was jubilantly singing old church hymns and war songs and enjoying every note. She didn't even hear Mukai enter the house.

"I'm home and let's share the glad tidings. You sound so happy."

She immediately put her cleaning rag back in the pail and quickly wiped her hands on her skirt. Before she could utter a word, Mukai hugged her, and she hung on to him for what seemed like eternity.

"I wasn't expecting you back so soon."

"I have been gone a month now. It shows that you didn't even miss me." He sat down, slipped off his shoes and removed his green jersey that Ruva knitted for him years back. "Have you heard from the girls yet?"

"I haven't even had a chance to check the mail."

"What have you been up to? I thought you would have lots of time on your hands now that the girls are out of your hair."

"Let me check and see if there is anything in the mailbox now. I'll come and tell you of the many changes in my life."

"I can't wait."

When she went outside, he noticed an English textbook on

the coffee table. He picked it up and opened it carefully, and on the first page was her name written in capital letters. He dashed to their bedroom to quickly scout for more clues. He saw a well-ironed maid's uniform spread on the bed.

"Mukai, I have letters from both girls. They must have been in the mailbox for a few days because they are a little damp. We had a good downpour the other day. I don't know why I never even thought of checking after the girls promised that they would write. Read them please, I can hardly wait."

"You can read too. I'm sure the girls are fine. First, I want to hear what has been happening in your life that is keeping you so busy. Are we not important anymore?"

"That is not the point. I only forgot to check the mail. Now that the letters are here, I'm anxious to know how my girls are doing." Ruva was ready to open one of the letters, but Mukai snatched it away from her.

"Ruva, you promised to fill me in about the changes in your life. Those letters can wait." Mukai planted a kiss on her forehead and put his arm around her. They both sat down on the sofa. Ruva crossed her legs on the sofa, and Mukai stretched his long legs onto the coffee table.

"Where should I begin? After you and the girls left, my life was empty and lonely. I thought I needed to do something to fill the void. I went to the employment agency and got a job as a domestic worker. The lady pays me more than the going rate, gives me bus fare and allocates food rations for me every week. What more can I ask? Since I'm working, I thought this would be the right time to start going to evening school. I can afford to pay for my own fees. You've Hilda's fees to worry about and many other things."

"I hope you're not taking so big a bite that you can't chew. You need to slow down."

"I'll let you know if I can't do it."

"You look much happier than I've ever seen you in a long time. Go for it, but don't let anybody push you around."

She closed her eyes and breathed a sigh of relief. She shifted focus and asked, "How was your journey with the girls?"

"I'll leave it up to them to tell you all about it. They can narrate better than me. I'm sure it's all in their letters. I can only say, I look forward to many more journeys with them."

"Now let's hear from them, please? Which letter do you want to read first?" Ruva was getting excited.

"It doesn't matter. Maybe Hilda's letter will be loaded with surprises," he hinted.

"Do you know something?"

"Let me read, and we will find out."

St. Theresa's Secondary School,
14 January 1979

Dear Mama,

I just want to let you know that I am fine. Everything is going well. I am enjoying my studies. It might be of interest to you that we had tests already and I passed all of them.

What I do not like is I have to wake up very early to have a warm shower and if one lingers in bed, warm water runs out quickly.

The nuns can be mean at times, but I am always on my best behaviour so that I do not cross their paths. We are assigned duties for Saturday mornings, and this term, I will be cleaning the nuns' residence with four other students. I look forward to the treats they give us when we are done. In their enclosed compound, the nuns can surely let their guard down. They behave differently. They do not put on those ugly veils. They let their hair loose and cut each other's hair. They listen to rock music, and Elvis Presley is their favourite. They show that they are human rather than the holier-than-thou personalities they portray when in public.

Father and I had a wonderful journey. He will tell you all about it when he comes home. We celebrated his birthday in a nice restaurant. It is a pity that you and Matie were not there to see Father in his tender moment when we sang happy birthday for him. It is an unforgettable occasion. I learned a lot of things about my father. He said a little about our grandfather and has promised to shed more light on his childhood.

I promised Matie that I'd write first, but she has not responded to my letter. The girl must be having a good time and has forgotten her only sister. I miss her lots and you too.

Love you, Mama. You are the best.
Hilda

"Now I'm trying to remember what date that was when you left with the girls, since it happens to be the famous birthday. I'm glad you celebrated with your daughter. Those are memories she will treasure forever. We should all start celebrating our birthdays, but we don't need to go to restaurants and spend money that we do not have."

Mukai sensed some jealousy, and he quickly tried to defuse that feeling. "When is your birthday, my dear? Today we are going to celebrate all your past birthdays. How's that for a treat?"

"I don't know the exact date. I once asked my grandmother, and she said she had no record of my birth. But she remembered that it was end of the rainy season when I was born. I have always given March 25, 1944, as my birthdate."

"Now that you have straightened out your birthday, you should get a birth certificate and a passport."

"What do I need a passport for? I don't travel at all, as you do. There must be more surprises from Matie. Oh, by the way, what were you telling her about your father?"

"What is there to tell? Matie might have something interesting to share too," he said as he opened the second letter, evading the question. Ruva rested her head on his shoulder and listened as he read the second letter.

Lord Armstrong Secondary School,
19 January 1979

Dear Mama,

My journey to school with Hilda and Baba will be something to always remember. As exciting as it was, I would rather come back home on the bus with the other students.

I managed to spend a short time with Hilda at my dormitory where I live with 19 other girls. Thanks to Baba who gave us 30 minutes plus to say our goodbyes.

Being in a boarding school is surely an interesting and unique experience. Imagine sharing the open shower room with 20 other girls from the adjacent dormitory. It can be chaotic in the mornings.

I am enjoying my lower sixth year classes. There are some intellectually gifted boys and girls here. It is competitive, but I intend to stay in the top mix.

Hilda promised to write me first, but I have not heard from her. I miss her so much. You must be lonely by yourself. You should find something to fill your time. You can volunteer at our old school. There are local women who come here to help with so many things around the school. In a way, they are like our mothers away from home.

I'm going to keep this short, as I have a science test tomorrow and need to study.

Love you always,
Matie

"Poor Matie is always concerned about my welfare. Helping out whenever I can is something I'd like to do when I have lots of money in the bank."

"The more money one has, the greedier he becomes," said Mukai.

"You have provided for us. It'll be good if I can bring in a bit of extra money."

"I won't abdicate my responsibility. Next time, I'll take Matie to St. Theresa's so that she can see Hilda's school," said Mukai.

"Can I come along too?"

"That can be arranged. You have to be extra nice to me."

"Let me finish doing the chores, and then we can celebrate all my past birthdays. How exactly are you going to do it, if I may ask?" She understood very well what he meant. She went back to her chores.

"Wait and see."

Mukai slipped out of the house and went to the shops to buy something to eat. He bought a barbecued chicken, wedged potatoes, Madeira cake, a red candle and a small bouquet of flame lilies.

While Ruva was having a bath, Mukai cut the flowers short and arranged them as best as he could in a three-legged pot, which they rarely used. He placed it on the coffee table. It turned out to be an interesting and creative piece that could easily have evoked a conversation. There was no way Ruva was going to miss the flower arrangement. Mukai sliced the chicken and put it on an enamel dinner plate. He put the potatoes in a smaller round dish and dug the candle deep into the cake.

"Wow, the flowers are beautiful. I could never have thought of doing what you did with that pot. You get full marks for effort."

While she was wowing about the flowers, he brought the dinner from the kitchen. To make it interesting, he put on a red apron that Hilda had sewn in her primary home economics class. It looked as if he had worked hard to put everything together.

"Sit down, Ruva, let's feast. We have a lot of celebrating to do: past birthdays, new job, going back to school, the beginning of bigger things to come, being a wonderful wife and the best mother there is. Anything I left out?"

"You said it all." Ruva was really touched. Mukai had never praised her like that. She became emotional. Tears started streaming down onto her lap as she bowed her head. Mukai stood up and knelt in front of her. He dabbed her eyes with his cigarette-smelling handkerchief. Ruva was immune to the smell. Mukai's love was all that she longed for at that moment, and all other things were irrelevant. She positioned her head daintily on his chest. Mukai gently pulled her up and they hugged. Ruva drew away slowly from Mukai and said, "Let's eat first, and then we can play. Oh, I mean celebrate."

They sat down again and impulsively started kissing and cuddling on the sofa. It was too much for both of them. Mukai picked her up and carried her into the bedroom. He gingerly placed her on the bed and pulled her skirt up, and before she knew it, Mukai was on top of her. Ruva responded lovingly. When they were done, Ruva said, "I like the idea of merely having sex for our own intimate pleasure and not being stressed about making babies."

"I thought you declared that discussion closed. Let's live in the moment and make the best of it. I'm enjoying you more. I think you're now more relaxed and patient with me. We are done making babies."

"You're right, but I want you to know that tension and stress gripped me for years. It's all behind us."

"You made your point. Case closed."

Back in the living room, he lit the candle with the lighter that was always in his shirt pocket. He tried to sing "Happy Birthday" but his voice let him down, so he abandoned the idea, laughing at himself. Ruva applauded the effort, regardless.

In April, the girls arrived home on the same day but by different modes of transportation. Matie came by bus, as she had requested. She wanted to be part of the end of the school term fun and to enjoy the company of her schoolmates. Hilda came home by train, and it was the first time that she had travelled on one, so it was altogether a whole new experience for her. She and her ecstatic schoolmates kept moving from coach to coach on the slow-moving train watching the changes of scenery as the world went slowly by. Although the girls had made new friends, they were looking forward to seeing each other again. Matie and Ruva waited at the station for Hilda, who looked relieved to see them.

The girls and their mother sat down for dinner and talked about life at school. Ruva retreated to her room early because she sensed that the girls had a lot to catch up on, and it was going to be a long night. She was happy to see that they were still close. Time and distance had not taken that away.

"Matie, I see you're reading *Animal Farm*." Hilda picked up the book and leafed through it. "Do you know that they use that book in literature classes at my school? Maybe I should read it too when you're done."

"How is school for you?" Matie asked.

"School is great. You'd think a girls' school is boring. Not St. Theresa's. There are some very interesting girls and naughty ones too, if I may add. But I try to avoid troublemakers."

"How long are you going to remain a saint?"

"What do you mean?" asked Hilda.

"Never mind! Do you have friends?"

"I have many roommates and classmates but Lindiwe is one good friend. She is down-to-earth and somewhat laid back. Okay, how about you? Have you lost your virginity, since there are boys galore?"

"No. Right now, I'm not interested. I see all these girls being dumped by their boyfriends and getting depressed. I don't want to join that group yet. But having said that, there is this boy who is interested in me, Toby. However, I've become good pals with Wilma, who is also a twin, but I sense that her sister doesn't like me."

"Oh, what a coincidence that you befriended a twin! Are you saying the sister is jealous of you?"

"She certainly is. I don't know what her beef is. I don't pay much attention to her. Otherwise, school is good. School is good," she repeated for emphasis.

"You're stealing her sister away from her, can't you see?"

"Oh! She's just jealous."

They chatted non-stop well into the night until Ruva called from her room. "Ladies, let's catch a few hours of sleep. Tomorrow is another day." The loud, laughing voices reverberating through the thin walls had broken into Ruva's sleep, since she was a light sleeper.

"Were you listening to our conversation all this time?" asked Hilda.

"She was not. Mama, we're sorry for disturbing your sleep," Matie said. With that they finally went to bed.

When they woke, their mother was sitting outside on the veranda, basking in the Saturday morning sun. They joined her. Ruva could not take her eyes off her girls. She noticed that they had matured, their arguments had conviction and they were beginning to show signs of independence. She even commented on their drooping eyes. "You girls need your sleep."

"Mama, this is not from last night, but from the whole term when we had to put in countless of hours of study. Otherwise, it becomes a struggle between sleep and high grades," explained Matie.

"A struggle indeed, but one with rewards," agreed Hilda.

Mukai came home from one of his trips a few days after the girls had arrived. He was happy to see his three ladies. During that break, Ruva noticed that Mukai was not drinking beer.

Usually, whenever he came home, he had three or four beers daily.

"The beer stores must have run out of beer. I have not seen you drinking since you came home. What is happening?" Ruva sarcastically asked.

"My dear wife, you made a few changes in your life for the better, and I have decided to follow suit. There are other things I'd like the girls to remember of me besides drinking beer. Let me be frank, it hasn't been easy. I'm having cravings, but I'm determined to stay away from the bottle. I'm not saying I had become an alcoholic like you know who." He was referring to his father.

Ruva continued to tease him. "We'll be able to save a bit of money now."

"It's not about money, but good health is important, and being a responsible parent is what I'm striving for."

"I'm with you." She gave him a high five.

The next day, Ruva came back from work and told them that Beth wanted to see them. Ruva had mentioned to her that Mukai was going on another trip, and the girls were not going to be home for long before they went back to school.

"Tomorrow will be good. You do not have to come with me early in the morning. But I can give you the address and the directions on how to get there. Before lunch would be the best time."

"Of course, we'll visit tomorrow. What do you think, girls?" Mukai said.

"I'd love to meet her," said Hilda.

"It's good to know where you work, anyway, and we have to

see this lady for whom you have such high regard. From what you have said, there is something special about her," Mukai added.

"We'll be there for you, Mama. Do we need to be dressed in our Sunday best?" Matie asked.

"Make it casual. Beth is not going to expect you to be starchy. You're not going to one of their parties. It's a short get-to-know-you visit. That reminds me, I found a nice second-hand shop at the shopping centre near Beth's place. Some of the things have never been worn. We should go there before you go back to school," said Ruva, who was always penny-pinching and looking for a bargain.

The following day, there was much anticipation about what was going to happen. Mukai put on his only suit, which had brown stripes. He was from the old school and he believed in suiting up for any occasion. Because of his height, the suit hung well on him. He wanted to leave a lasting impression.

From about 11:30 on, Ruva kept on running to the gate to check on her family. The excitement was making her jittery and giddy. "I hope they are not going to get lost. They have never been to the suburbs."

"Ruva, don't worry, they'll be here. Harry will watch out for them," said Beth.

"They might not know what to do when they get here. I forgot to tell them about the bell."

"Okay, I'm going to ask Harry to go out there and wait for them, or he can leave the gate open. I don't want you to fret so much."

As they finished that conversation, Beth looked through the window, trying to locate Harry somewhere on the premises. She saw Ruva's family coming through the gate with Harry, who had gone outside to collect the mail.

"They are here. Now you can relax." Beth moved back and watched Ruva rubbing her hands together with nervousness. Ruva quickly opened the front door and was not sure of where they were going to sit. She had never received her own visitors and was confused about letting them sit in the living room where Beth normally received her visitors. She wondered if she should take them to the TV lounge where it was less formal, or the veranda where they could appreciate the beautiful garden.

"It's okay for them to go into the main living room," Beth said after noticing Ruva's hesitation.

Ruva fidgeted with her hands and introduced her family first. She stood up and brushed her husband's hand, which was resting on the wing chair where he was seated, and said, "This is Mukai, my husband."

"Glad to meet you, Mukai. Ruva has told me a lot about you. Good things, by the way," Beth said.

"Thank you. I suppose she says good things about everybody. You should hear what she says about you. She admires you a lot." He was right; that was Ruva's nature.

Ruva moved in between the girls, who were seated on a big sofa, and she put her arms around them. Their eyes were darting everywhere, taking in the beauty and splendour of the décor. It reminded her of the day she arrived there and saw what money could buy.

She turned to her right. "Hilda goes to St. Theresa's Girls High School." She didn't give Beth a chance to jump in. She quickly turned to her left and said, "This is Matie, short for Matilda, and she goes to …" Ruva paused and looked at Matie, who she expected to come to her mother's aid.

Hilda said, "Mama, it's called Lord Armstrong."

"Thank you. Don't you hate those moments when your mind just goes blank?" Ruva stood up and kneeled next to Beth. "Beth is the owner of this amazing house and a wonderful employer. Larry, her husband, is in England on a work assignment. She has three beautiful children. Where are they, Beth?"

"I'm glad to meet you all, and welcome to my home. Now that you mentioned the children, I'll get them from the playroom." Beth left at that moment because she felt that when they entered the house they looked intimidated. She wanted them to settle down and make themselves comfortable.

"Mother, I agree with you that this is truly an amazing house. I can only dream of living in a house like this," said Matie in a whisper. "Dreams have been known to come true."

"Shhhhhh. Lower you voices."

"I can see you living luxuriously like this one day." Hilda believed that this lifestyle was indeed achievable.

"Girls, to get to this point you have to work hard at school first. Let's get that straight."

"Why don't we have more pictures on the wall, especially in our room?" Matie asked her mother.

"It will only distract you from your studies. This is not the place to have that kind of discussion," Ruva reminded her.

"It would make it more exciting," Matie persisted.

"You heard me." Ruva looked stern.

Beth walked back in with her kids in tow. She hadn't told them there would be visitors coming, in case they got too excited. It was a surprise for them. "Here are my children. Kyle is the oldest, then Keith and Keira, the youngest." Matie and Hilda made small waves to the children.

There was silence, and then Beth said, "I understand you girls are attending boarding schools. How is that going?"

Matie's confidence began to shine. "All is going well. I like my school, and I'm leaning towards a career in science."

"And, Hilda, what kind of subjects are you taking?"

"I have a mixture of arts and sciences. I'm keeping my options wide open."

"I thought you wanted to be a teacher," said her father in a surprised tone.

"That's still an option, Baba, but you never know. I have since discovered that there are other things to do besides teaching."

"I know for sure that your mother is very proud of you both. I hope you will not let her down. She is working just as hard at her evening classes. She wants a better life for all of you," said Beth, smiling. She turned to Mukai and said, "Ruva has told me that you go to all the surrounding countries with your job. Where do you feel at home?"

"I like visiting Malawi because that's where my forefathers came from. I'm hoping that one day I can trace my roots and discover my history. The problem is both my grandfather and my father are dead, and the other remaining family members have no clue of our clan."

"Baba, I didn't know that we are Malawians. That's another revelation. You're beginning to slowly peel off your own layers," said Hilda, giggling.

"The fact that we were all born in Rhodesia makes us Rhodesians. Beth, is that not correct?" Matie said.

"I totally agree with you both, but country of origin is also important in terms of one's roots."

"Mukai, you're in trouble. Anyway, Ruva, can you offer everybody drinks, for you know what they like," said Beth.

Mukai felt uncomfortable and embarrassed, since the girls had never openly challenged him.

Ruva asked the girls to go into the TV room to keep the Sanderson kids company, and so she could defuse the discussion that was heating up. Beth was trying hard to engage Mukai in conversation, but he had suddenly become reserved.

Ruva sensed her husband's discomfort, and she took the opportunity to ask Beth, "Can I please take my family to the shopping centre up the street and grab a quick lunch with them?"

"Sure! Take the whole afternoon off and go and spend quality time with your family. I'll see you tomorrow, and unfortunately the laundry will still be waiting for you." Beth then excused herself and went looking for her purse. "Take this money and go and have lunch. There are a couple of restaurants at the shopping centre that serve good lunch. Treat yourselves."

"Beth, please, I have some money," pleaded Mukai, who found it embarrassing to accept money from a lady.

"It's okay. Add to what you have. I want you to go and have something different."

"Thank you," said Mukai, humbly bowing his head and putting his hands together, as was the custom.

"Let me tell the girls that we're ready to go," said Ruva.

Beth's kids had taken the girls to their bedrooms. Matie and Hilda were envious of what they were seeing. They didn't have that kind of furniture and never had so many toys when they were young. They could only wish they had that many books.

While they were waiting, Brian, Larry's younger brother, arrived and Beth did a quick introduction.

"Meet Ruva, our new domestic worker and her family."

"Checking on you, are they?" Brian asked.

"Here you go again. I invited them," Beth answered. "And don't mind him."

"Beth, we've got to run," said Ruva.

Everything seemed fine as they were walking, until out of the blue Mukai said, "That Brian looked at me as if I'm a piece of trash."

"I didn't see it that way. I'm not here to defend him, but we're too quick to judge people we don't know," Ruva retorted.

"Are we talking of the same person we just met?" Mukai asked.

"Of course, but don't create monsters out of nothing." The accusation upset Ruva.

"Can't you see through their deceptions?" Mukai replied.

When they walked into Corra restaurant, which was recommended by Beth, Mukai and Ruva put their squabbling aside. They took their time eating and savoured every moment of the fine dining. It brought back treasured memories for Hilda.

"This reminds me of the lunch I had with father on my way to school. But this is even better because we are all here as a family."

"We should go out for a movie and make this day special," Ruva suggested, since they had money left over from lunch.

"That's a good idea, for we'll have something to talk about at school when people ask the usual question, 'What did you do?'" said Matie. "I have never been to a cinema. At school we sometimes watch movies on Sunday evenings in the dining room. The last one we watched was *The Sound of Music*."

"So what are we going to watch?" Hilda asked, knowing fully well that nobody had a clue.

"We don't know yet. It has to be age-appropriate." Ruva was concerned about what she had heard regarding some movies that had unsuitable content. She was determined to protect the girls. With peer pressure from all directions, she knew it was an uphill battle. When they got to the cinema, they looked at all the shows that were listed.

"We're almost eighteen and can watch anything we want."

"Wait a minute, age is not a factor here. We're going to watch what is appropriate for us all."

"You girls mind your manners. I don't like the way you are talking to us, do you hear me?" Mukai admonished.

Matie made the final decision on the movie, and she chose *Chariots of Fire* after reading the review on the poster.

They managed to slip into the theatre a few minutes before the movie started. They were ushered to their seats, which were down in front. When the lights were turned off and the movie started, they were all surprised by the utter silence that descended over the room. Mukai and Ruva did not understand the plot but they found the races entertaining and on the whole the movie was enjoyable. Matie and Hilda both followed the story and understood the driving forces behind the main characters, who were determined to run in the Olympics, in order to fulfill their strong and yet different beliefs, which compelled them to compete. Matie drew a parallel between the two main characters and herself, because she saw poverty as a social force that propelled her to work hard in her studies and the effort she put into her schoolwork as the preparation for the major prize.

"I liked the competitiveness and perseverance shown by the characters," said Matie.

"It teaches us to stand up for what we believe in," added Hilda.

"Matie, that was a good choice, and you girls have learned something, from what you're saying," said Ruva.

Since Mukai had to leave for work before the girls' holiday was over, Matie and Hilda joined the other students for their trip back. The girls had so much to brag about when they went back to school, things like the delicious lunch, going to the movies and the visit to the Sandersons' beautiful home.

Ruva's classes were going well. Her school holidays corresponded with her daughters'. The following term, she took three classes: mathematics, biology and history. She needed to be more organized, and with a good plan and schedule, she felt she would cope well. She attended classes four days a week. This seemed to be too much, but she was not going to be deterred. Beth was a great help in her education plan. She offered to pay Ruva's fees and extended her lunch hour so that she could study or catch up with her homework. Beth tutored her whenever she needed extra help with her homework.

Beth had a master's degree in mathematics, and that was not her only forte. She could also figure out science problems with ease. Upon graduating, she married her prince charming and started a family soon after. Her mother passed away a couple of months before her wedding. She cried throughout the ceremony. Her father, Dr. Blyton, gave her away. He was a clinical psychologist who worked part-time both at the university and his private clinic. Beth's father had moved from England to Southern Rhodesia when he was a young man. He left for a few years to study for his doctorate in England and did not spend a day longer after he was done. He went back, since he loved his adopted country.

Beth made the decision to be a stay-at-home mom and to revive her career when the children were older. She was raised as a Baptist, and her parents instilled in her a belief in giving, loving and respecting all human beings. She volunteered for many assignments at her church. She loved to teach, so she became a Sunday school teacher. She participated in food drives, and her list of what to do outside the home was always long.

During the midterm exams, Ruva asked Beth if she could have a week off. Beth readily agreed to the request. The day Ruva was supposed to write her biology test, she woke up sweating with a fever. She went to the hospital, hoping that she would be given something to make her feel better and able to write her test in the evening. The news she got from the doctor was not what she wanted. The doctor suspected malaria and she was admitted to the hospital.

In the ward, she asked the sister-in-charge to phone her boss and let her know that she was in the hospital, but it was nothing serious. She phoned Beth, who sounded concerned.

"I'll come over and see her this afternoon. May I ask what is wrong with her?"

"We are not sure yet. We'll have to wait for the blood tests." The nurse didn't want to divulge the illness because of the Privacy Act.

At the hospital, Beth saw Ruva's face buried in her history textbook. "This is not the time to be studying," she said as Ruva lifted her head.

Beth noticed that Ruva looked tired but seemed comfortable, since they had managed to lower her temperature. Ruva hadn't suspected that Beth would come to see her.

"You should be resting and not studying, for you will not be writing any tests soon. I'll go and tell the school of your absence and that you will not be there for the whole week and maybe longer. It depends on what the doctors have to say."

"That would be a good idea. In fact, I am not retaining

anything. Can you please ask them when I can write the tests?"

"No! When you go back to school, you will sort that out with them. Take it easy and stop stressing yourself." Beth sat in the chair for about fifteen minutes, and there were no words exchanged, since Ruva was tired and had dozed off. When Ruva looked at her and smiled, Beth felt it was time to give her a little advice then leave.

"You should take lots of water. It's good for you, especially when you have a high temperature. Is there anything else you want me to do?"

"No, I'll be out of this place in no time. I feel better already. I don't like hospitals. I would like to share something with you. I had a number of miscarriages and ended up in hospital. Mukai and I always wanted a big family, but it was not meant to be."

"I'm sorry to hear that. Thank you for sharing something so personal with me," Beth said. "If you need anything, please let me know."

"See you in a few days," said Ruva.

Beth looked hard at her and said, "Not until you're a hundred percent better."

Four days later she was discharged. Before she left the hospital grounds, she decided to phone Beth. There was a long queue at the only telephone booth, and she waited her turn patiently. She pulled from her purse a piece of paper with the telephone number, which she dialed twice before a man answered.

"Hello."

"Is that Larry?" she enquired, for the voice did not sound familiar, and she almost put the phone down, thinking she had dialed a wrong number.

"Yes, it's Larry."

"I've been discharged. Can you please tell Beth that I'll be at work tomorrow?"

"No need to rush here. Beth will manage." Larry could be distant and cold at the best of times.

The following morning, Ruva arrived at the Sandersons' at her usual time and saw a girl in the kitchen talking to Beth. She thought Beth had found a replacement and might not need her. She waited outside, trying to figure out what she was going to say.

Beth glanced at Ruva through the kitchen window and noticed that Ruva was upset. She invited her in. Ruva pulled a chair and sat down

"Ruva, you don't look well. Turn around and go back home," said Beth. The malaria had sapped her energy.

"Am I fired? When you came to visit at the hospital, why didn't you tell me that you were hiring somebody else." Ruva normally had a calm personality but at that moment she had to keep her temper. She was aware that there was always someone ready to take that job.

"You come back in a week's time. You look lethargic. Your job is safe. Chipo is Harry's sister and she's stepping in temporarily for you. That will also give you time to get stronger and prepare for the tests that you missed."

"I'm sorry, Beth. What a relief. Glad to meet you," said Ruva, patting Chipo's back. "If you're as hard-working as your brother you'll be fine."

"Is Mukai back?" Beth interjected.

"Not yet, but he should be home any time soon. See you in a week's time, since you insist."

"Wait, I'll drop you at the bus stop. I'm going to church to pick up some big bins for our food drive."

"Who gives this food?" asked Ruva.

"Anybody can give, but we rely mostly on farmers to donate maize and vegetables, and companies donate money, which we use to buy other types of food. This country has enough food to go round. Nobody should be going hungry. Even you can buy a loaf of bread and give the other half away."

Ruva looked at Beth in surprise and couldn't fathom how she could do that, since she considered herself relatively poor. It was a concept that went beyond her imagination. Beth left her confused, but she knew that she would figure it out eventually, if she could look beyond that loaf of bread.

On her way home, she passed through the school to reschedule her tests. Ruva was not somebody who procrastinated. She was eager to have this done.

"Good morning. Can I help you?" the clerk greeted her.

"Morning. I'm Ruva Ganda. I missed my tests because I was in hospital."

"Oh yes, your boss phoned. How are you feeling now?"

"I'm well enough to write my tests?"

"Whenever you're ready. You have two options. One is to write them all in one day, and the other is to write them on separate days. It's up to you. We are quite flexible here."

"I'll take the first option. I want to get this over with. How's today?"

"I expected you to choose the second option. You must have been studying."

"If I don't do it today, tomorrow there'll be something else."

The clerk went to a back room and pulled out the tests.

"Can you come with me to one of the classrooms? Which test do you want to write first, since you have three subjects?"

"Let's start with history and get those dates out of the way."

"Hand me any textbooks you might have. I'm not accusing you of cheating, but that's the policy."

"I wouldn't dream of doing that. I'd rather fail than cheat."

"Some students don't see it that way. They come here with answers written all over their bodies."

"So what do you do? Tell them to go and scrub themselves?" Ruva laughed.

The clerk laughed too and said, "You're funny. We don't give them that option. If we catch them, they are automatically disqualified and they're given a zero. The new principal is very lenient compared to the old one, who left three years ago. He was a no-nonsense man. He would expel them, and they would never be allowed to set foot in this school again."

"There's pressure to do well academically, since we're all anticipating to get better jobs when independence rolls in," Ruva said and took her seat.

Chapter Six

When she got home, Ruva was so tired that she needed a power nap to refresh herself. She slipped into her flannel nightdress, since she did not want her dress to get creased. She had planned to go back to school later for her evening class. An hour into her nap, she heard a knock at the front door. She jumped out of bed, wondering who could be at the door. She opened it slightly and peeped through. Standing there was a policeman with a file in one hand, chewing on a pencil.

"Give me a minute, sir. I'm coming." She went back into her bedroom and put on top a white-and-blue floral dressing gown, a hand-me-down from Beth. Then it dawned on her that the policeman might be bringing bad news. Could Mukai or one of the girls be in trouble?

"Are you Mrs. Ganda?"

"Yes. I hope you're not the bearer of bad news?" Immediately, she felt a shiver run down her spine. She had a suspicion that something had happened to Mukai, because he had been gone longer than usual.

"Can I come in, please?" asked the policeman.

Ruva opened the door wider to let him in, and she began to tremble with fear. She knew something was wrong when the policeman kept on looking at her and his notes.

"Can we sit down?" The policeman also looked uncomfortable.

Ruva signalled him to take a seat. She put her right hand on her tummy because her stomach was already rumbling and churning. She sat down slowly near an open window, trying to compose herself, but she expected the worst.

"I'm really sorry, Mrs. Ganda. Your husband, Mukai, was murdered in Lumba. We are not sure yet when this happened. When they found his body, it was badly decomposed. His remains were discovered floating in the river. We do not have all the details yet, and investigations are still going on."

Ruva kept on staring at the policeman in disbelief while he was speaking. She suddenly fainted and went down with a thud. She lay there for a little while before the policeman went into action. He opened the door to let in fresh air and started fanning her vigorously with his file. She quickly recovered and began reorienting herself. He helped her get back onto the sofa.

"Are you all right, Mrs. Ganda? That was a bad fall."

She felt the bump on her head and said, "Slight pain, but I'll be fine. My husband is dead?"

"Yes."

The sad news finally sank in, and she let out a wail that was so loud, Shungu could hear her from her house. She had seen the policeman going into Ruva's house and soon after she heard the cry. She went over to see what was happening.

She barged in and sat next to Ruva. "Sir, can you tell me, who is dead?" She had made the deduction from the wailing.

"Mr. Ganda." The policeman looked relieved that there was someone else to comfort Ruva.

"What happened?" Shungu began to wail too, uncontrollably.

"He was murdered in Lumba. I can't give you any more information."

"Have you made any arrests?"

"As I said, ma'am, I don't have all those details. This is a police case, and things are going to take time. You will be dealing with main police station because this is an international case. I'm sorry; I have got to go now."

"Ruva, where do we start?" Shungu asked.

"I have to get hold of Beth and let her know. Surprisingly, she kept on asking me if Mukai was home, as if she had some premonition of his death. We must also inform Batsirai."

"Who is Batsirai?"

"He's Mukai's oldest brother. You wouldn't know him. He doesn't visit us at all."

"Do you have their phone numbers?"

Ruva started rummaging through her handbag, looking for her notebook.

"Please go and phone them and tell them that we are going to the main police station to arrange for the body to be brought back home."

Shungu trotted to the nearby shopping centre to make the phone calls. She entered a phone kiosk. The clerk was seated behind the desk with her head bobbing up and down, wearing a cap that covered her face.

She looked up and asked, "Local or long distance?"

"Two local calls," Shungu responded.

"Pick up phone number 3, and tell me when you're done with the first call."

She picked up the receiver and dialled the number. The phone rang a couple of times, and Beth picked it up.

"Hello, can I help you?"

Shungu took a few seconds before answering and then said,

"My name is Shungu. I'm Ruva's friend. Her husband, Mukai, was murdered in Lumba. Ruva and I will be going to the main police station in the city to get the details."

"Oh my! How is Ruva doing? Tell her that I'll meet her there at 4:00 p.m."

"Bye." Shungu hung up.

She looked at the clerk and said, "I'm done with the first call. Can you set me up for the second one?"

"Pick up the phone again and go ahead."

Shungu dialled the number, and the operator on the other side said, "Good afternoon. Can I help you?"

"I would like to speak to Batsirai Ganda?"

"I'll have to take a message. He is not allowed to leave his work station unattended."

Batsirai worked on big steel machines that moulded pipes for the gold mines. He did not do any better than his brother financially, although his job had the potential of paying more money. He was underpaid.

"Please tell him that his brother, Mukai, died."

"Since it's a relative who died, can I put you on hold while I give him the message?"

"Pass on the message. I've to go." Shungu didn't want to wait, for she would have paid more for the call.

She put down the receiver and asked the girl for the cost while counting her coins. The clerk didn't answer. Her head was resting on the desk; she was asleep. Shungu moved closer to her, shook her by the shoulder, and the clerk opened her eyes slightly. Shungu lost her patience and repeated, "How much are the calls?"

"Seventy-five cents."

"Do you know that I could have walked away without paying? I wonder if your boss knows that you sleep on the job.

Get enough sleep at home and come here refreshed to serve your customers," Shungu snapped.

When she got back, she escorted Ruva to the main police station. Beth was waiting in her Mercedes-Benz, looking at her watch, since they were running late. She was reflecting on the misfortunes that had recently befallen her employees. She spotted Ruva crossing the street, got out of the car and moved towards her. Ruva saw Beth and was overcome by emotion. She walked to the stairs at the police station and sat down, covered her face with her hands and wept buckets. Beth sat on her left side and Shungu on the other. She actually alternated leaning her head on their shoulders. In the midst of her weeping, she said, "I'm glad that you're both here with me today. On my own, I wouldn't know what to do."

Beth took charge because she knew that her racial profile would carry a lot of weight when negotiating. "We should discuss what the immediate needs are after talking to the police."

Shungu confirmed what Ruva knew already. "I don't have the means, but I promise to be there when you need me as a friend."

"Any kind of support is important in time of bereavement. Are you the one who called earlier on?" asked Beth.

"Yes, I'm Shungu."

After a while, Ruva stood up and said, "I need a moment to gather my thoughts." She clasped her hands behind her head with her head tilted down. She looked up to the heavens and prayed.

When she lowered her head, they joined hands with her, forming a circle, and Beth broke the silence. "Can we go in and see if somebody can help us before they start packing up for the day?"

Ruva nodded.

They walked a few stairs up into the hall of the big building. Beth started looking around to see where they could get help. She approached the receptionist and asked for directions. The receptionist pointed to her right without saying a word. Beth noticed the direction arrows pointing to a homicide office, and she led the way. The office was around the corner. The door was closed but there was a sign that read, "Come in. Door closed on account of the weather." Beth had always wondered why they put the sign up inside the buildings, for it didn't make sense. They knocked and went in. There were two white detectives who simultaneously looked at the clock.

Beth assumed the spokesperson's role. She put her arm around Ruva and said, "We're here for Mukai Ganda, who was murdered in Lumba and his wife was told to come here for more information."

"Do you have the docket number?" asked one of the detectives, who was perched on the desk with his legs crossed.

"Ruva, do you have the papers?" Beth asked.

"In the confusion, I forgot them at home."

The other policemen stood up, placed one leg on the chair and rested both hands on his waist and said, "Our filing system is in numerical order. Come back tomorrow with all the paperwork. Where do you live?" He glanced again at the clock.

"Highfield, sir."

"Sorry, it'll have to be tomorrow."

As the ladies stood there open-mouthed in disbelief, another white detective walked in and heard Beth saying, "I'm sure there are other ways of finding that file so that we can start the process."

The detective who walked in asked, "What is the name of the person?"

"Mukai Ganda, who was murdered in Malawi." Beth moved closer to him. He looked friendly and helpful.

"I'm familiar with that case. I'll bring the file." Meanwhile, the other two detectives had put on their jackets and slipped out of the office, leaving the three women standing there.

The detective noticed that his colleagues had left and said, "Nobody stays a minute later than five o'clock. Moral obligation doesn't exist any more in this place."

The three women could not believe their luck. Shungu said to Ruva, "It's the prayer you said out there that has been answered, my friend."

"Here will be a good place to sit," said the detective, directing them to some dirty and worn-out chairs. "I'm Detective Guy Miller, and you must be Mrs. Ganda." He guessed right, since Ruva's eyes were puffy from crying and she kept wiping them with her hand.

"I'm really sorry for the loss of your husband. I'll do what I can to help. I must warn you that it was a heinous murder. What we know so far is that his body was found naked floating in the river, decapitated. He had multiple stab wounds all over his body. There were signs especially on his hands, which showed that he went down fighting. Whoever murdered him had some evil motive. His truck was found completely burnt out about ten kilometres from where the body was discovered." He had his eyes down on the file.

While the detective was explaining this gruesome scene, Ruva had her eyes closed, but tears were running down her cheeks, her teeth were clenched tightly together and her hands were resting on her tummy, clasped into tight fists. The scenario caused her terrible pain. At one point she stopped listening and shut it out.

"When were you informed of his death?" Beth asked.

"We knew some time last week, and we sent a policeman to this address twice, but there was nobody at home. Today was his third visit."

"I don't remember him saying that. Anyway, everything is so blurry," Ruva replied.

"I doubt if it was the same policeman who came before. They are supposed to leave a note for you to contact the police," said the detective.

"I didn't check my mail."

"It's the time she was in hospital," Beth explained. "How does the process work?"

"What you have to understand is that this happened in another country, and the homicide department there is going to perform an autopsy and more investigations before they can release the body. Hopefully, it's done soon. It might take days, weeks or months to complete their own investigations, and it all depends on the leads they have. From my experience, there will be delays, twist, turns and frustrations on your part."

He paused to give Beth a chance to ask a question, since he noticed that she was impatiently waiting to say something.

"Will you be doing your own investigation from this side?"

"Definitely, we'll be doing our part. You never know, maybe the killers are from here. They might have followed him or travelled with him. We shall cover all bases in order to solve this case.

"Mrs. Ganda, you should go home and get some rest, but I'd like you to come back tomorrow morning so that I can ask you more questions that can give me an idea of who Mukai was. Can you be here at nine in the morning?"

"How is that going to help?" she asked.

"Knowing the company he kept and some of the things that he did on his trip might help us with the investigations. You might never know."

"I never accompanied him on his trips, so I wouldn't know. However, I'll be here tomorrow and I'll answer and cooperate as best as I can. Do you know if Rothwells is aware of his death?" That was the company that Mukai worked for, and she was hoping that it would help with burial costs.

"The company was contacted, and I understand they sent a representative to your house last week too. Would you like us to postpone our meeting to 1:00 p.m. so that you can go and see them in the morning? I'd like to do this as soon as possible. If we've witnesses, we can move faster when things are still fresh on their minds."

"I agree, sir." She didn't want to be the one slowing down the process.

"Ruva, I think you should come with me tonight so that you can have a good sleep, and then I can bring you back here tomorrow," Beth said with concern.

"That's not the way we do things," Shungu said.

"Thank you, Beth. I can't desert relatives and friends and the twins have to be informed."

"We should spare the girls for now until we know when Mukai will be home. I'll go and pick them up, if you can give me permission. You don't want them to miss school, especially when we don't have a clue of how long the investigation will take."

Beth turned and addressed the detective. "Sir, we would like to express our gratitude for taking this case on, and we look forward to working with you. We trust justice will prevail. Your compassion will not go unnoticed. We'll be back tomorrow. Thank you again." She extended her hand to him, and they left.

When they stepped out of the building, Beth said, "We should get a lawyer to be present tomorrow when the detective asks you questions. My brother-in-law, Brian, is a lawyer. You've met him at my house before. I'll contact him as soon as I get home and give him a rundown of what we heard today. I'm sure he can help us out. Let us meet at the cathedral at nine in the morning and then go from there. You need legal advice when you approach the company so that you can get all that Mukai is entitled to. You don't want the company to take advantage of your vulnerability."

"I can't afford to pay those huge lawyer's fees," said Ruva.

"Don't you worry, I'll talk to him and see what he says. He is a good man. I trust that he will help us."

"I'd like to come back tomorrow. I'll be there till the end. Please count me in," said Shungu, who had been unusually quiet the whole day.

Beth drove them home. This was her first time in the townships. Shungu directed her, since Ruva had a lot to sort out mentally.

When they arrived home, there were people waiting to show their sympathy. Shungu became Ruva's caretaker and shielded her from all these inquisitive people. The next morning, they slipped out of the house undetected and went back to meet up again with Beth.

"Ruva, you look so worn out. Shungu, did she sleep at all?"

"She didn't. People sang and danced the whole night."

"Lack of sleep, plus you hadn't recovered from malaria. It's taking a toll on you," Beth said with concern. "Is that what your custom demands?"

"You've a lot to learn about black people," said Shungu.

"Excuse my ignorance. Let's go across the street into that cafe and find something to eat. I didn't have anything to eat myself because I was running late. It wouldn't do us any good going around with grumbling tummies."

An alert waitress received them as they came in. "Good morning! Our special menu today is two fried eggs, sunny side up, one boerewors sausage, tomato and two pieces of toast. I'll give you a few more minutes to browse through the menu."

"No. We don't have much time. Ladies, would you like to order now?"

"I'm not hungry. I'll have toast and tea. You two can have the special. Oh, by the way, Beth, you do not like fried eggs. I should know that." Ruva remembered her first lesson at the Sandersons' house and also that Beth was not a big eater.

"No, I'm going to have fruit salad and black tea. Shungu, what are you having?"

"Is that all you're eating? I'll take the special and coffee. I always feel hunger pains in the mornings, I don't know why." Shungu was patting her tummy. They were served their beverages. Shungu took her coffee and started blowing on it to bring the temperature down.

"It's too hot, is it?" Beth asked, hoping to interrupt the annoying noise. She turned to Ruva. "I talked to my brother-in-law, and he will be joining us at Rothwells at ten today. He said he is going to waive all the fees for you if the company fails to pay. He'll accompany us to the homicide office too this afternoon. It's wonderful to have him by our side for advice."

After a while, Shungu asked, "Isn't it time to go?" after glancing at the clock on the wall. She scooped the last bit of food onto the fork with her finger and stuffed it into her mouth.

"You're right. Let me go and pay, and we can start moving. Remember, we don't have an appointment. Let's hope the person in charge of these issues will be available to see us."

"You nibbled at your food. We don't know when we'll have a chance to eat again," Shungu whispered to Ruva.

Ruva did not answer. She covered her food with a serviette before standing up and heading for the door.

The ride to Rothwells took fifteen minutes. Beth parked her car in a shady spot and looked for Brian's car, but it was not there despite them running ten minutes late. A few minutes later, they saw him pulling into the parking lot.

"He's here." The three women got out of the car.

"Sorry, ladies, to keep you waiting. Before we go in there, I would like to ask Ruva a few questions. Is it all right if we chat in my car?"

"Go ahead, Ruva," Beth said, pushing her lightly.

Brian removed a pile of files from the passenger seat and apologized for the mess. As she sat down, she noticed a little plaque on the dashboard that read: "BMW will take you anywhere safely." She wondered if this car was better than Beth's Mercedes-Benz, for she remembered Harry telling her that Mercedes was the best car make when he was meticulously cleaning it.

Before Brian got into the car, he removed his jacket and placed it on the back seat. He pulled a notebook and pen from his briefcase.

"No introductions, since we've met before. I didn't want them to join us in this conversation, since this is a private and personal matter. Beth understands the law and client privileges, and if you want to tell her later, it's up to you."

"I'll take your advice."

"Let's get on with the questions. Your husband's name is Mukai Ganda, right?"

"Yes."

"How long did he work for this company?"

"I don't remember, but it was a long time."

"They'll tell us. Do you know how much your husband earned per month?"

"I've no idea. He never revealed that information, but he saved a small amount of money."

"That's common, unfortunately. Do you know where he saved the money?"

"I can't remember. I never paid any attention when he showed me the savings account book." She lifted her brow and there was uncertainty in her voice.

"What about an insurance policy, did he say anything about that?"

"I remember him saying, 'When I die, you'll be a rich widow.' I didn't ask for more information because I never thought this day would come so soon," she said regretfully.

"Do you know whether it's personal insurance or company-initiated? Whatever it is, that's a plus for you. What would you want the company to do for you and the children?"

"I'd like the company to pay for Hilda's school fees. Matie has a scholarship until she finishes high school. First and foremost, they must pay for the funeral expenses." She could only come up with two demands before she had a mental block. She could not think of what she would like the company to do for her. She touched her forehead and started massaging her temples to relieve the mounting stress.

Brian said, "I'll tell you what I'm going to ask the company on your behalf. You must know that they do not have an obligation to agree to everything, but we'll try our luck. We'll ask them to cover the funeral expenses, pay fees for the twins until they are done university and give you a one-year salary. I'm sure he has accident insurance, since this was a high-risk job, and a sizeable pension. Let's not forget to ask them to pay for all the legal fees. Anyway, let's go in and see what they are prepared to put on the table."

"What's going to happen if they refuse to pay for all these things that you mentioned, especially the legal fees?" She remembered that Beth had said he was going to waive those fees.

"We'll cross that bridge when we come to it."

Brian went to Beth's car and said to her, "Can you two wait here? I don't think it would be a good idea for us to invade this company. Ruva and I will go in and talk to them."

Shungu came out of the car and yelled to Ruva, "Can I come with you?"

"Don't you worry, she'll be fine," Beth said. "Brian is here to protect her legal interests, and we're here to give her support."

Brian and Ruva approached the receptionist. "Good morning. Can we talk to somebody regarding my client's husband, Mukai Ganda, who died in Lumba?"

"Please take a seat. I'll find the manager."

It took a while before the manager appeared. "I understand that you're Mrs. Ganda," he said, extending his hand for a firm handshake. "I'm Willard Ngoma and I was his manager." Then he sat on the adjacent chair. "Sorry for the long wait. When I got the message, I was in a meeting. We were shocked and saddened by Mukai's death. He was one of our most committed employees. He'll be missed. This must be hard on you too."

She nodded. "This has been a nightmare, and as it sinks in, it's becoming real and unbearable."

He turned to Brian, who was seated opposite them, flipping through *Time* magazine, pretending not to pay attention but following the conversation. Mr. Ngoma asked him, "Have you been attended to, sir?"

Brian stood up, placed the magazine back in the rack, and straightened his tie, which was perfectly straight. He said, "My name is Brian Sanderson, and I was retained by Mrs. Ganda as her legal representative. I'm with Sanderson and Cox Law Firm."

Brian was flamboyant and had a dash of arrogance in his character that showed in his mannerisms. He put his hands in his pockets, rocking back and forth on his heels.

"Oh! Mrs. Ganda, I didn't think you'd be retaining a lawyer for something as straightforward and simple as this. However, let's go into my office?" Mr. Ngoma led the way.

"She retained me as her lawyer since this is new to her," Brian said before Ruva had the chance to reply.

They went upstairs to his office, where Mr. Ngoma apologized for its size. "Three people are a crowd in this office, but let me get an extra chair, and we should all be able to squeeze in."

Ruva was happy that Shungu and Beth hadn't joined them, for there was not even standing room. Mr. Ngoma offered the chair to Brian, who was standing.

"Mrs. Ganda, have you been in touch with the police?"

"Yes, I've been, and we are meeting the detective in charge of this case this afternoon." She looked at Brian to check whether that information was all right to divulge.

"They have been keeping us in the loop. Mukai was with us for sixteen years, and he had a clean driving record, was the longest serving driver in the company and his attendance record was impeccable. We never had any problems with him," said Mr. Ngoma with pride. "We appreciate his service to the company. In his honour, we have put together a package for you. Definitely, the first thing we are going to do is pay for all the funeral expenses. We have a capped amount to give you. We cannot give you a blank cheque, for we are running a business."

"Excuse me, Mr. Ngoma, that language deserves an apology. This lady is grieving. Sensitivity is required in this situation. Nobody is expecting a blank cheque, but only what she's entitled to." Brian's reprimand was firm.

"I'm sorry, I didn't mean to be rude. As for the funeral expenses, we'll ask for your input when the time comes. Secondly, we'll give you a six-month payout. Thirdly, we'll initiate payment of his accident insurance policy. Here is a form that you can sign consenting to its contents."

"Not so fast. My client will not be signing any form now, because she has other requests, which we trust will be honoured. I don't know whether you're aware that Mukai had two daughters in boarding schools. We are asking if the company can pay their fees throughout university."

"Mr. Sanderson, the payment from the insurance policy can be channelled towards their education."

"I don't know how much we are talking about here, but my experience tells me that it's not a substantial amount. Hence, we've made this special request. Instead of six months' salary, a year's salary would be appropriate. She might need psychological counselling for this horrendous crime. For how long, time will tell. I'd like to believe that after sixteen years, there is a reasonable pension and substantial payout from the insurance. Lastly, Mrs. Ganda has already accrued legal bills. We ask that the company cover that as well. Can I have a glass of water?"

As Mr. Ngoma was pouring out the water, he said, "I'm not in a position to grant those requests. I'll consult with my boss, who will definitely present it to the board. I'll get back to you as soon as I've all the answers."

Mr. Ngoma seemed taken aback by these developments. He had expected her to come in, sign the consent form, and leave without any objection or further demands.

"On behalf of your committed employee, I trust that you'll fulfill his wishes by providing for his family. Mukai sacrificed a lot for them, and I expect the company will respect that by showing generosity and compassion. I suggest that you communicate with me rather than my client, who is in mourning. Here is my card with my address and phone number for you to contact me." Brian, being a lawyer, laid out his closing arguments with conviction. "Mrs. Ganda, we should be going, unless you have any other questions." Ruva had never been addressed as Mrs. Ganda as many times in one sitting as these two gentlemen had done in that meeting.

"Thank you for meeting with us promptly without an appointment. I hope I'll hear from you soon, through my lawyer, of course," Ruva said, reinforcing Brian's statement.

Brian stood up, buttoned his jacket and guided Ruva out first. Beth and Shungu were anxious to hear what had transpired in that office. Ruva and Brian were not saying much.

"Did they give you money?" Shungu asked as she got back into the car.

"Not yet. It's not as simple as that but they'll let me know." Ruva was uncomfortable telling her the finer details.

"How are you going to feed all those people gathered at your place?" said Shungu with some concern. She cleared her throat and spat on a handkerchief, which she shoved back into her handbag.

"Shungu, please don't put pressure on her," said Beth.

Shungu was a very high-strung woman and could be pushy. Surprisingly, during those two days, she was holding herself together.

"Talking about feeding people, do we have enough time for a quick lunch?" said Brian, looking at his watch. He placed his briefcase on top of his car and took out Ruva's file, which he started updating. "I might as well work until you ladies decide. Choose the place, and lunch is on me."

"Let's go to Cathy's Restaurant," Beth suggested. "We can walk to the police station from there." The three ladies left together in Beth's car. They had lunch and left in time for the next appointment.

Beth led the way. She peeped through the window to see if there was anybody in the office. Guy Miller, the detective, was also standing on the other side of the door, waiting, and their eyes met. He opened the door and said, "Good afternoon. It's best if I talk to Mrs. Ganda in private. You can all wait for her in the hall. We'll not be long."

"I'm Brian Sanderson, her legal representative. If you don't mind, I'd like to be present." Brian always made his presence felt.

"Of course, you can come in, sir. Take a seat and make yourselves comfortable. Mrs. Ganda, I would like to let you know that I haven't heard anything new since our discussion yesterday, but can you tell me what he was like as a husband?"

"He was a loving father and husband. He provided as best as he could for us."

"What kind of things did he share with you regarding his trips, especially in Malawi?"

"He didn't say much except that he met some very nice people along the way. Some of them accommodated him and treated him like family. It was a blessing, for it helped with the loneliness that he felt on the road."

"Where exactly were these people that treated him like family, and did he share their names with you or what they did to make him feel accepted?"

"You know, when somebody welcomes you into his or her home, you feel the warmth and you know it. But to answer the first part of the question, I don't know."

"Did he mention any enemies at all?"

"He didn't have any close friends as such. As for enemies, I don't know. He used to say at times that boys stopped him and demanded cigarettes. As long as he gave them what they wanted, they didn't bother him, and they would let him go. The soldiers, on the other hand, used to stop him and check his truck inside and out. They always asked him if he was in contact with the boys."

"When you say boys do you mean the freedom fighters?"

"Yes, sir."

Brian was listening and noted that Ruva had given information that made Mukai look like an accomplice, by giving cigarettes to the freedom fighters.

"I have been following the interview. Is there something in particular you're trying to zero in?" Brian eventually asked.

Mr. Miller ignored Brian's question. "Mrs. Ganda, that's it from me. Do you have any questions?"

"I'm anxious to know when the body will be here."

"I'll phone them this afternoon. I wish I could do something to expedite it. I know how dreadful the waiting can be. It brings back vivid memories of my brother who was killed in Mozambique when his military plane was shot down six months ago. By the way, he was a soldier in the Rhodesian forces. His body was burnt beyond recognition. Up to this day, I don't know if we buried the right man. It took more than a fortnight before they brought him home. The waiting felt like ages. I've been in your shoes. I know exactly how you feel."

There was dead silence before Brian said, "Those are the consequences of war. But all we hear is propaganda about how many freedom fighters they have killed. White soldiers have paid the price too. I hate wars."

"Mr. Sanderson, how will I get hold of you if something comes up?"

"Here is my card."

Ruva and Brian left the office and met up with Shungu and Beth, who were eager to know if there was anything new.

"That was a good hour wasted," Brian reported.

While they were discussing the next move, Brian whispered something into Ruva's ear, and it left a smile on her face that showed her beautiful teeth.

Shungu pulled Ruva aside, and they walked behind Beth and Brian. "If you're not careful, that lawyer will take all your money. You're putting too much trust in these people."

Ruva kept quiet, since she didn't see the point in arguing. She appreciated Brian's contribution.

Beth drove them home. As people saw Ruva, they began wailing and running towards her. Shungu directed her inside the house. Beth followed them, feeling very much out of place. Ruva sat down, acknowledged the condolences and began to sob uncontrollably.

Shungu looked at the crowd that had gathered and said, "Beth, you see the number of people gathered here? We need money to feed them."

"I think you should tell them to disperse for now. We don't know when Mukai will come home. People will have to be patient with us. Do you think Ruva should be here? She isn't going to have any rest at all."

"Beth, you do not understand our culture." Shungu was getting agitated, and she kept cursing under her breath. "That's not done. We do things differently from you white people." People stopped singing and their eyes were fixed on Shungu. She became aware of the instant audience and continued exercising her authority. "Who are you to tell them to leave? Ruva is not going anywhere. This is her home. You're not the decision-maker here, and these are her people, who'll be here supporting her when you're long gone to your white world." Beth recoiled from Shungu's abrasive words.

Ruva did not stir while Shungu was ranting on and on. When she had heard enough she pointed a finger as ammunition and in a firm, strong and commanding voice, she yelled, "Shungu!" The echo of her voice resonated through the brick walls and could be heard outside.

These two women had become friends when Ruva moved into her house two or three years after the girls were born. During all those years, Shungu had never heard Ruva raise her voice with that kind of fury, frowning at her with such intensity and calling her name with so much outrage. She instantly knew that she had crossed a line. She didn't attempt to redeem herself, for Ruva made it obvious that this behaviour was not tolerated. She gestured for Shungu to leave her house.

Beth was standing frozen, confused and blushing. She stretched an arm over and patted Ruva on the back to get her attention. Ruva looked back, and Beth handed her an envelope with money. She cautiously manoeuvred her way out of the crowd, walking slowly and looking over her shoulder, because she was scared she might be mobbed.

For two weeks, there was no word from Beth or Brian. Ruva wondered if she had a job or whether Brian was still her advocate. Shungu had let her down, and Mukai was lying in some mortuary. She felt abandoned by everybody she trusted. While waiting for any word and with those grim thoughts flooding her mind, she became more desolate.

As she sat on her veranda in the morning, looking back at the times she and Mukai had spent there, she saw Harry checking her address from an envelope.

"Harry, you're at the right address," Ruva called.

He walked closer and said, "Hello, Ruva. My condolences." He gazed at the obvious sadness in her eyes. "Beth is worried about you. She asked me to come and keep you updated. You have to meet her and Brian at Rothwells at nine in the morning, tomorrow. They were informed that Mukai's body is on its way today, but paperwork can only be done tomorrow at Harare General Hospital. Beth is also asking for permission in this letter to go and fetch the girls." He paused for a minute then continued. "You have to sign it and write names of the schools. She said you have to be prepared for a long day."

"When is she going to fetch the girls? I don't know, how I can ever repay her," Ruva said with deep gratitude.

"Maybe this afternoon. Beth's dad is visiting, and I heard them talking about him accompanying her," Harry said. "I'll confide in you, because I went through the same emotions that you are going through now. Anna and I were so much in love, and we were planning on telling Beth that we were getting married. Anna was four months pregnant. After her death, I didn't see the point in explaining all that to Beth. I would like it to remain our secret. Don't say anything to her."

"Trust me on that one." Harry didn't know that Beth

suspected something, and Ruva kept her word. "They say time heals all wounds. I hope that will apply to both of us. Tell Beth that I'll be there tomorrow." She signed both letters and handed them back to Harry. "My poor girls, I can't imagine how devastated they'll be."

"I've to rush back. Beth said not to bring your friend. I guess you know whom she was referring to."

That night Ruva could not sleep. Her mind was in turmoil. Mukai was in the mortuary, the girls were now aware of their father's death and relatives were waiting in the wings with their demands.

Beth left with her father on her journey to fetch the girls. They picked up Matie first at Lord Armstrong. At the school, Beth explained the situation to the principal, and Matie was tracked down. Upon seeing them, it quickly became clear to her that something was not right, judging from the sombre expressions on the faces of all three people in the room.

Beth took Matie's hands and looked her in the face. She took a big breath and said, "Matie, I'm sorry, your father was killed while on one of his trips, and your mother wants you home for the funeral."

Trying to process what she had just heard, Matie asked, "When is the funeral?"

"Thursday." Beth turned to the science teacher who happened to be there. "Can I go to the dormitory and help her put things together?"

Matie finally buried her face in Beth's bosom and started to cry, and after composing herself she asked, "Does Hilda know?"

"We're going to her school now."

Dr. Blyton took some time before introducing himself since he waited for Matie to calm down. "I'm Dr. Blyton. I'm sorry to meet you under these circumstances." Matie kept quiet.

Beth's father was a good storyteller. Throughout the journey, he talked non-stop about his experiences, which Beth had heard numerous times. Matie was periodically switching him off and sinking into her own sorrow.

It seemed as if they had been travelling forever when Beth finally said, "We made it in good time. I wonder if we have to go to the nuns' residence or principal's office. No, let's start at the principal's office." She parked in the visitors' parking.

To their amazement, they saw Hilda sorting mail outside the office. "Matie, what are you doing here?"

Matie embraced her sister and said, "Baba is dead, and we have to go home for the funeral."

"What happened to him?"

"I don't have all the details but Beth said he was murdered in Malawi. It's ironic that he died there. That's Beth's dad in the car. Bring earplugs if you have some because the man talked non-stop all the way here. I mean it," she whispered.

Beth got out of the car and watched the girls standing there as if there was a mirror reflecting one image. She folded her arms and said, "Hilda, I'm sorry."

"Thank you, Beth. How's Mama doing?"

"She's holding her own. She's a strong woman." Beth cupped Hilda's face in her hands and placed a light kiss on her forehead, and that is when Hilda started to cry.

One of the students ran to the nuns' house to tell them about the tragedy. Sister Leah came and prayed for the girls and their family before seeing them off.

The girls cried themselves to sleep in the car, and Beth woke them up when they arrived at her house.

The following morning, she took on the role of counsellor. She talked about the grieving process, which could manifest as fear, guilt, anger, pain, sadness and despair, and how to deal with it. She advised them to take baby steps to recovery. Their sorrow was consistent with the deep pain they were experiencing, but the support and comfort they were shown lifted them up. They admired this beautiful and loving woman who gave them not only tools to help them navigate through their time of mourning, but lifelong lessons.

The next morning, Ruva left with Batsirai and an uncle who insisted on tagging along. Upon arriving at the company office, they found Brian waiting.

"Is Beth bringing the girls? Do you know?" she asked Brian.

"Everything is fine. They will join us later. Beth reported that the girls handled it better than expected. Of course, they are sad. She didn't think it would be a good idea to drag them along with us today.

"Gentlemen, can you excuse us? Ruva and I will go and see Mr. Ngoma, and hopefully everything will be settled today," said Brian.

The gentlemen were upset, since they wanted to hear for themselves what was included in the package. They believed they had a stake in it. They were looking at it from the cultural point of view that automatically made them inheritors of the estate.

The company met most of the demands, except that it would pay out full salary for six months and half salary for the remainder of the year. They made her sign an affidavit declaring that she would never reveal the contents of the offer to anybody.

"Ruva, that offer is not too shabby. Let's take it and run."

"I can't run, for I've never been an athlete, but I'll walk from here with my head held up high."

Brian laughed. "You misunderstood me. It doesn't matter anyway. We should scoot to the bank and open an account for you before you're robbed by your in-laws," he added humorously.

The next stop, the hospital, was the most difficult. Ruva, Batsirai and the uncle went into the mortuary to identify the body. When Ruva saw the nametag tied to the foot with a missing baby toe, she was satisfied that it was Mukai. A snake had bitten his leg when he was a young boy, and his toe was amputated because of gangrene. That was enough for her, and she left.

Mukai's brother and uncle the torso examined closely, counted the number of stab wounds, looked at the hole left by the decapitated head, and the examination confirmed the gruesome murder. When Batsirai went to sign papers for the release of the body, he was visibly angry. They seemed more upset with Ruva than with the murderers, because they felt she did not care any more since she was given the money.

Ruva and her brother-in-law went to the funeral home to make the final arrangements. Ruva chose a casket, which the brother-in-law thought too expensive.

"We know you have money to burn, but he doesn't need that fancy coffin. For goodness sake, the man is dead."

"That's not up for discussion," said Ruva.

"You're on your own, but we'll see." Ruva was left to finalize the details on her own, since Batsirai was upset.

As she walked towards the parking lot with her hand shading her eyes from the bright sun, she saw Beth and the twins waiting. The moment of truth had come when she had to tell the girls herself that they no longer had a father. She suddenly became tongue-tied. She was still thinking about Batsirai and his frayed emotions.

"Are you okay, Mama?" Hilda asked, but it was plain that her mother was in a daze.

Matie did not say anything, but when they looked each other in the eye, they both began to cry. Ruva pulled a white lacy handkerchief from her bra and started wiping away their tears. She found her words and said, "Yes, we'll miss him, but we'll survive this together." She fished an envelope with money from her handbag and handed it to Beth.

Beth looked her right in the eye and said, "Be strong. Let me know if you need anything. I'm sure you have arranged everything the way you want it to be. Where and when is he going to be laid to rest?"

"The service will be on Thursday at two in the afternoon at the Methodist Church on Highfield Road, and we'll lay him to rest at Highfield Cemetery nearby."

The girls spoke at the funeral, and surprisingly, their voices were as clear as a church bell. As they stood at the altar, the eerie silence in the church didn't deter their composure. Their tears dried up for that moment as they gave a short and moving tribute to honour their father. Matie spoke about the void he had left in their lives.

"Our father was a man who had strong ambitions for us. He worked hard so that our lives could be better. His love for us had no limits, and his generosity knew no boundaries. He truly cared for my mother, sister and I. People who have no respect for mankind cut his life short. They took away our father and a husband prematurely, but justice will prevail. We shall miss him."

At the end of her speech, her voice quivered with emotion. She took a step back and gave Matie her place in the spotlight. She talked about what he meant to them.

"Although our dreams of spending time with you have been shattered, we'll hang on to the fond memories that you left behind for us. Whoever took your life is not a hero, but you'll always be our own honourable soldier. You stood guard for us, and we felt safe in your presence. We shall celebrate your life with zest, and you shall never be forgotten. Father, rest in peace."

The crowd applauded when they finished speaking. They put their hands behind each other's backs and walked away from the pulpit. These eulogies were encouraging to their mother, since they gave her strength to fight on their behalf.

Ruva, as heartbroken as she was, beamed with pride as the girls stood before the crowd of about 150 people who had come to pay their last respects, including Mukai's workmates and Beth with her own entourage that included Harry and two private detectives who did not make themselves conspicuous. Brian and Larry did not attend. Shungu was there and when people came out of the church, she went to Ruva and said, "The girls were great. I liked their speeches. Send them my way when I'm dead."

"Your boys will be there to do it their own way," Ruva replied.

"You're holding yourself together well. Is that the money you received?" Ruva looked at her scornfully and Shungu knew that she had overstepped her boundary again.

"That's something I'll not be discussing now or anytime

soon with you. If you'll excuse me, I still need to bury my husband." Ruva walked away. She had heard from her other neighbours that Shungu was spreading rumours about her having received lots of money from the company.

Ruva passed up Beth's offer to take the girls back to school. She opted to take them by bus and get acquainted with their travel routes. Ruva liked their schools, for she believed that they were teaching the girls to be positive, confident and articulate. She met some of their teachers, friends and nuns, who promised to do all they could to help them get back on their feet.

Chapter Seven

Ruva's ultimate goal was to be self-sufficient, and to achieve it, she had to make progress in her studies, encourage the girls to do the same and organize her finances.

Mukai's death took a toll on her. Getting over it was an arduous process. She notified Beth that she was going to take time off work. The amount of money she got from the company and the insurance payout was enough to make her comfortable for a while.

Mukai's discontented relatives continued to be a thorn in her side, and she phoned Beth for advice.

"I'm not going to let them get away with that nonsense."

"Contact Brian. He might give you better legal advice than I can. It's a pity that Mukai didn't have a will."

However, Ruva had mixed feelings about taking the legal route straight away. She still wanted to maintain a cordial relationship with her family, if only they could be reasonable.

"I'll see if talking to them can bring any positive dialogue, and if it's not resolved, then I'll certainly contact Brian. I don't have any other choice."

Negotiations with Batsirai and his uncle didn't resolve much, since Ruva was not changing her position. A year before Mukai's death, Batsirai had divorced his wife, who disappeared with their two young boys. He did all he could to find them but was never successful. He went into a deep depression. Although Mukai and Batsirai were never close, nobody would ever know if it was Mukai's death that eventually drove him to the edge. His behaviour changed dramatically and Ruva became a target. He started harassing and threatening her to the point that she was scared of him. He would visit at odd hours, making unreasonable demands and using obscenities. Because of his continued threats, Ruva was gripped by fear, and she became a prisoner in her own home. She wrote letters to the girls, warning them to be careful. She was scared that she would harm her or the girls. It became ugly, and she reported him to the police, but that didn't stop him.

Finally, she went to see Brian Sanderson in his office and sought his legal advice. "Brian, can you please help me to keep these relatives at bay, for they still want a piece of the pie."

"Why did it take you so long to come and see me?"

"I thought he would go away and leave me alone, since I had reported him to the police. Unfortunately, he has shown disregard for the law. What am I to do?" Ruva was sweating as she spoke.

"I'll ask the police to send summons for harassment. Meanwhile, work on having a phone installed so that you can phone the police if he comes to your place. Have you been in touch with Beth? I had lunch with them on Sunday, and she didn't mention it."

"Yes." Her voice was low. "She knows what's going on but not the severity of it all."

"We'll put an end to this," said Brian firmly.

In that period, when Batsirai was busy threatening her, she got news from Brian that there were three Malawian suspects in custody, charged with Mukai's death.

"The inquest is going to begin first week of February. You should go and hear what happened," said Brian.

"I would like to go, but I could be there for weeks, if not months, and what about accommodation? Will I be able to handle what is to come? I need time to think this through. On the other hand, I might regret it if I don't go."

"Hmm. As for accommodation, you can surely find something reasonable and you're also right that it could drag on for months. However, I do understand how you feel. It's not easy, but at times you have to work through your fears."

Ruva looked at him then nodded a few times and said, "From the way I feel, it seems as if nothing can be of any help right now."

"You should give psychotherapy a try," Brian said carefully.

Ruva thought for a moment and then said, "I'll pass for now. I'm not one to go and tell strangers about my life. Going back to my culture, one confides in their elders regarding those issues."

"You are selective about this cultural thing. Anyway, think about it and go from there."

"Surely, I've my work cut out for me," said Ruva. "Eventually things will fall into place."

During the school holiday, Ruva received a letter from Beth with a surprise offer.

Dear Ruva,

You and your girls have had a rough year, and I would like you to join my family and me on a two-week holiday in Cape Town. Larry's boss offered us a house, big enough to accommodate us all. My father is joining us. I am sure he would reconnect with the girls.

I am going to ask Harry too. He is going to leave us end of January because my husband found him a job as a messenger in his company. He has been with us for a long time, and this will be our farewell present to him.

If it's okay, we'll have to organize passports and visas urgently. I am sorry about the short notice. Please come and see me if you need help with processing of documents.

Beth

Ruva was literally jumping for joy. The girls heard the commotion while reading in their room.

"Girls, we are going on holiday to South Africa with Beth."

Hilda was concerned. "I wonder what the accommodation arrangements will be like, because I read a book about race relations in South Africa and the politics involved. The segregation there is worse than it is here. People have been killed because they have crossed racial boundaries."

"That's at the bottom of my list of worries. Let's leave it to Beth. I trust she knows what she is doing," said Ruva.

A few days before they left, they had their birth certificates, passports and visas in hand, because Beth had arranged it all.

On Christmas Eve, just before they were to depart, Beth said to Ruva, "We have one more passenger who should be here any minute now." As she said those words, there was Brian boarding the plane.

"Made it in the nick of time as always," said Brian, panting.

As soon as everybody had their seat belts on and ready, they took to the skies in a private jet that belonged to Larry's company. Ruva and the girls took their seats at the back of the plane and buckled up for the adventure of their lifetime.

Beth and her family, including Dr. Blyton, sat in the front. The children entertained themselves by screaming at every bump of turbulence. The doctor could not stand the noise, and he went into the cockpit and chatted with the pilots until they landed. Everybody was gabbing away except Harry, who sat quietly and confessed to Ruva that panic and anxiety were overwhelming him. He was sweating and threw up all over himself. He thought his death was imminent, and he kept his eyes closed to avoid looking outside. He held on to the seats for dear life, but he survived.

In Cape Town, they stayed at a secluded winery hidden by tall trees and high walls with their own private beach. Larry's boss, who was Rhodesian, owned the winery. The Sandersons had stayed there before and once took Anna with them. Beth knew the challenges of apartheid and had to be careful. She and her family and Brian stayed in the mansion. Ruva and the girls stayed on their own in a comfortable cottage, and they loved it. Dr. Blyton was supposed to stay in the main house, but the children were too noisy for him, and he opted to stay with Harry in a smaller cottage.

Dr. Blyton had taken to poetry writing in his spare time. He read it to Harry, who didn't get it but listened all the same. Matie and Hilda listened intently to his poems. They found them inspiring, especially Hilda, who had not yet made a decision on a profession. Literary writing all of a sudden became an option.

In some evenings, they sat together for dinner. The black cook could grill a piece of steak to everybody's satisfaction, broil a trout with spices that brought out the taste or roast a juicy chicken with steamed and crunchy vegetables. At times, the cook would share some African staple foods with Ruva, the girls and Harry.

Matie and Hilda helped Beth's kids build sandcastles, waded in the ocean waters, played hide and seek in the vineyards for endless hours and played soccer with Harry. Even Ruva joined in the fun. She found herself being a kid again.

One hot afternoon after lunch, Brian asked Ruva, "Can we go and sit on the beach? I have a few questions to ask you."

"It's too hot today to be out there," said Ruva.

"Excuse me, I'll go and fetch an umbrella." He brought one big enough to shade them both from the blazing sun. He had a small bag filled with drinks and fruit hanging from his shoulder. He had changed into his red swimming trunks, covered his balding head with a wide-brimmed hat and put on a pair of dark shades. Fortunately, Beth had picked some up for the girls.

"Are you going to put on a bathing suit?"

"A bathing suit didn't make it onto my list of things to pack, since I can't swim. I don't anticipate being out here that long." She felt odd sitting at the beach in her ordinary frock.

They sat with their feet in the water without speaking for what seemed like eternity, until Ruva cried out when Brian smacked her arm with his bare hands, trying to kill a bee that had landed there. It left a stinging pain.

"At last, I have your full attention. How are you doing? I've only talked about business with you and overlooked your well-being."

"I'm doing much better, and these few days of the holiday have done wonders for me. I'm relaxed and enjoying every bit of it, and trying to put the last few months behind me. You gave me a good smack," Ruva said, rubbing her arm.

"I'm sorry, I didn't mean to hurt you." He scooped water from the sea and poured it on her arm. He gently rubbed it. "Does it feel better?"

"If sea water is the only remedy available, I'll be okay."

"Good! Do you think you'll be going to Malawi for the inquest?" Brian cautiously asked.

"I'm not trying to be impossible, but I need a break from all that stuff. I only want to enjoy this paradise."

"Maybe you're right. What are we going to talk about?"

"We can talk about you for a change?"

Brian was caught off-guard, and he laughed out loud. "Where do you want me to begin? Ask me whatever, and I'll be as truthful as I can."

"When you catch your breath, tell me whatever you want, for example, family, job or hobbies," she said, digging her feet into the sand.

"Wow, that's interesting. By family are you referring to children and wife?" Brian turned and looked at Ruva, who nodded.

"I'm a widower." He glanced again at Ruva to see her reaction. "I married an Italian woman named Gisella, who I met in Florence. I was on holiday, and we happened to stay at the same hotel. We hit it off instantly, and what happened on that holiday is better left to one's imagination. Her beauty stole my heart. I came back home and kept on thinking about her. Six months later, I proposed over the phone, and she accepted on the condition that I returned to Italy. I was in love and I packed my bags and went back.

"We were married in a small old church in her hometown of Bologna. I stayed in Italy with her because she was at the pinnacle of her career as a professional gymnast in a circus. She performed daring tricks that were at times scary to watch, but I got used to it because I trusted her prowess. I toured with her and the troupe to different cities around the country. I put my career on hold for her sake. I worked in restaurants and bars to supplement our income and I learned to speak Italian, but I'm no longer as fluent now.

"I kept on hoping that, one day, I'd bring her home to meet my family. My parents were still alive, and I had my brother, Larry, of course. It wasn't meant to be."

Brian stopped talking, swallowed hard and continued again. "We talked about her opening a gymnastics academy in Rhodesia. Gisella loved life. Her energy was amazing. It rubbed off on me. We did things I'd never have imagined myself doing. She had a petite figure but when she was skiing or climbing those mountains, she attacked them with so much tenacity. Her passion for living her life on the edge always blew my mind."

He paused again and cleared his throat. He took a big gulp of beer and the froth left a white moustache. "Am I boring you?"

"No, keep on going. I'm listening."

"I haven't talked about Gisella to anyone for a long time. This is weird. Are you sure you want to hear about my past life?"

"There is no way you can stop now. Finish what you started." Ruva was immersed in the story.

"I'll continue, but the hardest part for me is remembering how much she suffered. She often complained of abdominal pains, and medical examinations and tests were always inconclusive. As time went on, the pain became more and more intense."

With that description, Ruva remembered her own pain

whenever she miscarried. She took a big breath and held it for a while before exhaling it. Brian saw her reaction. "What's the matter?"

"I can identify with that pain," she said, squinting.

"Are you hinting at something I should know, Mrs. Ganda?"

"No, continue with your story, sir. This is your platform."

"I'll continue if you can forget about the 'sir' part. You're so quick-witted. I love it. Where was I?"

"Intense pain," Ruva reminded him.

"Finally, they diagnosed her with an aggressive form of ovarian cancer, and it had spread to her bones. What did her in was the fracture she sustained in her hipbone. It became badly infected. Within six months of diagnosis, she was dead at the age of twenty-six, a few days shy of her twenty-seventh birthday." He took another gulp of beer and asked, "Are you still with me?" He stretched his legs and rotated his ankles before picking up a bottle of orange juice and handing it to Ruva.

"Thank you. I'm listening. Brian, you don't have to keep on going if you feel uncomfortable. It's a sensitive issue."

"It brings back good and bad memories, and as I said, it's my first time sharing it after a long time."

"It's unbelievable that you lost someone dear to you too. How did you get over it?"

"If I knew what I know now, I would have tried other avenues," Brian said.

"It's never too late, though," Ruva commented while rubbing the sting on her arm.

"True! Since I came back, I have lived with two other women, but in both circumstances the relationships didn't work out. I have no children. One girlfriend, Peggy, got pregnant, but the baby was born prematurely with multiple medical problems, and it died. She was never the same after that. She moved to Johannesburg and I never heard from her again. The other one, Clara, had a lifestyle that was too demanding, and she desperately wanted to get married, but I wasn't ready. We had a joint business venture that failed and later she claimed I owed her money. I decided to part ways with her before things got too entangled. She was very bitter. I'm not attached to anybody right now."

"You've had your share of heartbreaks. Does it mean these women didn't measure up?"

"They might not have measured up but I'm also to blame because I hadn't reconciled with my loss." Brian stood up and shook his cramping legs, and at the same time he saw something out on the water.

"There's a killer whale out there." He helped her get up quickly, but it had disappeared under the water.

"You've got to see one before we leave. Let's watch out for them. You wanted to know about my job. I love it and have great respect for my three associates in our law firm. We have taken some difficult and interesting cases, ranging from criminal, political, family to human rights. Our success rate has been impressive. I can't say too much about my job, but our law firm is one of the largest in the country. What else did you want to know?"

"Did I ask you about your hobbies?" said Ruva.

"Oh yes, I'm too busy defending people or fighting for what is theirs." He softly massaged Ruva's thigh then quickly withdrew his hand. "Including you. Therefore, I deprive myself of fun. I live on a small farm, and I breed horses. That's my hobby. By the way, you talked about pain. What was that all about?"

"Not now, please. My saga is still ongoing. When I write the last chapter, I'll let you know. Thank you for sharing. We should go back inside and join the others. I'd like to see what the girls are up to. With teenagers, you have to keep an eye on them or you lose them so quickly." As she stood up, she saw something from afar.

"Brian, look! There are two of them jumping up high."

By the time he took off his sunglasses and perched them on his head, they were under and blowing the water.

"You won because you saw two."

"I didn't know we were playing a game."

"Always be prepared for a gamesmanship. That's how you get ahead in life."

Ruva didn't understand and let it pass.

As they entered the house, Larry said, "You were out there for a long time. You must have covered a lot of ground in your discussion. Brian, would you join us for wine tasting and dinner up the coast?"

"Enjoy your evening," Ruva said.

"You're joining us too. We're leaving in an hour or so," said Beth, holding Ruva's hand.

Ruva pulled Beth aside. "Are you sure it's okay for me to come with you?" she whispered. "Larry extended the invitation only to Brian and you know here blacks and whites don't mix."

"Don't be silly, you're coming with us. Do you have something formal?"

"Fortunately, I packed a suit," Ruva said with a nod.

At the cottage, as she sat on the bed, locked up in her own conscience and going over in her head what Brian had shared with her, the girls came in and Matie said, "We thought we would see you getting ready for wine tasting and dinner?"

"I don't know if I want to go," Ruva said, rubbing her nose.

"Mama, it's a good chance to enjoy fine dining. If I were you, I wouldn't miss that. When you were sitting at the beach with your lawyer, Dr. Blyton asked the white manager for a mini tour. We accompanied him and saw how they make wine from succulent grapes. It's an interesting process indeed. He explained all we needed to know about wine tasting," Matie said.

"Something that bothered me is that the manager kept on swearing at the workers and calling them names. It wasn't called for. The workers were humiliated in front of us," said Hilda.

"Now you understand why us black Rhodesians have been at war for years now. We can't wait to self-rule, which will put an end to that unacceptable superiority. We can only hope that we won't be doing the same bad things to each other. You didn't drink his wine, for goodness sake?" Ruva asked.

"Do we look drunk? Dr. Blyton did more than wine tasting. By the end of the tour, he looked tipsy. The manager gave us some quick tips on how to enjoy wine tasting. Correction, he gave tips to Dr. Blyton but we were listening. In his eyes, we didn't exist but Dr. Blyton wanted us to be there. He kept his arms around us all the time. He was like a hen protecting its chickens," said Matie. "Nevertheless, if you're going we can pass on the tips."

"What was he saying?"

Meanwhile, Hilda picked up a wineglass and handed it to Matie for a demonstration.

"The important thing to know is that wines range from dry, fruity, sweet to tangy, and the list goes on. It's helpful if somebody asks you for your preference. Swirl the wine in the glass like this and sniff to gauge the aroma. You can sip if you want and savour the wine. Keep an eye on what other people are doing. But leave the rest to the experts."

"I can do that." As she was practicing, the girls were laughing and having fun.

"We'll see if you'll be able to stand when you come back," Hilda teased her mother. "Mama, rule of thumb, when you're dining, white wine goes with white meats, and that's fish and chicken, and the red meat goes with red wine. But this too is left to one's taste and discretion. In case you can't resist the pressure to take that sip, have a serviette handy to throw up on."

"Hilda, that's not ladylike. Mama, don't do that, you'll never be invited again."

"You two know way too much for my liking. Promise me that this isn't the beginning of the temptation to drink. It's time for us to discuss the negatives of alcohol consumption, and from the sounds of it, the sooner the better."

"The manager told us that the French serve wine to their children during meal times," Matie said and when she noticed her mother's piercing eyes, she protested, "It's true."

"You're not French and never dream of being served wine at the dinner table any time soon."

Soon Ruva was ready to go, dressed in a beautiful black polyester suit, which accentuated her figure. A snow-white blouse with a neck bow went well with the suit, which she had bought from a second-hand shop. It looked just like new. She put on black high-heeled shoes to complete her outfit. She looked chic with her hair coiffed in nice curls. Her beauty that seemed to have lain dormant due to years of hardships shone through.

"You look beautiful, but you applied too much powder," said

Matie, using a tissue to dab extra powder from her mother's face. "You don't want to look like a clay pot that has been scorched by the sun for years."

"Yikes, that's harsh!" said Hilda.

"I want her natural beauty to shine through. Mama, you're beautiful, but you have always downplayed your good looks."

"Add a touch of lipstick, and you will be good to go," said Hilda.

"I like the new you. This is the first time we have seen you with make-up," Matie said.

"Won't be the last," Ruva answered with pride.

"You were prepared for this holiday," said Hilda, lightly patting her mother's hair.

❧

Brian held the door ajar for Ruva, and she slid into the car sideways. "You look astounding in that suit." Ruva was embarrassed by the compliment.

"What a privilege to be in the company of such beautiful women." Brian's gaze lingered on Ruva.

Beth had on a red fitted dress with a round neckline, a multi-coloured silk scarf and black pumps. The men were dressed in black suits. Beth said she had chosen this particular restaurant because they had dined there before and she liked the ambience, the variety of music, and the service. They headed straight to the ballroom for wine tasting. Ruva scouted the room and noticed she was the only black person. She felt as if all eyes were upon her.

She tapped Beth on the back and asked, "Are blacks allowed here? Some people are giving me some dirty looks. I feel uncomfortable."

Beth whispered in her ear. "Ignore them. Today I enquired about that, and they said anybody is welcome. Therefore, my dear, walk with your head high, for you have all the right to be here." Beth gently pulled her back, away from a couple that gave them a cold stare.

The wine tasting tips from Matie and Hilda came in handy as Ruva walked around the room holding a glass of wine, which she kept on swirling and sniffing but not sipping. Brian hadn't noticed that she was not sipping the wine and said, "Have you tried this Cabernet Sauvignon?"

That threw her off. "No. I don't drink. Holding a wine glass wards off too many questions. The connoisseur gave me a sweet wine. How many have you tasted so far?"

"Not counting. The trick for me is to wash it down so often with water so as not to end up losing the true taste. Let's move on to the dining room." He put his hand on her back to guide her.

They had just ordered their meal when two white angry men approached their table. The men stood behind Ruva and demanded that she leave the restaurant immediately. Ruva turned round and one of the men said, "You, don't look at me," pointing at Ruva. "And all of you, if you want to enjoy your dinner get this *kaffir* out of here."

"What has she done to you?" asked Brian as the men continued to lob insults. "Somebody call the police."

Ruva was so petrified she stood up, wanting to leave. Brian asked her to sit down and the men moved closer to her.

"Go back to the townships where you butcher each other."

"I talked to management and they said it was okay for her to come here," said Beth angrily. "Who are you?"

"Shut up!" the man shouted at the top of his lungs.

A black waiter who had chatted with Ruva earlier on jumped on the man who was the most vocal and grabbed him from behind. He twisted his body around and punched him in the face. The man staggered to his feet before he went down hard. Complete mayhem broke out when some guests came to the white man's aid. The waiter was severely beaten up. Police were called to restore order and the badly injured waiter was handcuffed and taken away to the cells. Beth and her party were blocked off and could not leave until the police briskly escorted them out.

"This is South Africa and we know the racial policy very well. I'm angry about what has happened, but we brought this on ourselves. No more outings," said Larry as they were walking to the car.

On their way back, they were all quiet, reflecting on the evening. Larry stopped the car right at Ruva's doorstep. Brian, who was sitting in the front seat, quickly got out of the car and opened the door for her.

"Ruva, don't give it another thought. They are crazy men."

"They were more than that," she replied.

"Racists, I agree," Brian called out as she walked in without looking back.

The girls were anxiously waiting to hear what happened.

"Ehhhhhh, Mama, you still have your balance," said Hilda, who was lying on the couch watching television. "How did it go? You are early."

"Everything went so fast but it was a good experience. Your tips were very helpful indeed. I asked for a sweet one, swirled it in the glass like an expert and sniffed it like a hound. I sipped once and I didn't like the taste so I couldn't savour it."

"Wow! You might be converted if you keep this company," Matie joked as she came out of her bedroom.

Ruva pretended she hadn't heard. "I'm going to bed once

I take off these shoes. They are killing me. Speaking of that, I wish your father was here with us."

"Let the truth be told. We wouldn't be here if he was alive, but I'm sure he's here with us," said Matie.

"Say goodnight for me if he comes by your room," Ruva laughed.

"Mama, you don't look as excited as I would have expected," said Hilda, watching her mother struggling to undo the straps on her shoes. "Do you need assistance?"

"The straps need nimble fingers but I can do it. We'll talk about what happened tomorrow. Let's go to bed."

Ruva had enjoyed the holiday, despite the restaurant incident, which reminded her that racial inequality was part and parcel of their society. She did not tell the girls about the brawl that had left her frightened, because she did not want to spoil their happy memories. She looked forward to going back home.

When Ruva and the girls approached their front door, they knew something was amiss because the living room window was broken and the doorknob had been pulled off the front door. They stealthily entered and saw an empty living room. The culprits had used the paint, which was behind the sofa, to write vulgar jokes all over the walls.

"I'm going through a patch of bad luck," exclaimed Ruva. She moved into her bedroom, and the old furniture there was intact, but clothes and other personal belongings were strewn all over the floor.

Matie sneaked into their room and shouted, "Our school suitcases are gone with everything in them."

"They took our refrigerator and our stove," Hilda was screaming from the kitchen.

"Hello, Ruva," said Shungu. "Where were you? I woke up three days ago and saw that somebody had broken in. I called the police, and they haven't been here yet."

"We were in South Africa with Beth and her family."

"You have been going places?" Shungu was envious. "Why didn't you tell me that you were going away? I'd have kept watch on the house."

"It was a last-minute decision." Ruva turned away and continued what she was doing. Shungu got the message and left.

That day, they piled the girls' bed and dresser against the front door, and they huddled together on Ruva's bed. Ruva didn't close her eyes that whole night, afraid the thieves might come back. The following morning, she asked a neighbour who happened to be a handyman to fix the door, window and install stronger burglar bars.

Ruva reported the matter to the police, and officers finally came and did their little investigation. Ruva suspected Batsirai but he was never charged and nothing was ever recovered. To replace some of the stolen items, she went to a second-hand store. She chose to lead a frugal existence, for she was determined to finish school and help the girls until they were able to fend for themselves. She replaced some of the girls' stuff since they were going back to school.

"Mama, I'm worried about you being here alone."

"Matie, you've to stop worrying about me. I've no other place to run to. This is home. We'll all be fine." She put her arm around her daughter for reassurance.

The girls could not wait to go back to school, to brag about their holiday experience and to show off their souvenirs and the pictures that Beth had taken.

Chapter Eight

"I'm glad you came to see me, because the trial will begin in a week's time. I was talking to Guy Miller, and he said it's going to be rough for you. Do you have somebody to accompany you for support?" Brian asked. "Not that friend of yours. She might be more of a problem than help," he added.

"I have to learn to stand on my own two feet. I'm going there alone to gather the truth, and when that's done, I can start to live again."

"The experience is going to be painful, that's why I'm saying you need somebody for support. Detective Miller contacted somebody by the name of Sergeant Chobi, who kindly offered to accommodate you until the trial is over. Accept that offer. It's for your own good. As I said, you need to be with someone."

"Are you suggesting that I need a bodyguard?" Even in a serious conversation, Ruva could inject a light moment.

"Maybe not a bodyguard, but it's an option."

"There are still good people in this world. I'll take your advice."

"Take care of yourself."

She left the office and carefully closed the door behind her. She stood on the other side of the door for a moment, slightly opened it again and said, "By the way, somebody broke into my house when we were away."

"Oh, can you come back in?" Brian asked, walking towards the door and holding it wide open.

"I don't want to take more of your time with my unending problems. Everything is all right now." Ruva waved and walked away.

"As long as you're okay." Brian watched her disappear into an elevator. He sensed that she wanted to talk, but he hadn't given her a chance. He followed her down the stairway but could not find her since she had vanished into the congested streets.

❧

A few days later, Ruva boarded a bus for Lumba. She was over-anxious about the long journey ahead of her, and on the other hand she was determined to attend the trial and put the tragedy behind her. Sergeant Chobi and his wife were at the bus station to meet her as arranged by Guy Miller.

As she got off the bus, she went into the waiting area and found Sergeant Chobi waiting and their eyes locked.

"Are you Mrs. Ganda?"

"Yes, and you must be Sergeant Chobi?"

"Welcome, and please meet my wife Alile." She was caught rubbing the inside of her eye to remove little crusts that had formed overnight.

My city is more beautiful than this, Ruva thought as she looked around. Alile interrupted her thoughts by saying, "Glad to meet you. How was your trip?"

"It was a long journey, and thank you for hosting me." Ruva flashed a smile.

"It's our pleasure."

"How do you know Mr. Miller?" Ruva asked.

"A few years ago I went to Salisbury for training, and I stayed with him and his wife. They were wonderful hosts. We've remained good friends ever since," said the sergeant.

"I'm nervous about this whole trial," Ruva confessed.

"It's normal. I hope you don't think that all people in this country are bad. We're peace-loving, and unfortunately in our midst there are a few bad people that need to be weeded out from society. If it's a fair trial, those suspects should be locked up for life."

"Sergeant Chobi, how far from here is the river where they found Mukai's body?"

"It's about thirty minutes from here."

"Is it possible for me to visit the area before the trial, so that I've an idea of the whereabouts? I'd like to buy some flowers before we go. Will that be alright?"

"No problem! Let's go home and you rest for a while, and then we can go late in the afternoon."

"That's very kind of you."

"It'll give you a clear picture when they start describing the area where they found the body. It's going to come up for sure," said the sergeant.

Just before sunset, he drove her to the site where the body was found floating, trapped between rocks. The three stood there in silence and paid their respects. Ruva bent down and gently placed three roses she had bought on the way. The roses represented one for her and one for each of the girls. Before leaving, she reached into the water and picked up a small, round pebble, which she wiped with the hem of her dress and threw into her handbag.

On the first day of the trial, the charges were read to the three accused men. They were charged with kidnapping with intention to cause grievous bodily harm and murder. The men pleaded not guilty to murder, although there was a mountain of incriminating evidence. Their lawyer applied for bail, but it was denied. He also tried to have the case thrown out on the basis that the deceased was a foreigner who was involved in illegal activities like prostitution, which was a criminal act under the penal code.

A couple of weeks after the charges were laid out, the actual trial began in earnest in the High Court, presided over by a judge who was known for giving criminals second chances. When Ruva had gone to identify the body in the mortuary back home, she refused to see the whole body, but in that courtroom the pictures of the mutilated body created the backdrop of the horrifying scene. She understood why the judge had warned all the faint-hearted in the courtroom to leave because of the gruesome nature of the case.

The lead counsel read an opening statement, which sounded to Ruva as though he was talking about a different Mukai. She could not believe the hair-raising facts in those statements. The public prosecutor concentrated on the gruesome killing. It turned out to be a rough day for her. She knew the trial wasn't going to be any easier but she decided to soldier on. She went back to her hosts with her spirits crushed. They were supportive, but it was too much for her to bear. She went into her room, closed the door and cried herself to sleep.

Ruva had thought she was going to remain anonymous, but word went round that Mukai's wife was around, and she didn't realize that the courtroom was full of people who were curious to see her.

The hired killer was first on the stand. He was questioned for three days about the murder. He narrated how he was hired to kill Mukai by the kingpin of a prostitution ring, because he had failed to pay for prostitution services rendered on several occasions. The kingpin literally asked for his head for a fee. Mukai was a strong and tall man, so the hitman collaborated with two acquaintances to carry out the murder and deliver the head as requested. In the creepy silence that ensued, one could hear a pin drop.

The three men had approached him late at night when he was leaving a bar where he was known to hang out frequently. It happened that he had given one of the three men a ride once when the man was hitchhiking from Rhodesia. For a while they became friends, but then they went their separate ways over borrowed money. This was now a chance to get revenge. The accused provoked Mukai, and there was a scuffle. They overpowered him and dragged him into the woods, where they beat him to a pulp, and he died. They took all the money he had won on his gambling escapades, decapitated him and dumped his torso in a nearby river. They took the head to the kingpin and were paid as promised. They drove his truck to a secluded area, where they set it on fire using the gas they had siphoned from the tank.

While the accused was responding to questions, there were graphic pictures of Mukai's torso in full view on the screen, with his head missing and deep knife cuts, especially on his arms, which were covered in crusted blood. It revealed that Mukai must have fought hard to defend himself. At times, Ruva became so agitated that she rubbed her hands vigorously on the pebble that she had picked up from the river to ease the tension.

Before she left for Lumba, she had thought attending the trial would give her some closure. Instead she felt as though she was watching a horror movie, and the anger building inside her made her want to roar like a lion. She was scared that the experience would affect her forever, for she had never seen anything as horrific as this.

The legal counsel called two witnesses who revealed that Mukai had fathered two boys by two different women and reluctantly helped out financially. Mukai was a big gambler and he sometimes won big money, which he recklessly spent as fast as he earned it. The lawyer wanted to show that Mukai was neither an innocent victim nor a trustworthy player in this saga. Ruva saw it as a way of continually smearing her husband's reputation.

In the afternoon during a break, Ruva went outside with Alile for fresh air and to clear her head. To her amazement, she saw a toddler playing with his mother outside the courtroom who was a spitting image of Mukai. She just stood there and kept looking at him. "Alile, that child must be one of Mukai's children the lawyer referred to today. He looks so much like him."

"Yes, it is."

Ruva wanted to reach out to the mother, but to her surprise, Alile pulled her back by the arm. "I might as well tell you that I saw the other woman sitting at the back."

"How do you know them?" Ruva snapped without meaning to sound angry.

"Here we have that small-town mentality of wanting to know everything happening around us, and nothing passes us by. When your husband's body was discovered in the river, the story was in the newspapers and people came out of the woodwork with unbelievable stories. Of course, one had to sieve the chaff from the good grain. These two women appeared in one of the papers, claiming what you know now. I'm sure the papers will pick up the story again tomorrow. This death caused a sensation here that has never been seen before and that explains why the courtroom is packed. Nothing as horrendous as this has ever happened in our community. It exposed so many high-ranking people who were involved in monkey business. I did not want you to talk to that woman for I know there are people watching you, waiting to spread juicy gossip."

"Can you imagine, I was sitting at home not knowing that there was a circus going on here, and my husband was the ringmaster?"

She walked back into the courtroom and took her seat. Alile followed her quietly and sat beside her. They both sat bolt upright, staring at the judge's empty bench as if something was going on.

Ruva felt a sudden uncontrollable anxiety. "My head feels like it's going to explode. I need to get out of here."

"Let's leave now before the session starts." They stood up and walked out against a stream of curious people who were packing the courtroom again.

"Hello, Mrs. Ganda!" Ruva recognized the voice, and she looked up.

"Mr. Miller, you're here! How wonderful to see a familiar face. I'm leaving and will be going back home tomorrow, for this is too much for me to bear."

"It's hard, I know. I was subpoenaed and will wait my turn to take the stand."

"Did you find something of interest that I should know?"

"No. It's routine, since I was part of the investigation."

"Please go in there and be my ears," she instructed him.

"Will catch up with you back home." He patted her on the back.

In the evening, as they were eating dinner, Ruva said dejectedly, "Sergeant Chobi and Alile, please accept my gratitude for your hospitality. I can't bear any of this mental torture and heartache anymore. I have decided to leave tomorrow. I thought I had a thick skin. I was wrong."

"We wish you would stay for the whole trial, but we totally understand. This has been difficult even for us who are on the fringes of this case," said the sergeant.

She went back home with a heavy heart and regretted ever having gone to Malawi. She didn't contact Beth or Brian for at least a month because she was too distressed by the experience. She vowed never to let the girls know the truth about their father's double life. There was no need to make them hate him in death for letting them down.

Brian knew that Ruva had left early, because he was in contact with Guy Miller. When the trial ended, Brian informed her of the verdict that all three men were found guilty of first-degree murder. The legal counsel pleaded for leniency and their sentence was reduced to five years, less time served. Ruva thought the sentence was a slap on the wrist, considering the nature of the crime. She was there to see justice done but the criminal proceedings had failed her. The prostitution kingpin bribed his way out and was never tried, since he vanished into thin air with his treasure. Terrible thoughts haunted her each time she thought about what they had done with Mukai's head. When the trial ended and sentence was passed, Ruva received a letter from Mukai's company through her lawyer.

Dear Mrs. Ganda,

As a company, we would like to express our disappointment over the circumstances that led to your husband's tragic demise. We believed that he was one of our trusted employees, but that statement apparently was far from the truth, according to what came out of the trial.

However, we regret the hasty decision we made in paying you without waiting for the judicial process to run its course. We re-examined carefully the compensation package that we originally offered you and felt changes needed to be made. The directive to pay for the children's (Matilda and Hilda) university fees was rescinded. The company will cease to pay for your lawyer's fees with immediate effect. For compassionate reasons, the rest of the package will be honoured.

The company wishes you well. If you have any further questions please direct them to Mr. W. Ngoma.

Regards,
Ken Donald, Rothwells CEO

"Where do we go from here?" Ruva asked Brian as she sat in his office.

"We could challenge them because they told us what a good worker he was for sixteen years, and now they are changing their tune. They have power and resources to fight us for every penny. Now the guns are drawn, and they're ready to battle. Reversing the contract was wrong, but they know you'll not go after them because of the huge legal fees involved. They're not worried about public opinion. I'd advise you to take what's there and work with it. You don't need to drag this out. I'll respond to their letter and tell them of our displeasure, which is the right business practice. Do you have something different in mind?"

"Not at all. I've always appreciated your opinion. I'll definitely try to pick up the pieces and move on with my life. Will it be easy? No!"

"You're empowering yourself with higher education. That's

an achievement, and things will work out in the end," Brian reassured her.

"Thank you for helping me. Let's hope I won't have to seek your legal advice again soon."

"I wish things had worked out better for you. But be assured that our paths will cross again. Listen, why don't you get in touch with Beth? That woman's life is never dull. She's in the middle of a small crisis."

Chapter Nine

Ruva was so consumed with her own problems that she did not take heed of the intense excitement of victory going on around her. The fight for liberation was won, and in April 1980 Zimbabwe celebrated its independence, which opened doors for many blacks, who slowly moved into positions of power in government. The business world rushed in to invest after years of sanctions. However, those who didn't have much education got lost in the cracks.

Ruva was anxious to know the latest crisis in Beth's life, and she paid her a visit.

"Happy Independence, Ruva!" said Beth.

"It must be a happy one for you too. I know you did not like the direction the old regime was moving in. Hopefully things will work out for all of us. Forget politics and tell me what's going on. Brian told me that you are in the middle of another crisis. What is it now?"

"Nothing that can't be worked out." Beth changed the subject. "I heard that the trial was agonizing?"

"It left some deep scars that'll take time to heal. What you heard is the truth. It's not only painful to talk about, but it was a demoralizing experience. I'll leave it at that, for I know you heard about it all from Brian." Ruva was dispirited.

"Now let me tell you about my so-called crisis. Stella came

here a week after we came back from our holiday. She told me that Anna's two boys were living with a family member, who was abusing them, and they were not going to school. Apparently, Anna's mother, who always looked after them, passed away last year, and I didn't know."

"That's sad, and who is Stella?"

"Anna's cousin. It's upsetting that I kept sending money, and the uncles were lining their own pockets. Larry and I discussed this in detail, and we decided to adopt them. We weighed all the pros and cons. We consulted with Brian on the legalities of adopting the boys. To our surprise, Brian offered to adopt them himself. He said he had been thinking about it and an opportunity has presented itself. What do you think of the whole idea?"

"It's fantastic that you and Brian are so compassionate. Where are they now?"

"We asked Stella to bring them here. Brian contacted the Women and Social Services Ministry and they advised him to put them in an orphanage for now. She literally abducted them, and nobody has come forward to claim them yet. They'll live in the orphanage until the adoption process is through. Meanwhile, the Ministry is running through his personal records to rule out any sinister motives. He's pushing really hard to get it done soon. He doesn't want these children to experience any more psychological trauma. I talked to him the other day, and he said things looked promising."

"Brian needs a wife to help him raise those kids."

"I agree, but he isn't going steady with anyone right now. He's too busy making money in his law practice, and getting custody of the boys is his new undertaking. He asked me to run this by you and see if you would manage the day-to-day stuff of his farm and help him care for the boys. You don't have to give me the answer today. Give it some thought and let me know."

"That's a tall order by any means, Beth. I have never managed anything of that magnitude. He has horses and I've no experience." Ruva was getting comfortable with Beth now and could freely talk to her as a good friend.

"He's aware of that. You don't have to worry about horses. He has somebody who looks after them and has tremendous professional experience. It's a lot of work grooming and training them. He's particularly protective of those horses. Two of them race in competitions. He hinted that if you were to take the job, you would have to move into the cottage on the farm, which he has always rented out. It would be safer there than living in Highfield. This is an opportunity for you to move on and move up. Give it some thought."

"Without doubt, an opportunity is knocking on my door. But why didn't Brian ask me himself when I saw him in his office yesterday? He said you were in another crisis and didn't even mention that he's involved in the crisis himself. He's sneaky, that fellow."

"He wanted me to check with you first. That's Brian for you. If you're agreeable, I'll pass on the good news. I'm excited for you." Suddenly, Beth remembered something. "I had forgotten to ask you about the break-in at your house. Brian mentioned it as a matter of fact."

"They took everything from the living room, scribbled vulgar graffiti on the walls, took my stove and fridge, left with the girls' school suitcases and scattered everything else everywhere. They left a big mess. I have spruced the house up and life goes on."

"It's upsetting indeed," said Beth.

"Let me discuss this new proposal with my girls, and I'll

come back and give you an answer. They are home on holidays, and by the way, they sent their regards."

"Wonderful! The girls can say whatever they want, but let the final decision be yours."

"It's true. I'm doing it for courtesy's sake," Ruva laughed.

"Good enough. I'll wait to hear from you and then will pass your response along to Brian."

Ruva went home and digested the plan, which appeared to be in her favour.

"Girls, can you come here? I need your opinion on something that has come up." She and the girls crowded on the sofa.

"You're asking for our opinion, therefore, we must be a team," said Matie.

"I visited Beth and she told me that Mr. Sanderson, my lawyer, is adopting two black boys, and he wants me to help him raise them." Ruva stopped there, for she could see cause for concern in their immediate reaction.

"Mama, I'm confused when you say help him raise the boys. Are you saying there are marriage vows in the works?" asked Hilda.

Ruva laughed at the thought. "Oh no, I'll be taking a job as a nanny, and hear this, he wants me to manage the farm. That's not the end of the story. He wants us to move to his farm and live in our own cottage."

"Mama, you don't have the kind of management skills to run the farm efficiently. How are you going to do it?" Matie asked.

"Brian is aware of my lack of experience. He must have a good plan for me."

"Anyway, I'm for the move. Where is the farm?" asked Matie.

"Near Norton."

"Mama. Let's move to this farm, whether it's on Mars or Venus." Hilda jumped up and raised her tight fist in the air, fired up. "There's an opportunity here. I'm sure it's a beautiful cottage."

Ruva wasn't surprised by the enthusiasm the girls displayed. "Living in a beautiful house isn't all one needs to be happy, girls, but there are many factors that come into play. Material things can slip out of your hands at the blink of an eye. Always remember that."

"You've a point, Mama, but don't fret. Let's take this opportunity and run with it. Those other factors will fall into place. If it doesn't work out for you, we have our house here to come back to," said Matie, reasonably.

Ruva met Brian and Beth to discuss the offer. Brian laid it all out for her and took her with Beth to the farm. His house was big but lacked in style and cleanliness. It was scantily furnished with mismatched pieces. The farm had a beautiful garden with fishponds everywhere. The stables were on the other side of the farm, and horses freely galloped and trotted in the open fields.

"My house is not as nicely decorated as Beth's, as you can see. This will suffice for me and the boys for the time being." Brian sounded apologetic but quickly started on something close to his heart. "I like the peacefulness this place offers me after a day's hard work. I can walk in my garden and appreciate life in its different forms, like flowers budding, little ants building anthills, bees sucking the pollen, butterflies showing off their colours, spiders weaving their cobwebs in the midst of all this and worms digging into the dirt. The only noise I hear most of the time is the horses neighing, birds chirping away early in the morning when I'm sitting on the veranda sipping my cup of strong coffee and occasionally a gust of wind blowing through the avocado trees."

He waited for a reaction after that descriptive prose, but there was silence. "It might be a drawback for you since you're not used to this kind of life," Brian said.

"I grew up in the rural areas not too far away from here." Ruva looked down, embarrassed of her humble roots. "You have a beautiful garden."

"Thanks," Brian said proudly. "Gardening will be my hobby when I retire from practicing law."

"There are a lot of positives here, especially the tranquility of this place. Without a doubt it'll be therapeutic. I'll be too busy to notice the absence of the hustle and bustle I'm accustomed to in Highfield. I like it here."

Beth pointed in the direction of the stream. "There is a small stream down that slope with small fish."

"Is there? I'll keep away for a while," Ruva said.

Beth quickly realized the significance of the river. "I'm sorry, Ruva. It wasn't my intention to remind you of past incidents."

"Oh, I'm glad you mentioned it. It's good that I know it's there," said Ruva.

They toured the modest cottage she was going to live in, with its modern furnishings that Brian had inherited from the last tenant who ditched his lease and left a note to say he was leaving the country. It was bigger than Ruva's house and she liked that they would have an inside bathroom with a bathtub and separate shower, piped with hot water. The bathroom at Ruva's house was outside. There was a small fireplace in the living room. Ruva loved everything in it, and she knew the girls would be overjoyed too.

"Now that I have seen your beautiful place, I would like to meet the boys when you have time to escape from work."

"That's a good idea. Fortunately, today is one of the days I visit them. Beth, since you haven't seen them in a while, would you come with us?"

"I'm coming. Ruva, you'll notice that they're extremely withdrawn. We suspect that there was something seriously wrong going on," Beth said, adjusting her purse, which was sliding slowly off her shoulder. "This abuse might have been going on even when their mother was alive. We don't know."

"Yes. We have a lot of work cut out for us," agreed Brian. "I love them no matter what. They are mine now. I still have problems communicating with them, but it will happen."

"What are their names?"

"I know your next question will be how old. I'll answer both. Tawaka is nine, and Anopa is six. When I heard of the boys, I instantly knew that they were meant to be mine. They're small for their ages, but once they come home and we start giving them a balanced diet, love, hope and all the other things that sustain us emotionally and physically, they'll definitely fill up. Their growth spurt is still to come."

Ruva never imagined that fate would bring her back to Anna, whom she had only met through the eye of the lens of the camera. She remembered admiring how exuberant Anna seemed with Beth's kids. But seeing the woman's boys in this state saddened her.

Ruva hit it off with Tawaka and Anopa, and being as superstitious as she was, she believed Anna wanted her to look after them. Brian took comfort in their instant attachment.

"I'm certain there'll come a day when I'll be able to tell them how much you and Anna meant to me and my family," said Beth, turning to Ruva and giving her a half smile.

"Anna worked eight years for you, and as for me, it was a mere eight months. There's no comparison."

"I'll never be able to explain it clearly. It comes from the heart and the measure of time is irrelevant. You brought different attributes to my household," Beth said.

"That reminds me of Chipo. How's she doing?"

"She is hard-working but there hasn't been that deep connection with us as a family. I can't pinpoint why," Beth said guiltily. "Harry is doing very well in his job. He's staying in one of the townships, and he visited a few weeks ago to see his sister. Keith and Kyle miss playing soccer with him after school. Larry has slowly filled that void because the kids have been bugging him."

Ruva enjoyed listening to bits and pieces of other people's family stories.

Two months later, she sold most of her meagre possessions but kept her house in case things didn't work out. Mukai's life insurance had paid it off, and all the investment returns were hers. She grappled with her departure, for she loved the house where her roots were firmly planted, and she knew most of the people in the neighbourhood. Her church community had been there for her. But it was time to leave all that behind. She didn't tell them that she was moving but went over to Shungu to bid her farewell. She knew Shungu would spread the news. She found her friend in a foul mood and decided to tell her anyway.

"Brian offered me a job as a farm manager and nanny for two newly adopted boys. I'm moving tomorrow."

"You must have known for a while that you'll be moving, and this was an afterthought. Are you sure of what you're doing?"

"I'm sure. If it doesn't work out, I'll try something else."

"Like what?" Shungu asked impolitely.

"Another chance will come up. I believe that if one door closes another one opens. I promise to come and see you and let you know of my progress. I'll be renting out the house to a young schoolteacher. If she needs help, please be kind to her." Ruva thought it would be a good idea to give Shungu a small responsibility, for she didn't want to burn all her bridges.

"You don't truly mean it. If you did, you would have given me your address in case there are any problems. Are you ashamed to see us at your doorstep?"

"I don't have the full address yet. It's disturbing that you always think I have a hidden agenda. I could have left without bidding you farewell, do you know that?" Ruva nevertheless hugged Shungu, who stood there stone cold. Ruva left the house, and Shungu banged the door behind her.

"Oops!" Ruva exclaimed, for the sound was deafening. It was obvious that the farewell was not taken well. She was disappointed that their relationship had spiralled downwards so quickly.

She went back into her empty house. She sat on the floor and scratched her back on the wall, trying to get comfortable. Thoughts started rushing through her mind and she began to think realistically of what Shungu had asked her. "Are you sure of what you're doing?" It was a fair question and she wished she had said something that would help Shungu understand why she was taking this leap of faith.

She thought aloud what she should have said. "My beginnings were humble and I've nothing to be ashamed of. I'll always remember where my roots are and that will keep me well grounded. I can't change my past, but I'm thankful that I have the capacity to make better choices for my future.

"Things were not easy between Mukai and me, but we did

the best we could with what we had. The way he lived his life was not noble, and his death was painful for me. I was blessed with two beautiful girls and only wished that they'd keep their dreams alive.

"Along the way, Beth came into my life and gave me a new beginning. She is my bridge to another world. Brian is offering me something I can't resist. It's a change for the better, with endless possibilities. I'll treasure this opportunity. I'm not going to focus on failure but will look at each day with gratitude and how I can build success upon it. I have a lot to be thankful for and I'll work as hard as I can. I won't need a contingency plan, for I believe that my future is bright. Shungu, I know what I'm doing."

She finished talking then inspected the house for the last time, before she closed the door quietly behind her.

Chapter Ten

Ruva quietly moved to Brian's farm and began a new chapter for herself and her children. Her life was taking on a new dimension, and she looked forward to the change with great expectations.

Brian explained the disadvantages of living far away from the city. "Ruva, it'll be a good idea if you learn to drive, since this place is far away from shops, schools and Harare, and I know you like going to church on Sundays. I don't want you to live like a captive here."

"Something to think about. Anyway, I'll give it a try and see how I fare."

"I have another car locked up in the garage which you can use. It's an old Vauxhall. It drives like a charm."

"I'd rather go to a driving school and hone my skills. I don't want to bang it."

"You'll need it for extra practice," he persisted.

"Maybe I'll use it when I get my license. In the meantime, I've other important things to learn."

"I asked an old buddy of mine to work with you until you can stand on your own two feet. Definitely, there will be a lot of things to learn. How do you feel about that?"

"That's a good idea. I welcome the help, but patience on

their part will be a necessary requirement," Ruva warned him. "What exactly would they be assisting me with?"

"Basic bookkeeping, communicating with those you might be in contact with regarding farm business and relations with the farm workers. Beth told me that you're doing well at school, and this should be a breeze. You won't need help with looking after the boys. Am I right?"

"After raising my own children, I don't think so."

Brian gave Ruva a few days to acquaint herself with the farm, before he called all the workers to meet her. Preparation for the meeting was nerve-racking for her since she was charting new territory. Most of the workers were men and she was intimidated.

"Mrs. Ruva Ganda will be your new manager," Brian said when introducing her. "Now things will be dealt with quicker. You won't have to wait for me to come home and sort out problems. Give her time to adjust before bombarding her with all your demands. Ruva, do you want to say something?"

"Good morning! I shall be going around the farm getting to know each and every one of you and the work you do on the farm. Brian has told me that you're a group of hardworking people and we shall continue to work as a team. I want you to be fully aware of what is happening in your surroundings and report anything that is out of the usual. I'm looking forward to working with you."

"That was a good beginning," said Brian as they were walking away.

Ruva put a lot of effort into learning how things worked at the farm before making a few changes. She relieved Homba of his housekeeping duties because he failed to keep the house meticulous. She replaced him with Sphiwe, who used to do laundry once a week. She looked forward to seeing Sphiwe every morning, for she was the only other woman working at the farm.

Homba frowned at the changes but kept his cooking job. Cooking was his trade. He had worked in hotels before taking a job with Brian, who trusted him to whip up a dish on short notice, knowing it would be delicious. Ruva scheduled him to help either in the garden, stables or other extra odd jobs in the house, including looking after Shumba the dog, a Rhodesian ridgeback, and Bobo the cat. She kept a watchful eye on Homba, for he had a tendency to disappear for hours on his bicycle.

Hot on the heels of Ruva moving in, the children were fully adopted by Brian. Because he showed so much interest in the boys, the adoption was expedited, since the authorities recognized he would be a doting father. The adjustment was not easy for the boys, especially relating to Brian as dad. They could not get past the difference in skin colour, but Brian continued to work wholeheartedly to win them over.

Ruva was the surrogate mother who eased the situation and bridged the gap. She treated the boys as her own. She loved them but did not believe in spoiling them. She was firm and consistent, just as she was with her own daughters. The boys called her Mama, which she welcomed because she felt it would create a strong bond between them. Culturally, it was a sign of respect, and she encouraged it. Ruva prepared the boys for the girls' homecoming.

Matie and Hilda liked their new home, which provided a great deal of comfort and safety compared to their previous dwelling place. The girls took delight in listening to stories about the farm workers. Their mother was always mediating conflicts between the workers, which were frequent.

The girls took the boys under their wings and encouraged them to go and play with the workers' children, which they loved to do. Matie and Hilda found them to be very introverted and one had to push them to do something.

"Can you imagine yourselves in their shoes? The change hasn't been easy. They were taken from the only people they knew to an orphanage and now they are here. It's only a matter of time before they come round," Ruva explained.

One sunny afternoon, when the four of them were casting their fishing rods into the water and waiting for a catch, Tawaka asked the girls, "Who is your dad?" He was confused by the setup and was not sure if Brian was also their dad.

The girls looked at each other before Hilda responded. "Our dad died last year."

"Our mother died too," Tawaka said. Ruva had given the girls a short synopsis of the boys' past. Matie and Hilda were afraid to ask them too many questions in case they stumbled on sensitive issues.

Anopa, who normally didn't say much, opened up. "I like my new dad and my new mother."

What he said did not surprise the girls, since he preferred to snuggle next to their mother, who responded with affection.

"Do you like horses?" asked Matie, who was struggling to find safe questions.

"Anopa is scared of horses," answered Tawaka on his brother's behalf.

"What about you?" Matie asked.

"I'm not scared. I used to ride my uncle's donkey." At the mention of his uncle, the girls noticed that he cringed. They knew it was time to go back into the house and introduce something different.

Tawaka and Anopa were registered for the last school term of the year at the same school as Beth's children in Harare. Beth volunteered at the school, and she kept an eye on both children. Placement tests showed them to be in lower grades compared to kids their age. Brian sought private tutors for after school to help them brush up on their English. They had access to some of the best educational materials to help them catch up, as well as a psychologist who monitored their behavioural progress. Within three months, Tawaka showed remarkable progress, considering what he had been through. Unfortunately, Anopa displayed signs of learning disability. He was trying hard but was never able to easily grasp basic concepts.

The boys were slowly warming up to their new dad, who made an effort to spend more time with them. Over time, he taught them to ride bicycles and horses, swim and play lots of card games to stimulate their minds. He became a soccer coach for the under-six-year-olds team to help Anopa, who was extremely shy. He took them to playgrounds on weekends, where they released some energy. Ruva preferred to stay out of the way to allow them to bond.

One morning, Sphiwe and Ruva were having tea under a musasa tree, and Ruva asked a question she had been avoiding. "Are you married?"

"I'm divorced and have no intention of marrying again." Sphiwe laughed. "A few years have gone by, but I remember it clearly like it was yesterday. It was on a Friday evening, when my ex-husband came home and filled a small bag with his few and insignificant belongings that were still in the house. After packing, he stood at the door and told me that it was over, for he had found somebody else. It was no surprise, since he had long abandoned his conjugal loyalty."

"He must have broken your heart."

"The worst was over. I had already gone through all that. Instead, I felt as if I had finally been freed from a twenty-year bondage." Sphiwe laughed again.

"Were you married that long?" asked Ruva.

"Unfortunately, yes."

"You look so young to have been married for two decades."

"I married young. Listen to this." She shook Ruva's shoulder for attention. "I put on the gramophone and danced the night away to wild rock and roll music in celebration of my liberation. A new me had emerged from that ordeal."

"You are funny." Ruva could not help laughing too. "Do you have children?"

"No. I couldn't have children." At that question Sphiwe calmed down and looked sad. "That was the root cause of my failed marriage. I spent a lot of money going to witch doctors who actually did me more harm than good. I visited hospitals for test after test that left a deep hole in our pockets, and was also referred to the so-called prophets, who gave me false hope to no avail."

Ruva had not expected the whole scoop, but Sphiwe spoke candidly.

"Sorry to hear that. How dreadful an experience that must have been," Ruva said sympathetically.

"As difficult as it was, I finally accepted my barrenness and lost my marriage. He was a good man but family pressured him to have children outside marriage, and that drove him to infidelities." Sphiwe pinched her nose to stop a sneeze but was not successful, and she sneezed into her hands, which she wiped on her apron. She sniffed to clear her nostrils before she continued. "I have been living with somebody for a year. There are no expectations, no marriage talk and no strings attached. We're merely living partners who are looking for companionship." Sphiwe paused. "What about you? You don't look as if you have had it tough like some of us."

"It's all relative. My husband died last year." Ruva quickly ended the conversation. "I'll leave you to do your work without any more interruptions." She leapt to her feet and walked into the garden. The conversation had conjured up old memories and she could not believe the similarities with her own life story. Ruva respected people like Brian and Sphiwe, who could look back at their lives and narrate their stories with both humour and sadness. Ruva was not yet ready to tell her story, because her emotions were still raw.

Brian grew sunflowers on the farm for sale, mostly to international markets, and they accounted for half of the profits. The garden, with all kinds of hues, stimulated Ruva's passion for gardening.

She believed that the stables were run efficiently under the supervision of a devoted and experienced horse trainer, and there was no reason for her to make unnecessary changes. From her observation, the stable hands' love for the animals was evident. She allocated herself time working in the stables to learn as much as she could. At the beginning, Ruva was not a big animal lover, but as she spent more time working with these graceful animals, her appreciation and love for the horses grew.

The girls were home in December, excited about finishing high school. During the last two years they had gone on an emotional rollercoaster, and they were looking forward to a time of relaxation before continuing their studies together at the University of Zimbabwe. Matie was on course to study medicine, and Hilda had decided to study psychology. They were anxious when they were waiting for the results, but they were confident that they would pass.

One sunny afternoon, Matie asked her sister to go down to the river. Brian had built a cement bench where people could sit and relax facing the flowing river. The girls got down to their ritual of gathering little rocks and throwing them one by one into the water. They enjoyed the splashing and splattering of the water. Hilda could see that her sister was unusually quiet.

"You look tormented by something." Hilda took Matie's hand and squeezed it tightly.

"I'm pregnant," Matie said sorrowfully.

"What! How many months?" Hilda was astonished.

"About three. I've gone past the first hurdle, which is you, and telling Mama will be the toughest."

"Of course, how could you do that?"

"Did it once and for that I'm going to pay dearly. I'm not in the least proud of what I did," Matie said with tears in her eyes.

"I'm disappointed too, for I thought you were smarter than that." Hilda kept on firing questions about the father of the child, where the act had taken place and whether they had used contraceptives. The questions were answered with shame and Matie sobbed for a long time without stopping. Hilda calmed her sister down, and a moment of silence followed in which both were thinking of the implications.

"When are you going to tell Mama?"

"I'll do it tonight. If she gets angry with me, she will be justified."

❧

That day Ruva was happy, because she had passed her driving test. Brian gave her the keys for the old Vauxhall. After dinner, she asked the girls if they wanted to take a drive in the countryside and a stop at an ice cream parlour. Matie excused herself but Hilda liked the idea, since she had a sweet tooth.

"Something is not right with Matie. I can't pinpoint exactly what it is. Her behaviour has been off."

"Ask her. I'm not her mouthpiece." Hilda was pouting, still angry with Matie.

Ruva held off her questioning, for her maternal instinct kicked in and she suspected that Hilda knew something but would not tell.

❧

"Matie, I have brought you chocolate ice cream," said her mother, knocking on the door.

"I don't want any ice cream," replied Matie.

Ruva opened the door and removed clothes that were piled on the desk chair so she could sit down. She handed Matie the ice cream and said, "It's yours, and it's melting." Matie carefully licked it.

"We have to talk."

Matie looked at her mother and thought Hilda had snitched on her already. "It's true."

"What's true?"

"Didn't Hilda tell you?" Matie began to cry.

"Am I missing something here?" Ruva moved from the chair and sat on the bed. "Hilda didn't say anything. Was she supposed to have told me something?"

"I'm pregnant." Matie covered her face with a towel and peeped out to see her mother's reaction.

Ruva froze, as if a lightning bolt had struck her. When she recovered a little from the shock, she sighed heavily and went into her bedroom to digest the unexpected news and plan the right course of action.

Hilda saw her mother going into Matie's room and anticipated fireworks, but everything looked normal, since Ruva was not in there long.

Hilda slipped into her sister's room and in a low voice asked, "Did you talk?"

"I told her. You don't know how relieved I am. I expected her to go wild with anger, but she just walked out of here without saying a word."

"Don't get comfortable, because she is not done with you yet." Hilda heard the sound of a car, and when she opened the curtain she saw her mother driving away. "I wonder where Mama is going to now?"

"Where else except to Beth's. She has to report this," Matie pouted.

Matie's suspicion was correct. Ruva went to Beth's house and parked the car outside the gate. Chipo was standing there chatting with her buddies, and she opened the gate. Ruva stealthily went into the house and found Beth helping Kyle practicing the piano.

"You two continue with what you're doing. I'm in no rush," Ruva said.

"We were just about to call it a day. We've been going at it for a good hour. Beyond that, our concentration begins to wane." Beth stood up. "Good job, honey. Ruva, out at the poolside will be a good place to talk and enjoy a cup of tea."

While Beth was brewing a pot of tea, Ruva was agonizing about all possible misfortunes that could befall Matie, the educational opportunities she had thrown away, the burden of single motherhood, financial constraints and dependency on other people.

Beth returned with a tray of Royal Doulton china. It was a wedding present from her mother-in-law. When Ruva used to work for her, these cups were only for special occasions.

"Something is not right? Your face says it all."

"I know you're going to tell me it's not the end of the world, but it seems as if I'm sitting at the edge of the cliff ready to jump," Ruva said, grinding her teeth.

"I don't read minds. Please tell me, for I'm getting anxious."

"Matie is pregnant."

"Oh dear!" Beth was tongue-tied.

"I thought I would sleep on it first before I talk to her, but I need your help."

"You'll have to give her all the support she needs and be the source of the right information. This is going to be a whole new experience for her."

"I got pregnant when I was much younger than she is. The difference is, I had nothing going for me. Marriage was my only way out of that village, whereas Matie had a bright future. I'm disappointed." Ruva rested her chin on her hand.

"How many months?"

"I didn't even ask. It was still surreal."

"Congrats! You're going to be a grandmother. Grandchildren are a blessing."

Ruva picked up a biscuit and bit off a small piece. "Hmmm,

they're yummy. Although Matie's pregnancy is consuming my mind, I have some good news. I got my driving license today. Brian was kind enough to lend me his old car."

"Time flies. It seems only yesterday when you started learning how to drive."

"It didn't appear so to me. It took forever. It was the fear that set me back for a while, but here I am. Thanks for the cup of tea and for taming my anger."

"Be careful on the roads," warned Beth.

The following morning, she walked over to Brian's house. He was sitting on the veranda where he usually took his breakfast. She did not want him to hear about Matie's pregnancy from Beth.

"What brings you over here so early?" asked Brian. "Pull up a chair and get comfortable."

Ruva sat on the brick ledge facing him. "I'm fine here. I want to catch vitamin D from the sunrays. I'm here to tell you that Matie is pregnant."

"Oh, my gosh! Didn't you advise these girls on how to use contraceptives?" Brian sounded accusatory and he paused for a moment waiting for Ruva to respond, but he saw her face growing sad. "You don't have to look so upset. She's young, and she'll bounce back. She could have done something worse than that. Can I ask Homba to make you a quick breakfast?"

"No, I'll go straight to the stables and talk to the horses."

"Brilliant idea! Don't take it out on them, they pick up on misery and could give you a good kick."

"At least they're good listeners."

"Are you suggesting I'm not?" Brian asked.

She giggled like a small girl, and Brian gave her a playful goodbye wave.

Instead of going straight to the stables, Ruva went to Matie's room and held on to the door handle. "Are you awake?"

"Come in." Matie sat up, looking scared of her mother's wrath. "Good morning."

"Morning. If there is any problem with the pregnancy or anything else, I would like to be the first person to know." Ruva had softened her heart.

"Thanks, Mama."

Brian had given it a little thought and followed Ruva to the stables. He looked for her but she was not there. He walked towards the cottage and saw her on her way to the stables.

"You took a detour. I want you to know that pregnancy is not a sickness. She'll be fine. I'll check with the girls in the office; we might need an extra hand to help with filing. The idea is to keep her busy, unless you have something in mind."

"She has no other viable option right now," Ruva agreed.

The girls received their A-level results. They were excellent, and both girls were accepted at the University of Zimbabwe. Matie was encouraged by Brian to write a letter to the university explaining that she would be deferring her studies to the following year. Hilda started university before Matie had her baby. The day she left was a sad one, for it reminded her of the day she took her first trip with her father to St. Theresa's and picked up one or two pieces of information about him. She never got another chance to learn more of what he had promised her.

"I wish Father was here. He would have been proud to see

me going to university and happy to be a grandfather," she told her mother.

"I'm ambivalent about the grandfather part. His wish was to see you both going to university, and of course grandchildren have their own time and place," said Ruva, who was watching Hilda pack her clothes. She was wondering whether Matie would have been a letdown for her father too.

"I'll drop you at the university. It will give me a chance to see the place, since I've never been there before. In another two years, when I finish my high school courses, I'll join you. Wouldn't that be something, especially if we take psychology together?" Ruva lifted her head. "Ask your sister if she wants to come with us."

"I doubt it. If I were in her situation, I wouldn't want anyone to know that I'm pregnant. I'd leave them guessing," Hilda shrugged.

Ruva dropped Hilda off at Swinton Hall, a girls' residence, and she didn't stay long since Hilda was more interested in reuniting with her high school friends.

When Hilda was unpacking, she noticed a nicely folded parcel in red wrapping paper. She carefully untied the bow and unwrapped the parcel. In it was a dress Matie had bought with her first paycheque to wear at formal functions at work, which were quite regular. It was off-white and pleated from a high waist. The length came down to her mid-calf. Matie had asked her mother to slip the little parcel into Hilda's case and tuck it in with her clothes. There was a note tied onto the dress with a red ribbon.

Hilda,

You don't know how much I envy you. This favourite dress of mine is a sign of my love for you, and you will need it for those endless dances we hear about.

Mama has been extremely supportive; I'll find a way of paying her back. Baba would have killed me for letting the family down.

Do me a great favour, if you meet any of my friends, don't hesitate to tell them the truth, especially Wilma. I can't hide it forever. I will live with this badge of shame for the rest of my life.

Remember that your success will be my success too. Whatever you do, never make the same mistake. Don't rule me out. I'll make up for it.

Love you dearly,
Matie.

When Hilda finished reading the note, she knew that Matie had listened in again to the discussion she had with their mother. "That's Matie," she said. She held the dress close to her and looked in the mirror before hanging it in the wardrobe. She wore it to the school opening dance, where she turned heads. After she wore it once, its glamour diminished, but it remained her favourite dress for a long time.

Matie's pregnancy was uneventful. She worked in Brian's office until the very end. As her pregnancy advanced, she packed on extra pounds, and she hated her body and what was growing inside her.

On a Sunday afternoon Matie felt nagging pains and knew the time had come. She told her mother, and Brian drove them to the hospital where Matie was in labour for six hours before she delivered a healthy baby boy with her mother in attendance. She named him Ira, after her favourite science teacher, Ira Gibbs.

Ruva took charge of Ira from the beginning. Matie welcomed her mother's help and also took advantage of Auntie Sphiwe, who helped to nurture the baby. Matie was not keen on nursing Ira, despite encouragement from her mother.

She did not give up on pursuing her education. She had every intention of redeeming herself. She applied to a number of universities in the UK and received favourable replies from a number of schools, but she settled for the University of Southampton, where Mr. Gibbs had studied. He passionately bragged about the quality of education at the institution.

Her biggest challenge was to find a scholarship that would cover her tuition and living expenses. She could not dare ask her mother for an advance, since Ruva had Ira to look after, or Brian, since she did not want to take advantage of his sincerity. Eventually, she received a special Commonwealth scholarship that covered the entire medical program.

When her plan of going abroad, which she had kept a secret from her mother, was in place, she revealed it. She also told Ruva that Tongai, Ira's father, who had not been in the picture, was a lost cause.

"It's his loss. Ira will be fine. I never doubted your ability to pick up all the pieces together. Now go and do it." That encouragement buoyed Matie's spirits.

Ruva was filled with trepidation. She gazed at her daughter with sadness. Matie minimized her own pain by hugging Ira and singing to him. He was oblivious to the events that would take his mother away.

Matie went to England in June 1982 and billeted with a hospitable family, the Auburns, while waiting for school to start. They had a daughter named Allison. The two girls clicked and were destined to be friends for life. The school matched international students with local students who helped familiarize them with the area and the new culture. There were some similarities; they were both twenty and pursuing the medical profession at the university. Allison had taken a gap year to work at Marks and Spencer as a cashier and was hoping to raise money to cover some of her expenses, whereas Matie took maternity leave by default and also worked in Brian's office.

Matie had three months before starting school, and she asked the Auburns to help her find a part-time job. She landed one at a fish and chips restaurant owned by an old friend of the Auburns. She hated the job because at the end of the day she smelled like a fried fish. She persevered for a fortnight until she overhead two customers talking about job opportunities on a cruise ship. She listened to the conversation with keen interest. She ran to the back of the restaurant and jotted down what she could remember before asking them a few more questions. One of the customers had done a stint on the ship and had all the tips Matie needed to embark on the adventure. This was great timing, for she had seen these majestic ships at the Port of Southampton. She could only dream of sailing in one of them. She told the Auburns, who were not in favour of her decision. Nonetheless, in the middle of July she left on her first trans-Atlantic trip from Southampton to New York City.

After her second trip, she made the decision to postpone attending college. This was supposed to be a summer job, but instead it had turned out to be a full-time one.

She did not see this as a waste of time, for she was visiting places she would never have known. It was definitely a different learning curve. What she was learning on the cruises was valuable, and she would see the world. Her appreciation of the service industry would widen, and she would meet people from all walks of life. Matie's desire to study had evaporated and she was not in a hurry to commit to anything major. Her newfound freedom and independence took priority.

"In hindsight, I wasted a year working for a pittance. I don't want you to make the same mistake. Look at this new interest objectively. Don't walk away from a rewarding career for the sake of following your own instincts. It's a blind faith," Allison begged, but Matie was determined to do it her own way.

Chapter Eleven

During one of Matie's trans-Atlantic cruises, the *Blue Seadom* ship experienced a scary rough ride thirty-nine miles from the eastern seaboard of Canada. Before the storm, the sea was calm and the sun was reflecting beautifully on the water. The ship effortlessly glided through the calm waters. By late afternoon, the winds had picked up and the waves were ferocious as they built and rose higher and higher. The ship swayed from side to side, throwing everything into disarray.

The ship's skipper advised people through the public address to go down to safer places and to remain calm, but furniture and hanging gadgets on board were strewn all over, injuring passengers and crew alike. People were screaming while trying to hold on to immovable objects as tightly as they could, or taking cover in tight places and hoping for the best. There was utter chaos as people pushed and shoved or tripped on moving furniture or avoided falling items.

The ship's crew was unsuccessful in controlling the crowds and pandemonium broke out. The *Blue Seadom* kept on moving through the storm, battered for hours, and fortunately drifted towards the Canadian shore. It was wrecked and not seaworthy, although it finally rode out the weather.

The ship had radioed for help, and when it was out of the danger zone, passengers were ferried out in lifeboats that littered the sea. Despite the calamity, only five of the 2,700 passengers registered on board died. It was a miracle that the death toll was that low, and most of the passengers emerged remarkably unscathed.

The crew helped passengers first before disembarking themselves, but Matie's instinct was clear. She thought she had been to hell and back and was not waiting. She put her street clothes on top of her uniform, since she was on a short break in her cabin down below when the ship ran into problems. Wrapped in a blanket, she quickly slipped undetected onto one of the evacuation boats full of passengers and was also taken ashore. As soon as they hit land they were driven to a school, which now served as an evacuation centre. She entered the gymnasium and sat in a corner, afraid of being caught. A male passenger recognized her and knelt down beside her. "Aren't you one of the crew members who served me and my friends on the ship? You gave us interesting insight into different wines. Are you okay?"

"I would be fine if you leave me alone. I need to catch my breath, and I'll be in action again soon." She stood up and was about to walk away when the only male black passenger on the ship ran in front of her and blocked her path. "I'm Fred Adom. What is your name again?"

"Tilda."

She surprised herself in coming up with this name. She kept on walking, and although he was right beside her, she never looked at him.

"I'm only trying to talk a bit." Fred was animated. "No need to ignore me like that."

Matie left him standing there as she ran into the bathroom, where she found refuge and gathered her thoughts. She was thinking about what could have happened. The thought of dying weighed on her and she was terrified.

As she exited the bathroom, another waitress bumped into her. "Are you all right? You should go and report to the supervisor. He's doing a second head count of all the crew members."

"Have you been looking for me? I was giving a hand to some elderly passengers who had sustained some injuries," Matie lied to the supervisor. Guilt was written all over her face.

"You're now accounted for. We'll talk about it later." The supervisor was not the impolite and forceful type, but he documented everything.

While the distressed ship radioed for help, one news station intercepted the message and ran a story about "another *Titanic* going down." On that day, the world remained glued to radio and television, curious to know the fate of the ship and its passengers. But as the whole saga unfolded and the true facts emerged, the station was forced to recant its story. That network's credibility was in question for a while. All the passengers and crew members were put on another ship en route to New York. Hordes of journalists waited for them at the pier to interview those willing to talk about their ordeal. Matie saw Fred being interviewed. He was beaming and enjoying his five minutes of fame. After his interview, Matie passed by and Fred flagged her down and handed her a business card.

"Look me up next time you're in New York. I've business dealings there, although I live in Toronto."

Matie took the card and slipped it into her pocket without looking at it. She was not mature and sophisticated enough yet to make a move like that, but she gave the invitation some consideration.

Matie took three months leave of absence. In spite of the frightening episode, she decided to go back to work on the ship. She enjoyed what she was doing and she dismissed the incident as a minor mishap.

As soon as she got back to London, she met up with Allison at the university.

"Can I ask for a favour?"

"What are friends for?" Allison replied without any hesitation.

"I don't want my family to know that I ditched school. I don't expect them to understand."

"Do you think I'm going to write your mother and tell her that you're cruising on ships and working as a glorified waitress?"

"You wouldn't dare. Can you be my contact and alibi until I straighten myself out?"

"As long as it's not for criminal activities."

"It's not that bad. I need to use your address and telephone number. Remember to tell whoever wants information about me that I live in Southampton and not London."

Allison played along. "That's a small favour to ask of a friend. Trust me on this one."

"I met an interesting guy on the ship," said Matie.

"You already caught your big fish on Atlantic waters?"

"Only you could say something like that. It's nothing serious," laughed Matie.

She took advantage of the time off, and the Auburns helped her move into a small flat in London. With the little money she had earned and saved, she was dying to explore the brighter lights of a big city. She visited second-hand shops and bought bits and pieces of furniture for her bachelor flat. She liked

Beth's décor of new furniture mixed with antiques. She tried to emulate that style, but she found it costly.

Eventually, she wrote letters to her mother and Hilda. She was getting homesick and was missing her family.

Dear Mama,

Sorry for taking so long to write. I'm living with a wonderful family that received me with wide-open arms and has taken me under their wings. This should be comforting to you, for I know you worry incessantly.

I'm still trying to get my bearings right at the university, as it is a big campus. Things are hectic, but I'm keeping up the pace.

I miss Ira. There isn't a day that I don't think about him and all of you, of course. I hope he's not keeping you hopping. I feel bad that he'll grow up not knowing me, but I have no doubt that you're the best mother for him. I trust that he will be the beneficiary of your tons of experience. Thank you again, Mama. Give my love to all,

Matie

After she had written her mother a letter, she had no energy to continue, and it was another week before she picked up a pen and paper and wrote to Hilda.

Dear Hilda,

I love England, which has more to offer than I could have imagined. I pinch myself now and again to make sure I'm not losing touch with reality.

As for medical school, it is challenging, but all is going well. After I graduate, I'll come back home to serve my people.

I constantly feel guilty that I left Ira behind. I hope he will not hate me for the rest of his life. I would love to receive Ira's pictures every so often. I miss him greatly.

How are the boys at UZ? If you're dating, contraceptives are the answer.

If you happen to bump into Wilma, give her my address. I would like to keep in touch with her.

Love you all,
Matie.

Matie signed a new contract and went back to work after two months of rest. That period gave her enough time to get over her fears. She was delighted when she discovered that she would cover the Caribbean islands. She had become more inquisitive about the world at large and kept a detailed diary of the places she visited. Her mind was never idle as she went out searching for pieces of history. She bought a small camera for capturing memories and also collected postcards, which she kept in photo albums. Whenever they docked, she was on the lookout for a chance to explore surrounding areas.

After three months of going back and forth at sea, she visited the Auburns, since she had heard from Allison that Mr. Auburn was hospitalized due to a heart attack. He slowly made a full recovery. While Matie was visiting, Mrs. Auburn took a strange call.

"I'm sorry to bother you, but I'm looking for a girl called Tilda, who works on cruise ships."

"The person you're looking for might be right here. Not sure about the name, but hold on, please." Mrs. Auburn handed the phone to Matie.

"Who is it?" Matie asked Mrs. Auburn with her hand covering the mouthpiece.

"He didn't say, but it's somebody who knows that you work on the ship. Go into Allison's room. It could be a suitor for all you know."

"Hello! I happen to work on a cruise ship. Who's speaking?"

"You might not remember me, but we met on the *Blue Seadom* six months ago. I've been wondering how you're doing. You were quite distraught when I last saw you."

As he continued to speak she recognized the voice. She opened the window, fluffed up the pillow and comfortably stretched out on Allison's bed. Her heart was beating faster.

"Is this Fred?" she asked.

"Yes."

"That terrifying disaster is hard to forget. I'm doing well. How did you get this number?"

"I expected you to phone, and when you didn't, I looked for your number until I got it."

"That's rather bizarre that people would give you my contact just like that." The feeling that someone had been tracking her down sent a quiver down her spine, but she was flattered that he was pursuing her.

"I'm still anxious to know how you got my phone number. It's driving me crazy."

"Don't worry about it. I won't tell you how I got it, in case you slip out of my grasp again. I'm an ordinary guy who is interested in something special. I've been here in London for a few days on business. Can you make it to London today?"

"Unfortunately, I'm going back to sea tomorrow. I'd rather stay put. They changed my route to the Caribbean."

"Damn! The Southampton-to-New York route was perfect. I was hoping that we'd meet in New York on one of your stops."

"What type of business are you in?" Matie asked curiously.

"I design buildings. Who answered the phone?"

"A friend's mother. She hosted me when I came here. My family is in Zimbabwe."

"Oh, really? How wonderful. I'm originally from Ghana. I haven't been back there since childhood. Isn't it a shame? I should look at establishing something there," he said. "My father told me that things are looking up. It's worth looking into that market."

Fred's grandfather worked for an Italian company called Fendi Ferrari Construction. The owner of the company died and there was no next of kin to take it over, so Fred's grandfather bought it. His two sons joined him later and became part of the company. He decided to keep the name from the previous owner, who had a good reputation. By the time Fred joined the company his grandfather had passed away. Fred joined the family construction business after completing his architectural engineering degree. He did not stay long with the company because he did not get along with his uncle, who thought that Fred wanted to take over ownership of the business.

Fred, on the other hand, did not like their old-school style of management. They could not keep pace with modern changes as fast as he would have liked. He branched out and set up his own company, Adom Architectural Designing (AAD). His business acumen was strong, and he knew how to strategically manage his ventures. He won great acclaim for his designs and had a reputation as an astute businessman. He slowly worked his way into the inner circles of the big guns in the construction industry. His contemporaries knew him as a designing and construction tycoon. He made money from real estate by buying rundown buildings, which he bulldozed then modernized to align with modern styles.

Fred lived in New York, but he worked all over the world. Hence, he was frequently in London. When he met Matie, he was in his early forties and unmarried. He had become so involved with his career that he did not want to be slowed down by family responsibilities, but that did not stop him from being a ladies' man.

"If I want to get hold of you again, can I use the same number?" Fred asked.

Matie gave him Allison's number. She hoped he would keep his promise and phone her back.

Three more months had gone by when Allison received a call from Fred asking when Matie would be in town. The impulsive Matie was in London and she rushed to Southampton. She gathered enough courage to call him.

"Hello, Fred, Allison told me you are in town."

"I thought you'd never call. I'm in town. Can we meet up today?"

"Certainly! Let's meet at Chatters Cafe for lunch at 1:00 p.m.?" Matie gave him the address. She had been there with Allison and enjoyed their pastries. She had never gone on a date of any kind and did not know what to expect. It was all new and confusing for her. When she arrived at Chatters Cafe, Fred was already waiting on the patio, perusing the *Guardian*. She could not miss him because he wore a baseball cap with a Canadian maple leaf. Matie strolled cautiously towards him.

"My goodness, you look awesome! Why did I wait this long to see you?" He looked mesmerized.

She did look spectacular in a taupe above-the-knee dress, which suited her as if it was tailored especially for her. It complemented her youthful looks. Black heels made her even taller, and her little clutch bag showed sophistication. The seam on her black nylons was straight, adding to her sex appeal. Her hair was sleekly pulled back and secured with bobby pins, and her makeup blended well. She had dabbed on a spicy perfume. She was definitely well put together.

"Thank you." She sat opposite him and noticed his admiring glance.

"How have you been?" He lightly squeezed her hand.

"I'm well," she said, feeling awkward since she did not know what to say, but she continued to observe him carefully and liked what she saw.

"Are you ready to order?" asked the waitress.

"Tilda, go ahead and order, since you're familiar with the menu."

"Their pies are the best. We'll have two meat pies, garden salad and two glasses of red wine. Fred, do you have any other preference?"

"I'll go with your choice. One area in which I don't have a clue."

"I love South African wines."

"We don't carry South African wines. Would you like Australian Shiraz?"

Matie had acquired a taste for good wine at an early age when her family visited the vineyards in South Africa. On cruise ships, she had resumed the interest and used her good taste buds to explain the different types of wine she served.

"That would be okay," said Matie. "Have you cruised again since that time?"

"I enjoy voyages by ship, but time is of the essence. I haven't. I wish we could meet more often, but the logistics could be tricky."

"It's said that where there is a will, there is a way. Look at you having found my number by hook or crook," she teased. When are you flying back to New York or Toronto? I can't keep up."

"I'm booked to fly out tonight. I've a meeting in New York tomorrow morning, and then I fly to Toronto late in the evening. Recently, I have been insanely busy."

"I'm sailing in a couple of days."

"I have travelled extensively in the Caribbean and love the weather and the food. I'd like you to visit me during your holiday. Now that I have seen you, I don't want to let you out of my sight. This is crazy. Do you still have my USA number, or did you chuck it away?"

"Let me have it again." Matie was warming up to him.

"Lunch was delicious. I hate to say goodbye. I still have to put things together before I go to the airport." He pulled his watch from his jacket and checked the time. "It's getting late. Can you come with me to the station, and the taxi driver will drop you off." They quickly got into the taxi, and ten minutes later they were at the station.

"Five pounds even," said the taxi driver. Fred and Matie didn't realize they had arrived at the station, since they were busy chatting away. "We're at the station, sir. If you are going to London you better hurry. The train should be pulling out in five minutes," the taxi driver said loudly.

"Please take her home safely," said Fred, and he left forty pounds on the seat next to Matie. He jumped out, and as the taxi was pulling away, he held on to the door, reached out and planted a kiss on her forehead. They gazed at each other with mutual desire. He pushed his way through the crowds to the London platform.

"What's your address, missy?" asked the taxi driver.

"Going to varsity to see a friend."

"Not going home?" the driver verified. "That man's show of affection says it all. He's in love with you, young lady."

"I would like to believe that. With time, I should know the difference between infatuation and true love." Matie trusted Fred, but she had to tread carefully. She wanted to know him better before committing to a serious relationship.

"What's wrong with you, young girls of today? You analyze things too much and end up losing out." The driver peeked in the rear-view mirror to see her reaction.

"If you don't, then you end up making wrong decisions based on false assumptions and lose out more. I'm still sizing him up because this was our first date." She was slowly maturing and getting wiser.

"He looks mature. I hope he's not prowling around the innocent. Check him out thoroughly."

"That's the point I was trying to make, and you totally missed it, sir." Matie patted him on the back and said, "On second thought, he looks okay."

"It's my hope that my two lasses can look at life from that kind of perspective," said the taxi driver. "I've witnessed a lot in my years of taxi driving, and customers have told me unbelievable stories. Each time I talk to my customers, there is something new to learn. On a few occasions, I've wondered which planet they come from."

"Compile them into a book and reap your profits, sir," Matie told him.

"I'm not a writer. Instead I'm a taxi driver and I enjoy what I do."

"There are ghost writers who make a living from writing other people's stories. Nonetheless, I share your sentiments. I thoroughly enjoy what I do for a living, although I'm not paid what I'm worth," Matie added.

"I see why that chap is going nuts. You're smart, too."

"Thank you, sir. You're so kind. Unfortunately, you'll never know the end of this saga," Matie laughed.

"I have no doubt that it will be a happy one. Fourteen pounds will do it."

Matie stepped out and measured every step as she walked towards Allison's flat. She knocked on the door a few times, but there was no response. She scribbled a note and slipped it under the door.

I came by to tell you more about the chap I met on the ship. I fancy him.

Cruising in a couple of days.

Keep well,
Matie

Over a period of eighteen months, Fred and Matie communicated regularly and met whenever they could during her breaks or stopovers. Fred would fly over to an island and they would spend a day together or back in London if the ship was dry-docked for a few days or weeks. In London, the little one-bedroom flat was their hideout, and Fred did not mind staying there because Matie loved it.

Matie loved Fred not only for his glamorous lifestyle but because he was affectionate and she found him attractive as well. Fred was slightly taller than her. His head was clean-shaven, and he had a tendency of running his hand on his baldhead. He was handsome, with a dark complexion. He was an exercise buff, and his muscles bulged beneath his clothing. From their discussions over the months, Matie believed that they had the same mindset, although she had shelved her own professional career and was selling her talents short.

She went to New York one summer to visit him, and she had lots of fun. By day, she explored New York. Her daily routine was shopping in extraordinary boutiques, visiting museums and touring the city with the help of Fred's driver. By night they wined and dined in expensive restaurants, prowled the nightclubs and attended shows on Broadway and other elite events. She held her own as well as anyone in that lifestyle. This was the high life she had envisioned as a young girl, and she was living it to the fullest. After a month's break and living with Fred, who treated her like a princess and provided spending money, she went back to work.

By now, Matie was madly in love with Fred. Whenever she was missing him, she would phone him from one of the islands, and they talked for hours on end. During one of those phone calls, Fred decided on a whim to fly and meet her in Nassau, the next port of call.

"Tomorrow, I'll wait for you at our favourite hotel where we last stayed on our short holiday there. Hope to catch an early flight. You grab a taxi and meet me there."

The following day, Matie was scheduled to go out for four hours. They had lunch at Moran's restaurant, which served hot

Caribbean food. They booked into their hotel and overslept. When they woke up, Fred phoned for a taxi. By then, Matie knew that she would not be able to board the ship, which pulled out of the pier as they watched.

The captain had alerted the police when she didn't check in on board. She was reported as missing at sea. The news was plastered everywhere, especially in the Caribbean. Someone alerted the police and they were both picked up at the hotel. After an explanation, they were released.

Matie and Fred flew together to the next stop, for he wanted to be there in case she was fired on the spot. He waited for her until the ship departed.

"Matie, what happened?" asked the supervisor.

"I encountered problems that resulted in me missing the departure time. I can explain."

"It's not necessary. We're always emphasizing the importance of time, because it's easy to end up in this predicament. This should not happen again."

"I'll keep my word, sir." Matie thought she was off the hook.

At the end of that trip back in Southampton, there were new developments and she phoned Fred. "On board, it looked as if it would be a warning, but unfortunately it was more than that. Upon arriving in Southampton, I was suspended for three months, for missing the sailing time and something else on my file regarding the accident on the *Blue Seadom*."

"What was the reason?" Fred was concerned.

"They were quite petty. It's a blessing in disguise. I'll take that time off to go and visit with my family."

"When do you think you'll be back? You aren't going to be gone that long, are you?"

"Two months will be good enough to reconnect with them."

"I'm in the middle of closing a lucrative business deal, and I can't afford to be away. Otherwise I would have come with you," explained Fred.

"Just as well, I haven't been home for a long time, and I want to spend as much time as possible with my family."

"Why don't you hand in your resignation and move here with me on your return from Zimbabwe? It's time we made this official. I'd like to share a permanent setup with you, not this jetting here and there. I trust there's a strong enough bond between us."

"It's something we can discuss when I get back."

"Tilda, do you doubt my commitment? I love you dearly."

"We both need to think it over," said Matie, who was having cold feet.

"What do you have to mull over? I hope it's not some frivolous accusation." Fred hung up.

Matie phoned Allison, who was busy preparing for exams but always had time to chat with her about her fascinating life.

"How are you, mate?" greeted Matie.

"I don't have a life."

"You're a hard-working student, what do you expect. As for me, I'm taking a trip back home since I'll be out of commission. I've put things on hold between Fred and me. I need to re-examine the whole relationship."

"Girl, you never cease to amaze me. The last time we talked you were oozing with love, and now it's on hold. If I were a playwright, you two would feed me all kinds of writing material. Why were you suspended?"

"I take full responsibility for what happened. You're busy, so that discussion can wait."

"I have a friend who's looking for a place to stay in London. Would you sublet your flat for the two months you'll be away?"

"That shouldn't be a problem. Do I know this friend?" asked Matie.

"No, I met him recently and we're just friends. He's a nice chap."

"Good luck. Hope he's the right package that you're always talking about. I'll leave the keys with my landlord."

"Thanks, darling. When you come back and you decide to ditch Fred, I'm sure there will be a spot for you in medical school. Matie, don't waste your time and your talents."

"School is always in the back of my mind. Even Fred has questioned the rationale behind my life of toil on the ships."

"He's not alone. Thanks, my love, for helping my friend, and safe journey, *Tilda*." Allison roared with laughter.

Chapter Twelve

Ruva had been working for Brian for over three years when she asked him to convert one of the garages into a storage room where she could keep all the tools. She created an efficient system that kept a record of inventory on hand.

She worked closely with the horse trainer, who gave her riding lessons. At first, she was paralyzed with the fear of falling off the horse, and the fright restricted her progress. She found the whole process slow and tedious, but she was not giving up.

"Ruva, you have to relax and keep an upright posture. Don't pull so hard on the reins," the trainer reminded her as she cantered and entered a gallop.

"Maybe I'm trying too hard," Ruva shouted back as the horse galloped away.

Ruva was learning to ride at the same time that Brian was teaching Anopa, Tawaka and Beth's children, but Ruva would not take lessons from Brian. The children loved it, especially Tawaka, who used to ride donkeys in his village. Anopa got over his fears and over the years horse riding became his favourite sport.

One day, Ruva was riding and Brian came home to find her enjoying herself on the pastures. He took his favourite horse, Dark Ash, and followed her, feeling the gentle evening breeze.

He galloped past her, and when she saw him, she fought with her horse to stop. Brian came around her and said, "I must have disturbed your leisure riding. Why did you stop?"

"I did not want to be in a race with you. You are too good."

"You're doing extremely well. Let's canter around and talk. It seems as if I have to make an appointment to see you, busy lady."

"I prefer to keep busy rather than being idle."

"You're definitely a hard-working woman. You've so many things going, the children, school courses and running the farm with all its problems. The problems we have on the farm aren't big, but one has to spend time running kangaroo courts. At times I wonder how you do it." Brian shook his head. "Can you spare an evening tonight and we'll go for dinner?"

"What about the children?"

"Is it all right to ask Sphiwe to babysit Ira and keep an eye on the boys?"

Sphiwe was by then employed full-time as nanny for Brian's boys and for Ira in addition to her housekeeping duties. When Sphiwe broke up with her long-time boyfriend, she moved into the servants' quarters.

"She might have other plans since it's short notice," said Ruva, who had a cordial relationship with Sphiwe.

"No harm in asking. Let me go and see what she says, and I'll also ask Charlie to mind the boys tonight. I'll phone you back."

They rode back to the stable, then Ruva went to the cottage and stayed near the phone. She was looking forward to going out.

She jumped for the phone ten minutes later. "Hello!"

"I talked to Sphiwe and Charlie. They'll help out tonight. I made a reservation for 8:00 p.m. We can leave around 7:15."

"I'll be ready."

She put down the phone and memories from the restaurant in Cape Town came flashing back. She thought about the waiter and wondered whether he survived or was tortured to death in jail.

Sphiwe arrived right on time with her snacks and her knitting. She enjoyed knitting sweaters with intricate patterns that she sold to farm workers. Right behind her was Brian, who was formally dressed.

"I'd love to be chauffeured today. Can you drive the old jalopy?" Brian asked Ruva as he went round to the passenger side.

"Of course, I'll drive you." Ruva was a cautious and very patient driver. She took to the wheel and they went into town to Meikles Hotel for dinner. She parked in a well-lit area, pulled out the key and threw it into her little black bag.

"Have you heard from Matie recently?" asked Brian once they were seated.

"No. She hasn't communicated for some time, and yet when they were in boarding school, they used to write regularly."

"The other day the girls in the office were enquiring about her."

"I wouldn't know what to tell you about that girl."

"She's fine, don't fret." Brian plucked a budding lily from the flower arrangement and handed it to her. "Cheer up! The service here is slow but the food is worth waiting for."

"You're not starving, are you?" she asked.

"I'm spoiled. Homba has dinner ready by six. This is rather late for me," he admitted. "Today I went to the parents' day at the children's school. The boys are way behind the rest of the class, as expected, but they are making progress. Anopa is still struggling with math, and the teacher said it's not for lack of trying. She isn't giving up on him."

"Math is not for everyone. When I was their age, I could not add two plus two."

"That's a blatant lie. Of course you could."

"Okay, I could add two plus two, but it never made sense to me. If I had continued with that subject, I would have wrecked my brain. You have done what is expected of you as a father," said Ruva.

"Thank you for being the best mum for them. You've provided the maternal love they so yearned for and the stability they needed. Alone I could not have done it. Now do you understand why I asked you to come and live at the farm? Socially they are slowly adjusting, which is reassuring. I want to believe that nothing has been suppressed that will crop up in the years ahead."

"They're great kids and excellent company for Ira," said Ruva.

"I couldn't agree more."

The dinner did not disappoint them. Brian chose the wine. Ruva delicately held the wine glass by the stem and remembered the little rituals of swirling, sniffing and sipping her wine. Brian had always thought she was a teetotaller, but he did not comment and sat back and enjoyed his dinner.

"How is school going for you?" he asked.

"I'm thoroughly enjoying it. I still have a long way to go."

Ruva had finished A-level and had started taking university courses part-time, towards a sociology degree. "A big celebration will mark the day when I'm done." Her eyes lit up.

"I'll be there to share the day with you."

"It wouldn't be a celebration without my boss."

"This week Anopa has a sports day at school. Would you come with us?"

"Of course. I haven't participated much in that regard. What time?"

"It starts at 2:00 p.m., and then there is an early dinner at one of the parents' houses. It would be nice if we could also volunteer to do something like that," said Brian.

"Surely you can do it," said Ruva.

"I don't see any enthusiasm from you." Brian leaned forward.

"Because I have no say in your personal life," said Ruva, who bent forward and pulled on his chin. "Can we go now? I'm not used to being out this late. Thanks for dinner."

"My pleasure." Brian seemed to like the playful touch.

As they were walking out of the restaurant, he said, "We should do this more often. It gives us a chance to catch up on a lot of things without interference from the boys and everybody else."

"I totally agree," Ruva said, nodding.

She got back on the wheel. When they were in the outskirts of town, the car stalled and suddenly stopped. Brian took over the driver's seat and cranked the engine but nothing happened. They got out of the car, which was heating up. Brian carefully lifted the bonnet.

"I should have brought a little shawl to cover myself. It's quite breezy tonight," said Ruva, who was shivering.

"I can warm you up." Brian covered her with his jacket. It was perfect timing for him to make a romantic move. He rubbed her shoulder sensually, pressed hard against her, lovingly cupped her face in his hands and passionately kissed her.

Ruva was caught by surprise at this sudden display of affection. When she was able to speak, she said, "Wow!" She fanned herself with her hand and drew in a deep breath before exhaling. "At least the mechanical failure didn't happen when I was by myself. I wouldn't have known what to do."

"Some things happen for a reason," Brian said.

"True indeed."

Brian held her tighter and said, "I have been waiting for this moment." He kissed her again without giving her a chance to respond. Ruva felt an unusual excitement she had never felt before.

A car passed by, flicked its lights, reversed back and stopped in front of their car.

"I saw you two at the Meikles Hotel earlier on. Are you having trouble with your car? I see the bonnet is up," asked the farmer who lived near Brian's farm.

Brian quickly pulled away from Ruva and said, "It's overheating and I don't think it will be back on the road tonight."

"Would you like a ride home? You can attend to the car tomorrow, if it'll still be here. I have heard that they can strip the car overnight and have customers waiting for parts by daybreak. There has been a wave of crime, as a result of these blacks who are moving into our areas."

"You're so kind. Let me lock it and see what happens by tomorrow. I have seen you around, and your name again, sir?" Brian had never seen this man, since he kept a low profile and never attended local meetings.

"I'm Jeff Georges. I was recently elected chairperson of the farmers' association. We're a good group of white farmers. You should come to the meetings. We've a great networking system."

"When you decide to be inclusive, I'll come. We now live in a new Democratic Republic of Zimbabwe."

"You come to the front seat and we can talk about this."

"No, thank you! I'm fine back here. I would like to respond to this wave of crime. If we treated these black people better, there wouldn't be this crime wave you're referring to." Brian repositioned the jacket on Ruva's shoulders and kissed her again. "Keep warm," he whispered to her. "He's a bloody racist. I won't give him the time of day."

She whispered back in his ear, "With that language, we could be thrown out of the car and find ourselves walking the rest of the way."

"Then let it be. That's what he is," he said aloud.

When the man dropped them off, Ruva said, "Thank you, sir."

The farmer ignored Ruva's gratitude and said, "Mr. Sanderson, is this your lady? I've seen her driving your car."

"Excuse me. It's none of your business. Hope to see you around and drive safely," said Brian, stepping out of the car. Mr. Georges glared at him with disgust. He jolted the car and drove off, leaving a trail of smoke.

"The man is fuming like his car. Tomorrow he'll be whipping his farm workers in revenge over what you said," Ruva said.

"Hope not. That was in response to the insult he lobbed at you. Forget about him. How about a cup of coffee?" He gave her another big hug.

"I don't think we should be doing this, Brian." Ruva, being the traditional girl she was, saw the amorous advances approaching too fast.

"I'm not doing anything illegal, am I? I'm a man who is following his heart. I have suppressed my feelings for too long. I can't hide this any longer."

She took his hand and clasped it tightly in hers. "Can you give me time to think about all this?"

"How much time do you want?"

"I'll let you know."

"Stay for a bit and we can have coffee."

"I'm ready for bed. It was a nice evening."

"We should definitely do this more often. I'll walk you home."

"I'll be okay. Look at the beautiful moon shining and the stars twinkling. What can happen to me?"

"Miss Naive, let me remind you that we should be wary of the likes of Mr. Georges, who have their own vendettas. They like to strike in the dark, because they are cowards," said Brian. He put his arm around Ruva's waist.

"Mr. Brave, that's quite a scary thought. With their guns, we don't stand a chance," she shot back.

"That's what I love about you. You're quick to fire back. I promise you that I'll blow out his brain if he touches you."

"That's getting too dangerous. Do you own a gun?"

"I do and it's the most effective form of self-defense. I recommend that you take lessons on how to aim and shoot at a target."

"I'm not initiating a battle here, am I?"

"I didn't mean to scare you, but it's the truth." He squeezed her. Ruva was ready to unlock the door when Brian pulled her hand back.

"What about a goodnight kiss?"

Ruva gave him her cheek, and he planted a quick kiss on it then went straight for her lips. He pressed her hard against the door.

"You're my boss and my lawyer. We should not be doing this," she said.

"A-ha! There you go again. Don't look for all the excuses in the book. They don't apply here."

Sphiwe, who was minding Ira, heard the commotion at the door and began to tremble with fear. She thought somebody was trying to break in. "Who's there?" she shouted.

Brian took the keys from Ruva's hand, unlocked the door and gingerly opened it wide enough to put his head through. "It's us and everything is okay." He slowly pulled the door towards him and closed it.

He turned back to Ruva. "I'm in love with you," he said passionately and insistently. He pulled her head to his chest and stroked her hair. For a moment they were contented to be forever in that state of tranquility.

"This pace is too fast for me." Ruva was not ready to commit to anything and didn't want to give in easily. She went inside and slowly closed the door behind her, thinking he had given up and disappeared into the darkness.

"Ruva, what was going on out there?" Sphiwe asked, despite hearing snippets of their sweet nothings.

"Nothing of interest to you. Was Ira fussy tonight? He has been putting up a fight before bedtime." Ruva went to check on Ira.

"By eight thirty he was fast asleep. Lock the door," Sphiwe yelled as she went out.

"Thank you. Be careful out there," Ruva shouted back.

Meanwhile, Brian waited in the bushes and watched Sphiwe leave before he went back and knocked at the door. Ruva had stripped off her clothes because she was getting ready to jump into bed. She wrapped herself in a towel and opened the door, thinking it was Sphiwe, who had forgotten something.

"It's me, but you should know who it is before opening that door. What if it's Mr. Georges and his army?"

"You're right." Ruva adjusted the towel. Brian scooped her into his arms, and the towel fell off.

"Couch or bedroom?" he asked.

"Shower."

Ruva thought he would let her run a quick shower and she'd try to distract him, but he had other ideas.

Brian put her down in the shower and turned on the water.

"It's hot!" Ruva screamed.

"I'm sorry." Brian adjusted the temperature. "Is it good now?"

He quickly took off his clothes and jumped into the shower with her. For their first lovemaking, they had a perfect setting for a literally steamy love scene. She pressed hard against his body. She wrapped her legs tightly around his waist and her arms lovingly around his neck, for her body surrendered. As the shower sprayed on their naked bodies, Brian licked the water from her body like a puppy. He gently laid her down and put a towel under her head as a pillow. They writhed in amorous lovemaking. When they were done, Brian pulled down her robe that was hanging behind the door and wiped her dry before wiping himself. They rested on the bed.

"It was so good that I didn't want it to end," said Brian, snuggling close to Ruva.

"It was lovely." She was contented and was going to say something else, but Brian silenced her with a kiss and said, "Good night, sweetheart." Brian fell asleep, but Ruva stayed awake, thinking of their relationship that had suddenly taken on a new dimension. They lay entangled in each other's arms till morning, when they woke to bright sunshine.

"The boys! I'll see you later. I'm inviting myself for dinner today, and it's anybody's guess what will happen after that." Brian sped away.

As he got into the house, Sphiwe was already getting them ready for school.

"Good morning, sir."

"Morning, are you normally here this early?"

"Yes."

Brian pulled back the sleeve of his shirt to check on the time, and his watch was not on his wrist. He had forgotten it in Ruva's bathroom.

A few months later, Ruva's old tenant in Highfield moved out, so she drove to out there to meet a new one. When she pulled up to her house, she got out of the car and unexpectedly locked eyes with Shungu, who was coming from the market. Ruva had no intention of making a special visit to Shungu's house but in a way was happy to see her. Shungu looked older, heavier and dejected.

"Ruva, you look much younger. How are you doing it? Your dress has changed." She was referring to the navy blue pants Ruva was wearing. Ruva used to wear skirts only, as a rule. "Whose child is this?" She quickly put down her plastic bag and stretched her hands out to take Ira, who held on tightly to his grandmother, whimpering.

"It's Matie's son. He does not take easily to strangers." Ruva was cautious of what she said because Shungu always twisted the meaning to suit her own selfishness.

"She got married, and you didn't invite us to her wedding. I guess we're nobodies and couldn't fit into your new elite class," Shungu said.

"You didn't miss any wedding. Matie is a single parent."

"How's Hilda?" Shungu bent down to pick up her bag and grimaced as if she had pulled a muscle.

"Are you okay?" asked Ruva.

"It's nothing. It's nothing," Shungu said, rubbing hard on her lower back.

"Hilda is fine, and both girls are in university. I haven't seen you in almost three years."

"You know where to find me. Is this your car?" Shungu looked inside.

"It's Brian's car."

"That lawyer! I remember him driving a nice car. If it's yours, you don't have to lie to me." She peeped inside again, looking for a clue to something.

"There's nothing to hide." Ruva maintained her composure and politely enquired, "How are your boys?"

"Billy is in jail. They said he raped a little girl. I asked your tenants to give me your address, and they refused. I wanted to talk to your lawyer to see if he could help me. Joel dropped out of school. I didn't know that he spent his time pickpocketing at the Harare market. I'll never know what he did with the money." She paused and wiped her eyes with the back of her hand. "At one point he was arrested and was locked up in the cells for two days then was placed in juvenile detention. He managed to run away after being caned a few times. I don't see any way out of this pit." Shungu paused and swallowed hard. "Look at you, enjoying your husband's money. Mine left us desolate." Tears welled in her eyes again.

"I'm sorry to hear that things are not going well for you and the boys." Ruva couldn't believe the string of personal mishaps befalling Shungu and looked at her former friend with pity. "There's my new tenant coming. I don't want to keep him waiting. Hope to see you again." Ruva stood there riddled with guilt.

"You never have time for your poor old friends. You have allowed those white people to turn you against your own." Shungu was flying into a jealous rage.

Ruva tried to calm her down. "I understand why you're angry. You haven't been able to catch a break."

"You'll never understand." Shungu turned and walked away, wearing an ugly frown.

Ruva put down Ira, took his hand, and they walked into her house. Before she left, she pulled an old envelope from her handbag, scratched her name off and stuffed in a few dollars. She asked the tenant to give the envelope to Shungu. Ruva had heard the cry for help before, and she decided to put all their squabbles aside. She vowed to send Shungu money every so often. It wasn't a lot, but it could be enough to cushion her in hard times.

She drove back to the farm and got busy. In the country there were shortages of all sorts of things and Ruva was feeling despondent as she struggled each day to fill orders for her low inventory. She was in the middle of shuffling receipts and papers of past orders when the phone rang. It was Beth.

"How are things? We haven't talked for a while."

"Farm demands and social activities are keeping me busy, but I'm coping with everything else," replied Ruva.

"According to Brian you've extended an invitation to us for dinner on Saturday."

"I'm sure it's next Saturday."

"Glad you clarified that, for you would have found us at your doorstep this Saturday. Can I bring anything?"

"Homba and Brian always have something up their sleeves. They are taking care of that. It'll be in Brian's house."

"I thought you were planning the dinner." Beth was surprised.

"Not at all, but your trifle is always a hit. I'll let them know that you are taking care of the dessert."

"Good! We'll talk soon. By the way, there's a tennis tournament for the ladies this Saturday. Let me know if you want to go."

"I'll be available this weekend. I'll come to your house."

Beth had begun to slowly introduce Ruva to her circle of white friends. She took her to tea parties, to play card games, and to watch and bet on horse races on Saturday afternoons. Ruva's life became busier and she enjoyed the company of her new acquaintances. She broadened her social horizon, which helped her self-confidence, but she remained humble, private and committed to her family.

The call made Ruva wonder if Brian had told Beth something about the mutual feelings that had developed between them. Brian and Beth were extremely close and freely exchanged secrets. Ruva was aware of the trust they held for each other. She would not have been surprised if Brian told Beth about their romantic relationship.

On the Saturday evening, Ruva kept everybody waiting, since she had decided late to put together a flower arrangement.

"Now that Ruva has made her grand entrance, we can sit at the table and start our dinner." Brian sarcastically bowed to her and ran his hand down her back, guiding her to the seat next to him.

"My apologies for being late." Ruva turned away as she looked for a spot to place her vase of fresh flowers.

"They are beautiful," said Brian, gently touching the bouquet that now adorned the dining table.

"You have become adept at this craft," Beth said.

"There's room for improvement. I would like to learn to use props with my arrangements."

"I have something coming up and will need flowers. We'll discuss that later," said Beth.

"I hear you can ride a horse gracefully," Larry said,

"Don't believe everything you hear. The grace part is questionable and exaggerated," she laughed. "I'm still a novice at this skill."

"Yeah! Ruva will never give herself credit for anything." Brian began to praise her. "She is the best manager I could have wished for. She straightened things up and put a woman's touch all over the farm. There were doubters who thought I was taking a gamble, but it paid off." He winked at her. The doubter he referred to happened to be Larry, who had initially objected to Ruva filling the managerial position, since he didn't think she could do it without proper managerial qualifications. He had thought Brian was giving her too much responsibility. They had vehemently argued about that until Brian told his brother to keep his distance.

"Definitely, the attention is on me. Thanks for your amazing and flattering compliments." Ruva pulled her chair closer to her plate and straightened the placemat underneath it. She was obviously taken aback by Brian's compliments.

Brian put his arm around her and squeezed her tight. "It would be wonderful to wake up and see this beautiful flower every morning next to me." Their eyes met and he continued. "With my brother and my sister-in-law present as witnesses, Ruva, would you marry me and be the legal mother of my two boys?" The timing could not have been more perfect for him.

"Bravo, my dear brother! You do it better than anybody I know," Larry teased. "You couldn't wait until dinner was over."

Ruva was totally taken by surprise. She could not find the words to describe the moment. It was only six months since they had begun an intimate relationship.

She had a quick flashback of her marriage to Mukai, which was totally different, but she immediately blocked out that memory and put herself into the present. She shyly said, "Yes, I'll marry you." Her head was down and her voice quivered with disbelief as she said the words.

Brian handed her the ring. Ruva had never seen anything as beautiful as the gem she held in her hand. She stared at it, glistening in her palm, before closing her hand. Then Brian took it from her and gently slipped it onto her ring finger.

Beth and Larry looked lost in admiration of the beautiful ring. Ruva had no idea of the value of that diamond, but what moved her to tears was the commitment shown by Brian. Her tears ran down his neck. He picked up a serviette and dabbed her face as she hid it on his shoulder.

"Beth, thank you, for you are the one who brought her into my life. I owe you big time."

"Don't thank me. It must be the chemistry you two have," Beth said. "Thanks to the warming tray, the food is still warm. I'll say grace now, if we're all ready for dinner?" When she finished praying, they all lifted their heads and served the food.

"Now that I have the assurance, the food will go down well," said Brian, whose eyes were fixed on Ruva throughout dinner. She was still in disbelief as she nibbled at her food.

"Dinner was good. It's time to make our way home and leave you lovebirds to plan your bright future together," Larry said as he stood up to give his brother a high five and a firm handshake.

Beth went round to Ruva and hugged her. No spoken words

could describe the moment. They were both thinking about the day they first met at the employment agency and the events that followed and led up to this very day.

❧

"You take everything lightly. Is there anything that bothers you at all?" Ruva asked when they were lying on Brian's bed for the first time.

"Of course, there are some things that bother me. I resist worrying unnecessarily over things I can't control. Worrying is pointless and self-destructive. That's a lesson I would like to pass on to you, darling, for I've noticed that you have that tendency."

"I have a lot of lessons to learn. Will you be patient with me? My background didn't equip me with a lot of those survival tools, and there is always something out there waiting to cause anxiety and worry."

"It's me who should be asking for patience, since I've been on my own for a long time, and I'm set in my ways. I continually need to re-examine myself."

"I must confess that at times I feel as if I don't fit into your society. I have to get over that hump."

"You have done that already. For instance, in the company of my colleagues, you're relaxed and sociable, and Beth has told me that you enjoy the social clubs you attend with her. I can only advise you to be true to yourself, and you'll win them over."

"I've a complex. I've to struggle with myself about whether I'm doing the right thing."

"Many people hide their insecurities. They don't talk about them. It's good that we're having this open discussion."

"Do you think I'll outgrow it?" asked Ruva.

"You will, and now I know we'll work together." Brian dismissed the issue. "It's not my intention to bring up old memories, but we have to discuss this for the sake of our own marriage. When you were married to Mukai, you knew very little about his financial activities and other things. There was a lesson to be learned there. In case I die first, I don't want you to go through that pain again."

Ruva was surprised. "You're definitely opening old wounds. Go on."

"I'm an open book. I won't be hiding anything from you, and I don't expect you to hide anything from me. I'll make an appointment soon with my accountant, and we will go over all my finances with you. I'm not wealthy, but we will be comfortable for the rest of our lives."

"We don't have to do it soon. We have a whole life ahead of us. It's something we can do when we get married, maybe." Ruva was uncomfortable discussing finances, because she wasn't in it for money.

"Whatever you say. You're the boss from now on."

"As long as you leave me my adopted horse in your will," joked Ruva.

"I'm glad that you mentioned a will. It's of paramount importance." He'd had one drawn up years back, and his brother was the sole beneficiary to his estate. But now with a wife in the wings, four children and a grandchild, he had promised himself to change it. They both felt they were starting on a good footing.

"It's bedtime, darling." He yawned, turned off the lights and drew Ruva closer.

Hilda was enjoying university so much that she hardly came home. Every so often she would come to see Ira, her nephew. She usually met up with her mother at the university canteen after her evening courses.

"Hilda, I have something to tell you." Ruva was all smiles as they started their usual rendezvous.

"It better be good." Hilda pulled her mother to an empty table.

"I'm getting married," said Ruva, who did not wait for Hilda to settle in her chair.

"Married? Who is the lucky guy? Is it one of the stable hands? I noticed that you spend a lot of time with those men."

"Good guess. It's Brian, and we've set a wedding date. The ceremony will be at the farm."

Hilda was baffled. "I didn't know you were dating Brian. You kept this little secret well under wraps."

"I guess we were attracted to each other and did not have the guts to express it openly for some reason. I hope I haven't disappointed you." Ruva eagerly awaited a response.

"I'm happy for you, Mama. I never expected you to cross that fine racial barrier. I'm sure you thought long and hard about it. Go for it, if Brian is the right man.

"Can I be a bridesmaid?" Hilda stood up, pulled up her mother and gave her a big hug.

"Of course, you and Beth will take on that role. You should write your sister. Have you heard from her recently?"

"Not for a while. This will be a good reason to write to Matie. She has to hear this news. Things have moved at lightning speed." Hilda could not contain her excitement. That same night, she urgently wrote Matie a short letter.

Dear Matie,

You have been quiet. Hope all is well. This is going to come as a surprise to you, as it was to me. Mama and Brian will be getting married end of August, and we are wondering if you will be able to come. This is something not to be missed. Let me know if this will fit into your plans. Wedding preparations are already in high gear.

Ira is doing great and talks nonstop. Miss you and cannot wait to see you.

Love,
Hilda

Chapter Thirteen

Matie arrived in Zimbabwe unannounced, two years after she initially left. She wanted to give everybody a surprise, and she pulled it off.

"Hello, Auntie Sphiwe," she said as she got out of a taxi.

Sphiwe was standing on the veranda with Ira on her back. She was singing a lullaby and trying to put him to sleep. She stared at Matie, completely bewildered.

She was confused because Matie's sophisticated appearance threw her off. Nobody had told her that Matie was coming home.

"Is Mama home?" Matie asked calmly.

"No, she went with Brian to Victoria Falls, where he's attending a conference."

"Is she now Brian's assistant as well?" Matie remarked.

"Welcome home. Look at Ira on my back." Sphiwe's voice rose. She turned her back to show Matie her son.

"Oh, my poor baby." Matie literally tore him from Sphiwe's back. "When I left, you were crawling." She held him tightly for a while then put him down and knelt down to his level. "Oh my goodness! Let me get a closer look at you."

The child was confused.

"When are they coming back?" asked Matie.

"Tomorrow."

"The job seems to have grown, and it seems as if she's a travelling assistant to Brian as well as many other things."

"In a way, she is." Auntie Sphiwe chuckled.

"Just leave the luggage out here; I'll take them to Mama's cottage," Matie said as Sphiwe was pulling the luggage into the house.

"My dear, things have changed around here. Your mother moved in here a few months ago. They're going to rent the cottage after the wedding. It seems like you aren't aware of what is happening here. I might as well squeal. Your mama and Brian will be getting married in six weeks."

"I beg your pardon?" Matie pulled back.

"You heard me right, girl."

"Although I'm surprised, this was clearly in the cards. It explains why Brian did all these things for Mama. He wanted to watch her grow like a seed." Matie was taken aback.

"Aren't you happy for your mother?" Sphiwe sensed disapproval.

"No, don't get me wrong. I'm happy for her and she deserves all the happiness. I'm only trying to figure out when they started dating. I don't think this was a sudden thing. Maybe it dates back to when our father passed away and we were too young to notice what was going on?" She shifted in her chair and repositioned Ira, who was sitting on her lap. "Who would have thought they would be getting married, considering their different backgrounds!"

"The answer is they are truly in love," Sphiwe responded.

"Is it a full white wedding?"

"I'm not privy to all the details, but it will be a garden wedding, out there." Sphiwe pointed in the direction of the river. "They have started clearing the bush down there."

"Brian's idea, of course. But it's nice with the river in the background. Mama must not mind it now?"

"Well, I don't know what you mean, but I guess not!"

"Truly, things have changed around here. Who is doing all the decorations?"

"Don't underestimate your mother's creativity. She can put things together in a way you would not have imagined. She's doing all the flower arrangements herself. When she started her job she was timid, and I wondered how she was going to do it. Now she is full of confidence and works well with us. We respect her in return. What was I going to say before I got sidetracked? Oh, I meant to say Hilda and Beth would be bridesmaids. Brian's boys and Ira too will be pageboys. I'm sure your mother will be asking you to be third bridesmaid."

"No! I expect there'll be plenty of other duties for me to do." Matie shook her head.

"This place is buzzing with all the preparations. Beth is always here directing things. She is still very close to your mother."

"Is there enough room for all of us in this house? I can't remember the layout."

"Plenty. You won't mind sharing the visitors' suite with Hilda, would you? It's a fairly big room."

"Not at all. It will be wonderful to relive our childhood days."

"She's not here often anyway," said Sphiwe.

"I've shared a lot of things with her. That won't be the first or the last," Matie said.

"Are you back for good?"

"I'm here for two months. It's perfect timing, for the wedding. If I had known, I would have bought my mother a gown befitting a princess." Matie finally cracked a smile.

She didn't want to leave Auntie Sphiwe with a negative impression.

All this time, Ira was sitting quiet and still on Matie's lap, then he jumped down when he saw the dog approaching.

"What's the name of the dog?" Matie asked Ira.

"Shumba," he shouted. Ira loved the dog, and it was his constant companion.

"Does the dog bite?" Matie asked Sphiwe. Matie was not an animal fan. They never had pets around when they were growing up.

"Not unless you're threatening it. Otherwise, it's a well-behaved dog," said Sphiwe as she was going inside to fetch a ball. "The two of them can play with this ball for hours."

"Now that Ira has diverted his attention to Shumba, I'll take care of sleep first. I forgot to ask about the boys — where are they?"

"Do you mean Anopa and Tawaka?"

"Yes!"

"They're at Beth's place for the weekend."

Matie went into the visitors' suite, checked the bathroom and the little kitchenette, and threw herself onto the bed. She slept until dusk when Hilda woke her up by gently rubbing her cheek.

"Hi, sister! You don't come home often. How come you are here?" Matie sat up straight and they hugged.

"Grapevine is at work. I phoned Auntie Sphiwe, wanting to check on them, and she told me that you arrived this morning and so here I am. Move, please." Hilda slipped under the covers with her sister.

"What's happening around here?" Matie asked, despite getting the entire scoop from Auntie Sphiwe.

"Lots of changes, and did you get my letter about Mama and Brian's wedding?"

"No. But it's my fault, for I should have been communicating more. You know very well what it's like when you are at school. You keep on procrastinating and eventually lose track of time." Matie made a point of yammering about school so as not to leave a shade of doubt in that area.

"When you left, Mama didn't have a phone, but I assume you never thought of using Brian's number. It's another way you could have kept in touch."

"Never crossed my mind. Did you know that Mama and Brian were having this little fling?" asked Matie.

"I didn't, and it's Mama's feelings now that count. All I can say is she's smitten with Brian. First thing you'll notice is the glow on her face. And the amazing confidence she has that is bringing out her true character. She has been able to manage this farm with integrity. We should be proud of her." Hilda was emotional. "She has come far, and she knows that. Do you know that she's taking university courses now?" She stopped as she saw Matie flinching.

"Good for her. We knew she had the brains," Matie commented.

"Didn't she mention it in one of her letters?"

"I don't remember."

"What else is Mama doing with herself?" Hilda mused. "She has been horse riding, making flower arrangements and attending social events. She is living her life to the full. Be prepared to see a different woman in that respect, but she remains a loving mother."

"I'm happy she was able to make a smooth transition," said Matie. "I worry about her, though, for the Brian I knew could be intimidating. When I worked at his office, some of the staff could not tolerate him and others would not be caught dead talking to him."

"He's different at home, and Mama is attuned to dealing with his cockiness, his sarcasm or whatever you want to call it. She's grown tough, for she can stand her own ground. He loves her, and that should give us comfort and delight. It's not as if he's abusive."

"I won't argue with you, because we'll analyze the same picture differently no matter what." Matie was resigned to Hilda's strong arguments. "Does Mama have a dress yet?"

"Of course! There's a talented seamstress who designed the breathtaking dress. Wait till you see her engagement ring. It's gorgeous. The diamond is as big as the pupil of your eye. He must have paid a fortune. You have to see it to believe it and appreciate its quality."

"Is it real?" Matie was doubtful. "It could be fake, and Mama wouldn't know."

"Oh please, don't be silly. Do you see Brian giving her anything less stellar than that? That would be deceitful to all of us."

"Now that you mentioned the ring, we never saw Mama wearing a ring when she was married to our father," Matie recollected.

"I don't think it matters now. It would be pitiful to compare these two husbands and the marriages. It's like comparing apples and oranges."

"True!"

Hilda propped herself up with pillows. "Enough about Mama and her wedding. Girl, you look smashing. Auntie Sphiwe said to me, 'You won't recognize Matie when you see her.'

"And do you know what I said to her? It's like not recognizing myself in the mirror. She laughed herself silly. She's a wonderful person."

They talked till late, until Hilda said, "I have a couple of hours to sleep before I slip out early and go back to the university. I'll call you later to see how you're doing. Maybe you can come and visit. It's a great educational establishment. Do you know that I'll be done my first degree soon?"

"Some of us will still be at it a little longer. I'll come with Mama when she comes for her class, and you can take me around. See if you can round up Wilma for me."

"I rarely see her, but I'll see what I can do," Hilda promised.

Ruva arrived home and noticed that Sphiwe was in her best frame of mind, not that she ever showed much if she was unhappy. "I presume that wide smile means all is well," said Ruva.

"I have made some changes in the visitors' bedroom. Go and see?"

As they were talking, Ira came bouncing towards them and held on to his grandmother's leg. "Auntie is sleeping." He took her hand and led her to the visitors' suite. Ira, who was leading the way, pushed the door ajar as hard as he could.

"Matie!" Ruva belted out her daughter's name. She kneeled down at the side of the bed and smothered her with her body. "Why didn't you tell me you were coming?" She turned to Sphiwe, who was standing at the door, and said, "Tell Brian that Matie is home."

Matie immediately noticed the glow that Hilda was talking

about and for a second was tongue-tied. "Hello, Mama. You look amazing."

"Thank you. What a surprise!" Ruva looked behind when she heard the now-familiar footsteps of Brian entering the room.

"Matie, welcome home." Brian stretched out his hand and gave Matie a firm handshake and a light tap with his left hand. "Thank goodness you didn't give your mother a heart attack."

"Wouldn't want that to happen."

"How's everything with you?"

"Everything is good, and medical school is going well. I'm on holidays for a while and will be back to the grind again end of August."

"You brought your medical books. Still studious?"

"I have to. Lots to review." She had borrowed Allison's books and had placed them on the night table where they were clearly visible.

"I'm glad you came back to visit. Your mother worries about you. I keep on telling her you are a big girl and can take care of yourself," Brian said nonchalantly.

"She still does?" Matie was surprised. "I heard that you two will be tying the knot soon." She darted a glance between her mother and Brian.

"I'll leave your mother to fill you in on that. She's in the driver's seat and is the superwoman here overseeing everything." He patted Ruva on the shoulder on his way out of the room. "Good to see you, Matie."

"Did you get the letter Hilda wrote to you?" Ruva asked.

"I don't know what happened to that letter. It was mere coincidence that I decided to come home."

"The wedding date is set. I can't wait." Ruva stood up and

walked to the window. "Let's keep the cold breeze out." She closed the window and leaned against it.

"Wait till you get to London. The temperatures can be frigid." Matie got out of bed and took her mother's hand, which she had tucked behind her, and examined the ring. "Beautiful ring! I didn't know that one could find such high quality and top craftsmanship here."

"Brian designed it himself. He even got the correct ring size." Ruva gleamed with joy.

"What does the wedding band look like?"

"It's plain and simple. It clicks here." She showed Matie. "If left to me, I would have chosen a ring with a small diamond. But I shall wear this one proudly. Let's go and see what's for dinner."

A few days later, Ruva and Matie were in the stables grooming the horses when Matie asked her mother, "How long have you two been dating?"

"Long enough to be sure of what I'm doing." Ruva was surprised by the question, but she was frank. "Why do you ask?"

"Just wanted to know. Is this Brian's first marriage?"

"No, he has been married before."

"I thought you were going to show him the ropes of married life."

"He knows all about it. Maybe more than I do. He was married to an Italian lady. Unfortunately, she died young. He came back home and lived with two other women. Things didn't work out with either of them," Ruva explained.

"I'm just worried that Brian can be aloof and has an annoying arrogance."

"I agree that he can be brash, but deep down he's a loving and generous man."

"I don't want you to be hurt again," said Matie.

Ruva thought really hard about what to say next. "You shouldn't judge him so harshly, because you have been away for two years, and there has been a remarkable change in him."

"If he has changed, that's a bonus for you."

"Matie, be open with me. You're making me nervous, because I feel some resentment." Ruva was concerned, since Matie didn't appear as excited as Hilda.

"You're being too sensitive. Nothing is going to make you change your mind?"

"Is that your intention?" Ruva smiled and shook her head. "It's too late now. I gave Brian my word that I would marry him. There's no turning back."

"Gosh, you're smitten, as Hilda said."

"Matie, when you love somebody you see things differently. We should resume this discussion when you truly fall in love."

"As long as you're clear about what you want, that's all that matters."

"I love Brian passionately. At times, it is difficult to explain it to somebody who has never fallen in love. Wait your turn, and we'll talk."

Before responding, Matie wondered if she should tell Ruva about Fred but decided to hold off. "It would be wonderful to compare notes with my mother." She laughed loudly.

"I missed that hearty laughter. On a serious note, I would like you to be the third bridesmaid."

"You have two bridesmaids already, and they're too many

for a second wedding. Out of a gazillion things waiting to be done, there must be one or two things I can help with."

"It's my first white wedding," Ruva said.

"How come it took you so long to ask me?"

"I've a lot on my mind. Forgive me. And each time I wanted to ask, you had a question about this and that. We had a lot to catch up on. Would you mind helping Beth with the planning? She has a tendency to overstretch herself. She has been a one-woman team."

"Sure, I can do that,"

"I'll talk to Beth, and the two of you can meet and go from there. She'll appreciate an extra hand."

Ruva got back into the house and excitedly phoned Beth. "Guess who's home?"

"Tell me."

"Matie."

"When did she come?"

"On the weekend, and she is anxious to help you. Let her know what needs to be done, and she'll do it."

"I'll come and meet with her. The earlier the better." Beth had a list for herself and she revised it to see what she could delegate to Matie.

"Welcome home, Matie. You sneaked up on us, didn't you?"

"That's the only way to do it so people won't go crazy with anticipation."

"That was a wise idea. Do you like England?"

"I haven't had many chances to explore much of it, but what I've seen is beautiful."

"Are you getting used to the English weather?"

"Of course, the weather is another story. Complaining about it is pointless. Besides that, I love the history and rich culture."

"And medical school is going well?"

"Yep! Mama told me that you need help. From my understanding, you have already put most things together singlehandedly."

"I have two lists with me. One is for the things that I have done and the other is for things that are pending."

"You've covered a lot of ground. There isn't much to be done," said Matie, looking at the lists.

"On the wedding day, you need to coordinate everything and most importantly to keep time. That's where I'll need your help the most. Your job is to make sure that everything runs smoothly."

"Consider it done," Matie promised without any hesitation. They went through all the items that needed to be completed and the run-through of the actual wedding day.

That August day, the sun was shining, but there was a slight wind that gently blew through the beautifully decorated tent where the reception was held. The sounds of the flowing river and of the song that was playing were in harmony. Ruva wore a simple off-white chiffon dress with cap sleeves and a wide band on the waist that showed her slim waistline, and it flowed to full length. The dress tightly followed the contours of her body. She could not have chosen anything more striking. Instead of a veil, she jauntily placed a small, attractively arranged bunch of three roses on the side of her head. She wore a string of pearls with matching earrings that Brian had given her as a wedding present. Later on, she threw over her shoulders a light velvet shawl to ward off the August evening chill.

Ruva was walking down the aisle, holding on to her uncle's arm. He tripped since he was distracted by his nervousness. She kept her balance and quickly pulled him up. The pageboys who were right behind them giggled uncontrollably. Beth and Hilda managed to quieten them down.

"My beautiful flower," Brian said softly to Ruva as she joined him. He squeezed her hand tightly as they stood side by side.

She turned to her uncle, who had given her away, and nudged him to draw his attention. He was partially deaf. "You can take a seat," she whispered, but he didn't hear. She asked Hilda to escort him to his seat. He was her only living and favourite uncle to whom she continued to periodically send parcels of food. She was honoured by his presence. He had never been in the midst of people of so many diverse backgrounds, and he walked in a daze throughout the ceremony.

The pastor conducted a short and beautiful ceremony, as requested by Brian, who did not want it to drag on. Ruva and Brian had written their wedding vows, which they exchanged as a commitment to their love for each other. The pastor blessed the rings then joined them in holy matrimony. They were pronounced husband and wife and Brian kissed the blushing bride.

From the wedding ceremony they moved to the reception. The sun was going down and the majestic lighting loomed over the beautiful setting, creating a romantic ambience. Everything was tastefully done. The guest chairs were arranged in a half-moon shape and faced the raised podium where the wedding party sat. Ruva's flower arrangements made a great impression, adding elegance to the décor.

To start off the celebration, Larry toasted his brother. "My dear brother, I was beginning to wonder if women in your past had put a curse on you. Little did I know that the woman who captured your heart lived amongst us. Today, you officially declared to friends and family what is rightfully yours. Remember, a flower always needs lots of sunshine and water to blossom." Brian gave him a thumbs-up, for he knew exactly what Larry meant. "Let's toast my brother, who is adding a new problem to the many he's been attempting to solve." The crowd laughed. Larry gave Brian a nod of approval.

The last time Matie had stood before a crowd was when she gave the eulogy at her father's funeral that signified the end. On this day the toast to her mother marked a new beginning.

"Mama, congratulations on your marriage. Hilda and I know how much in love you are, for you have confided in us. Give up your sweat and tears, for they belong to a bygone era. Instead, enjoy the honey and milk while it flows. We will give you permission to love Brian with all your heart as long as your sanity remains intact. Always remember that Hilda and I are your best advocates. Consultation for any advice will be free, but continued services will be charged accordingly. Let's rise and toast to this remarkable woman who is my mother. To a long marriage," Matie said, and the popping of champagne from the crowd blanketed her last words.

At the end of the toast, Matie flashed a smile and waved to her mother, who was relieved, for she did not want any embarrassing comments. The reception was full of sumptuous feasting, and people danced to music that catered to all ages. They danced so much that the improvised dance floor cracked.

Workers who were at the wedding had duties assigned to them. At one point, they all gathered together and showed a placard that said, "Congratulations to Mister and Madam Sanderson."

Matie had executed the wedding plan well, and in between her duties she would reach for a glass of wine. By the end it was evident that she was tipsy, since she was doing some weird dance moves with wild movements, staggering all over and slurring her words. She was putting on her own live sideshow.

Ruva witnessed Matie's new behaviour, which she abhorred, but ignored it. She didn't want to engage in a humiliating confrontation. "I'm embarrassed by Matie's behaviour," she said to Brian.

"What were you expecting? A saint? At times independence brings freedom. She's a true free spirit."

Instead she called Hilda. "Keep an eye on your sister. I hope things won't get any worse."

Before the end of the evening, Matie had consumed more than she could handle, and she finally put her head down on the head table and fell asleep. Hilda saw Dr. Blyton walking towards her, and she went over. They both helped her walk, with difficulty, to the house. Dr. Blyton was holding Matie with one hand, and in the other he had his cane to steady himself. Hilda was bearing most of Matie's weight.

"Matie, you can drink, but you shouldn't make a fool of yourself."

Matie mumbled some gibberish, and Hilda didn't understand a word.

"Don't waste your energy, Hilda. She's intoxicated," said Dr. Blyton.

She helped her sister into bed. She managed to remove only Matie's shoes, and then she covered her with blankets fully clothed.

As they walked back, Dr. Blyton concentrated the

conversation on Hilda's studies. "How are your psychology courses going?"

"Going well, and I would like to seek your guidance on what to do with a psychology degree."

"You would be a dynamic clinical psychologist. I'm now a retired old horse, but it was a rewarding profession for me." He added, "Let's discuss it more when you get a chance."

"Thanks. I'll get in touch after the wedding," Hilda said gratefully.

Matie slept through until the next afternoon, and when she woke up she did not know how she got into bed fully clothed. She remembered last dancing to The Rolling Stones, and everything after that was blurred.

"It's a shame that you didn't see the end of the celebration. You were totally drunk. How do you manage on your own when you're in that drunken stupor?" Hilda had frustration painted all over her face.

"Loosen up, Hilda, and have a life. I'm capable of looking after myself. Whatever happens to me, let it be."

"I'm not trying to pick up a fight. Would you like to hear what happened when you were sloshed?" Hilda fired back.

"I get it. Go ahead."

"Mama and Brian went and quickly changed before their last dance. While they were changing into riding gear, farm hands handed out lighted candles to all the guests. The truly amazing part was when the bride and groom came in riding the horses, which were beautifully decorated with ribbons. Brian did a little show with his horse. All the lights were switched off, and we lit the candles. The happy couple rode off into the night. It was such a romantic exit. Mama reminds me of Cinderella. We could only hear the sounds of horses' hooves fading in the far distance, where the getaway car was waiting to take them to the hotel. It was magical."

"Nobody told me there would be horses and candles," said Matie, knitting her brows because of a throbbing headache.

"I don't think even Mama was aware of that one. It was Brian's secret and he pulled it off."

The way Hilda described the ending of the ceremony left Matie feeling guilty and filled with regret.

"Did Mama see me drunk?"

"What do you think? She happened to have been present at her own wedding." Hilda was being hard on her sister. "You missed an opportunity to even say goodbye. Won't you be going back in a couple of days?"

"Unfortunately, we know the answer," said Matie as she left the room.

After Ruva and Brian left for their honeymoon, Matie helped clean up, out of guilt. As she pretended to tidy their bedroom, she went through her mother's drawers.

Sphiwe caught her in action. "Anything specific you are looking for? Can I help?"

"Not really, but this looks interesting," Matie said as she looked at a brown envelope tucked inside an old sweater. It had school reports from when she and Hilda were in primary school, letters from boarding school, documents pertaining to the trial of her father's murderers and letters from the company. She spread them on the bed. The discovery shocked her. She couldn't believe how her father had conducted his life and finally met his death. When she was done, she put them back into the envelope. "Please don't tell anybody that I was snooping into their drawers. Anyway, I found exactly what I was looking for." Matie bribed Sphiwe with some money before she left, and Sphiwe zipped her mouth.

When Matie got back to England, she phoned Allison in Southampton but couldn't get hold of her. She remembered her friend was on a short holiday and suspected that she might be in London at her flat with her friend. Her gut feeling was correct.

"Oh, Matie, you're back. Why didn't you phone?" said Allison, blocking the door.

"I tried your number at your flat. Since I couldn't get hold of you, I decided to come here. Can I come in?"

"Sure you can, but excuse the mess."

Matie looked around. "My goodness! This place is like a pigsty. Has anybody cleaned it since the day I turned the key?"

"I was going to do it today."

"Ally, do you live here?"

"Now and again, I make unannounced visits," she laughed.

"Your friend should have been picking after himself." Matie knew that chores were not something Allison did willingly.

"I'll go on my hands and knees and clean this place. But first, tell me about your holiday."

"How about I go across the street for a bite while you clean up the place?"

An hour later, Matie went back to the flat and saw some semblance of order.

"Now that you're back, I can take a short break. I still have to do my dusting." Allison looked busy with her pants turned up to her knees, her t-shirt tied in a knot at her waist and a headscarf around her head.

"You look the part of someone on a cleaning mission. As for my holiday, it was exciting to say the least. My mother married her old lawyer. They claim to have sent me an invitation, but I didn't get it."

"You have a pile of letters here, and I saw one from Zimbabwe, probably from your sister. Your tone isn't convincing me that you are happy about the marriage. Would you like to share?"

"My mom found her soulmate but I'm not fond of the guy. On the whole it turned out to be a beautiful wedding." Matie did not go into her own personal embarrassment. "Are you an item now with this guy? Why am I even asking? The signs are written all over you. You look comfy here."

"I'm in love, but I'm in no rush to be his maid, as you can see. Playing house will have to wait."

"That's what I like about you. You're always sure of what you want," said Matie.

"Fred called me a fortnight ago, wanting to know if you were coming back to London. That guy is serious about you. You better have a plan."

"I missed him. Unlike you, I'm set to move wherever he wants to take me. I had enough time to think about marriage."

"Why were you playing hardball before you left?"

"Immaturity, I guess. Will your boyfriend be interested in subletting the flat or taking over the lease? I'm already planning ahead."

"Colin is his name. I'll see what he says."

A few days after she arrived in London, Matie phoned Fred and they talked at length about their commitment. They agreed that they were ready to live together. To Matie's surprise, Fred expressed interest in moving to England due to promising opportunities and wanted to expand his business into European markets. By the end of the autumn, he began to tie up some loose ends in preparation for his big move.

Matie was quite happy to stay in London.

As soon as he got to the city, they looked for a house. They focused their search in Mill Hill, an affluent part of northwest London. Living there meant he continued to go back and forth to America for his other businesses.

One evening at a friend's party, Fred surprised Matie with an engagement ring. Instead of just being a get-together it turned out to be an engagement party. They celebrated the whole night. In the morning, when they got home, Fred went down on one knee and asked Matie for her hand in marriage. She accepted the proposal, and a month later they were united in a civil marriage at the Registry Office. They invited a few people for dinner at a hotel, including Allison, who was a witness to the ceremony.

Matie and Fred slowly joined the entrepreneurial circles of London. They became true socialites by associating with the elite. They lived a glamorous life criss-crossing between continents. This lifestyle went on for at least two years before Matie gave birth to twin boys. With the birth of the boys, she had a difficult time adapting to the idea of being a stay-at-home mom. Fred carried on with his flashy lifestyle and left all household responsibilities to Matie, and it put a strain on their marriage.

During those years, Ruva and Hilda wrote letters through Allison's address, and Matie sporadically contacted Hilda with very little information about herself. The letters were all written in generalities.

Chapter Fourteen

Since Ruva hadn't seen much of Zimbabwe and the situation had politically stabilized, they decided to drive around the country and make it both a honeymoon and get-to-know-the-country adventure. They had three weeks, and they started in the Eastern Highlands, where they visited the Nyanga mountain ranges and part of Chimanimani Park. They made their way down to Mutare and visited the Hotsprings Resort, where they stayed for a couple of days before heading west to the Great Zimbabwe Ruins. It was a lot of history for Ruva to take in. Brian had made these trips many times as a young boy with his parents and as a boy scout, but the countryside had changed tremendously because of the war. Bridges were damaged, roads were potholed, and historical landmarks were destroyed. Ruva truly acquainted herself with her beloved country.

A few days after Brian and Ruva left for their honeymoon, disaster hit their house. It was late at night when Sphiwe, who was left in charge of the children, heard a loud bang and then an explosion in the kitchen area. The smoke and fire spread quickly to the bedrooms. Sphiwe, realizing the gravity of the situation, hurriedly gathered the screaming children and pushed them outside through the main bedroom sliding door. They were coughing and spluttering from smoke inhalation.

Sphiwe and the children crowded together outside and watched the house burst into orange-red flames. The farm hands came out and stood helplessly. By the time the fire brigade was notified and rolled into the farm, there was nothing to save. In a matter of an hour, the house was a huge pile of rubble with charred furniture still smouldering and the glass cracking from the intense heat. Shumba the dog and Bobo the cat had perished in the raging blaze.

In the morning, Beth drove to the farm to check on the cleaning and clearing up of the tents and other standing structures. As she was driving down the main highway she saw smoke billowing into the sky, coming from Brian's farm. She put the car into high gear. What she saw was a beehive of activity. Police were interviewing the farmhands, the fire brigade was hosing any flare-ups, and people from the neighbouring farms were milling around to catch a glimpse.

Beth was gasping with anxiety as she wondered about the fate of the children. She nervously looked around for a familiar face. She saw Charlie the stable hand and ran toward him. "Did Sphiwe and the children make it?" she asked, unbuttoning her jersey, since she was sweating and her heart was pounding.

"Yes, they are in Sphiwe's room," Charlie said.

Beth ran towards the workers' compound. Another worker saw her running and pointed to Sphiwe's room without saying a word.

"We made it out safely, but the children have been coughing. The smoke was bad," Sphiwe reported as she and the children huddled together.

"I'll take you to the doctor and you'll stay with us. Wait a minute, I'll go and talk to one of those policemen and see if they are done with you.

"Do you know what caused the fire?" Beth asked a policeman who was standing nearby.

"It's too early to say, madam. We think somebody threw in some type of grenade, from the statement given by the maid. Are you related to the owner?"

"Yes! It's my brother-in-law's house and they must have told you that they are out of town."

"We'll be contacting you, if we find anything to report. Can we have your contact number?"

"And the children, are you done with them?" Beth asked as she provided the contact details.

"They are good to go."

Beth took them to the doctor and they were cleared of any complications. She went back and took measures to tighten security around the farm. She protected Brian's horses, his most coveted investment, by renting a horse barn fifteen kilometres away until Brian and Ruva returned.

Brian and Ruva were gone for more than a week and needed to check on their family. Brian attempted a few times to phone home but failed. He finally phoned Beth.

"Hello, Beth?"

"Brian, nice to hear from you. How's everything?"

"It couldn't be better. We're enjoying ourselves immensely. Listen, my dear, I've been trying to get hold of our brood. There's a problem with the phone."

"Yes. The phones in your area are down. You can phone here, and I'll pass along the message, but they are all well and everything is fine. Sphiwe is doing a fantastic job. I saw them this morning." Beth lied because didn't want them to cut short their honeymoon.

"I'll be in touch soon," said Brian.

"Regards to Ruva."

"Hold on for her."

"Hi, Beth! Matie must have left by now?"

"Yes, I took her to the airport. I haven't heard from her yet."

"Thanks a million. What would I do without you?" said Ruva.

Brian and Ruva made their way north to Bulawayo. Ruva liked the city and its wide roads. At Matopos National Park they visited the gravesite of Cecil John Rhodes. Ruva left armed with important Rhodesian history. They finally reached Victoria Falls, a bustling little town on the Zambezi River.

They walked deep into the woods and were soaked by the mist spraying from the falls. The majestic, thunderous falls flowing down into the Zambezi River were a wonder to behold. From a distance, the rainbow they saw looming on the horizon was picture-perfect. They went on an adventurous late afternoon boat cruise during which they saw congregations of crocodiles basking in the sun along the river bank, hippos dipping in and out of the water and different types of wildlife drinking and looking out for their prey.

In the evenings, the tourist village had a party atmosphere, and people danced to tribal music.

They took unforgettable memories away from their honeymoon, but the driving took its toll on them. In the end they decided to fly back home. They had kept Beth and Larry abreast of their change of plans. Brian and Ruva were surprised to see Larry and Beth at the airport, because Brian had asked his driver to pick them up.

"Good to see you, folks," said Larry.

"Where's the driver?" asked Ruva, who sensed that something was amiss.

"We missed you so we came instead. Can we go to Meikles Hotel for tea before we proceed to the farm? We're anxious to hear about your honeymoon," Larry said. "Who thought about this idea? I expected you two to have chosen some exotic place."

"We can do that some other time. It's important to know your native land first," said Brian.

Brian and Ruva told them about their honeymoon and described in detail all the places they had visited. Larry and Beth did not give any other hint that they had bad news.

As they settled down for tea Brian said, "You heard all about our honeymoon, and now it's your turn to tell us why you are here." He had a sixth sense that allowed him to take the suspense, since he sometimes went through that in courtrooms.

Larry went straight to the point. "Your house burned down."

"What? And the children?" asked Brian hesitantly and Ruva could only let out a gasp of despair.

"Sphiwe acted quickly. She pulled the children out of the house, and they are fine. They have been staying at our house," Beth reassured them. "Larry and I decided that we would let you enjoy your honeymoon and then deal with the consequences when you returned."

"Did this happen after Matie was gone?" asked Ruva.

"Yes, a few days after. Why?"

"I just wanted to know if she was okay." Ruva did not

want to expose her daughter's smoking habit. She thought if it happened when she was home, something might have caught fire from her cigarettes.

Brian jumped in. "Do you know what started the fire?"

"When I talked to the police they said they suspected that somebody threw a hand grenade into the house through the kitchen window. Actually, it was partly Sphiwe's account. They haven't gotten back to us yet. I'm sorry, Bobo and Shumba perished in the fire," Beth said sadly.

"What about my horses?" he asked.

"They are all right. I moved them away, but we can talk about that later," Beth said.

"I wonder who could have done this to us. They must have known that we were away and wanted to harm the children," Brian growled.

"I agree that the children were the target. They wanted to hit where it hurts the most," Beth said.

They drove to the farm, where an eerie silence hung in the air. It was a forty-minute drive from the city centre, but to Ruva and Brian it seemed as though they had been driving forever.

"Wow, it's only a shell," Ruva cried out upon seeing it.

"Whoever did this did not win this war!" Brian said as they all got out of the car.

"They already won. Can't you see what they have done? It's us who will be picking up the pieces from the devastation. They must be having a good laugh wherever they are."

"You can come and stay with us while you're sorting things out," Beth offered.

"Thank you. We can use the cottage. Thank goodness it's still furnished and not rented out. We'll stay here as we rebuild. Thanks, my sister."

"I agree with Brian. We don't want too many changes for

the kids," said Ruva. "I missed them so much. We should go see them now."

"Wait, I've got to check on the cars. The garage looks intact from here." Brian walked over and peeped through the window.

The garage had miraculously not caught fire because the wind was blowing in the opposite direction.

"I'll take the car and bring the kids home with us."

"I would have preferred to see you guys back here when the culprit is in jail. He's still at large and can strike again."

"If you live in fear, you give the devil more ammunition to keep on tormenting you," Ruva said.

"There is an element of truth to that," said Beth.

"Tomorrow, I'll go to the police station and see where they are at now," Brian said.

"Keep us in the loop, but meanwhile, you need to be careful."

The kids were playing soccer and ran over when they saw their parents. "Mama, Mama, they burned our house," Anopa shouted.

Brian knelt down and huddled with the children as if they were going through a rugby ritual. Even Ira found it fascinating, and as small as he was, he crawled into the centre and stood there laughing.

"Okay, let's go home. I don't expect them to have many things to take back to the farm," said Brian.

There were expressionless faces when Brian mentioned home. Ruva got out of the car last and stood there without moving a muscle as she watched the children. Then they ran to her and clamoured for attention. On the way home, the children posed a barrage of questions. Ruva and Brian answered them as truthfully as they could.

Life on the farm went on as normally as possible. The investigations were still ongoing. Ruva and Brian were called to the police station and they gave names of people they suspected. Mr. Georges and Batsirai's names were right on top of the list. Meanwhile, they started planning and rebuilding a bigger house to accommodate their growing family.

❧

A month after Brian and Ruva returned from their honeymoon, Beth instead received a call from the police notifying her of the progress they had made in tracking down suspects and that it was a matter of time before they would make an arrest. She quickly gave them Brian's number and straightaway relayed the information to Brian.

The messenger of court spoke to Brian, who had not heard from the police for a good two weeks from the time they left a message with Beth.

"Good morning, Mr. Sanderson. You'll be happy to hear that we've two people under arrest. You'll be receiving a letter specifying the dates of the trial in a matter of days," he said.

"Do we know the arrestees?" asked Brian.

"You might know them, but wait for the letter."

At the trial, Ruva did not experience the same emotions she had at Mukai's trial. It was different in the sense that Brian would be there to walk her through the workings of the criminal justice system, to hold her hand, and she would be on her own turf.

The prosecutor opened the session by calling to the stand Mr. Mathias Chigwende, who looked terrified. He had turned himself in because he could not live with himself and was tired of running and looking over his shoulder all the time.

Mr. Chigwende was charged with throwing a grenade at the Sandersons' house. Through a translator, Mr. Chigwende was asked to tell the court about his involvement in the crime.

"Mr. Gordon asked me to firebomb Mr. Sanderson's house in the middle of the night. I don't know if he assembled it himself, but he showed me how to set it off. He instructed me to throw it into the bedroom wing, where it would do the most damage. I got scared and threw the bomb through the nearest window and ran back to the farm. When I looked back there was a huge fire. He ordered me to leave at dawn, without telling anybody, and to go to Kariba and never return back to the farm."

"And then what happened?" asked the lawyer.

"He organized everything, including accommodation for me, and he gave me lots of money," said Mr. Chigwende. "He promised to keep paying me."

Mr. Archie Gordon was the white farmer charged as an accomplice. The defense attorney for Mr. Gordon painted Mr. Chigwende as a pathological liar who stole money from the little farm store and was fired but was seeking revenge by involving Mr. Gordon in a conspiracy.

When Mr. Gordon took the stand, he denied all of Mr. Chigwende's testimony. He clearly laid out, in his own defense, that there was no reason for him to harbour such passionate dislike for the Sandersons. The lawyer brought in a number of his workers as witnesses, who spoke well of him.

"Mr. Gordon was involved in the crime, despite his denials," said Ruva forcefully.

"He might have done it, but he will likely walk out a free man, because there's no obvious incriminating evidence. They searched his farm thoroughly looking for bomb-making materials but came up with nothing. "

At the sentencing, Mr. Chigwende was given six years, despite having cooperated with officials. Mr. Gordon was acquitted, just as Brian had predicted. He sold his farm and moved away, which gave the Sandersons some peace of mind.

Chapter Fifteen

Shungu had secured a little stall at the Machipisa Shopping Centre. One early morning as she was settling down after spreading out her vegetables and wares on the table, she heard one of the ladies reading aloud to her friends an old article about an explosion on a farm that happened when the owners were on honeymoon. It was front-page news.

At first Shungu did not show much interest until the lady started reading the part where the article described Ruva in detail. She became interested and paid great attention before acknowledging her acquaintance with Ruva.

"She is my friend and was my neighbour when she lived here in the township," Shungu said enthusiastically.

"We have never heard you talk about that friend or mentioning anything about the wedding of such a friend. Knowing you, you would've boasted about your friendship," said the lady who was reading the article.

One of the ladies in the next stall came to Shungu's rescue. "Stop attacking her. It's none of your business."

That remark caused Shungu more embarrassment. She couldn't defend her position on the matter, since she had no clue of the marriage between Ruva and Brian.

In the evening, she visited Ruva's tenant. "I misplaced

Ruva's address. I would like to send them a little gift for their wedding. I'm a little behind, but I don't think she'll mind."

He gave her the address and the name of the farm. "It's never too late from an old friend," he said.

"Thank you. Oh, by the way, were you invited to the wedding?"

"I didn't expect them to invite me. I don't know them that well."

"I was invited but I couldn't go. I will be in touch with her. Do you know when she will be coming to collect her rent?"

"I'll give it to Mr. Sanderson, whose offices are not far from where I work. If you give me the parcel I can deliver it for you, and then you won't have to spend money on postage."

"That's a good idea, I'll bring it over."

The following day at the market, Shungu was looking around at other peoples' wares when she saw an old chest full of knickknacks. She dug deeper and saw a small, badly tarnished jewellery box. It was the rich blue velvet lining that caught her eye. She liked it and was oblivious of its value. She paid very little for it anyway.

Shungu had seen a man welding and tinkering with metals on the other side of the market. She was not sure if he could bring out the colour of the little box.

"Can you clean this little box for me?" she asked.

The old man examined it and he knew right away what it was. "You won't recognize it when I'm done polishing it."

As he had promised, the silver sparkled under the morning sun as he handed it back to her. "No charge for you, but think of me when you sell it for a little fortune."

"You'll get your reward from above. I'll give it to a dear friend as a wedding present. It's just like new. Thank you." Amazingly, she had not even been looking for Ruva's gift when she came across it.

For weeks, Shungu agonized about whether or not to go to the farm. She finally made the decision to go on a Tuesday, since it was one of the slower days at the market. She was determined to track Ruva down.

Ruva was riding her horse when she caught sight of Shungu walking briskly up the driveway, as if she was marching into battle. She'd never imagined seeing her old friend at the farm. Ruva pulled back on the reins and the horse came to a sudden stop. She jumped off the horse and walked it towards Shungu, who stood still, looking frightened.

"It's okay. It won't harm you."

"You're riding horses too?"

Ruva nodded and forced a smile.

"So this is where you are?"

"Where are you coming from?" Ruva immediately regretted asking the question. "It's a little far out to come."

"Where you used to live before all this," Shungu shot back, with her arms wide open, referring to all that she could see on the farm.

"I'll take the horse back to the stables. Come with me." While they were walking, Ruva knew that she had to be careful in her approach. "How are you doing?"

"The struggle continues and I'm alive. I was worried about you. I heard that your house burned down."

"It happened when we were away." Ruva wondered how Shungu knew, but she dared not ask.

"Charlie, this is an old friend of mine. Can you tie the horse for me?"

"You have servants and all?"

"They are workers who offer their services and are paid wages."

Ruva took her to the garden. "Take a seat. This is my favourite spot, for it is peaceful. I'll go in and ask Sphiwe to put together a quick lunch."

As they were eating lunch, Shungu asked Ruva the question that had been nagging her. "How come you didn't invite me to your wedding?" Her accusatory tone made Ruva very defensive.

"I didn't invite you because I felt insulted each time I talked to you. You never gave me a chance to explain myself. You never considered my feelings. You kept on accusing me of being brainwashed by the white people. When was the last time we parted ways amicably?" Ruva had her brows drawn together.

As Ruva was talking, Brian appeared. "Look who's here! Long time no see. Your name just slipped my mind," he added, tapping his head lightly.

"Shungu," she replied.

"Pardon me?"

"Shungu," she repeated loudly.

"Yes! How can I forget it?" He clicked his fingers. "Is all well with you?"

"Yes," she answered shyly.

"Would you join us?" Ruva asked.

"I'm not staying. I just came back for some documents that I was working on yesterday. Just as well, I've met your friend. You didn't tell me she was visiting today."

"It's a surprise visit. Lucky for her, because normally this is a day I would be out and about."

"Good to see you, Shungu." He dropped a kiss on Ruva's forehead. "Have to run." He strutted away.

"Nice guy," said Shungu.

"He's the same guy you thought was going to steal my money." Ruva picked up where she had left off. "I'm sorry, our relationship had soured."

"Even the best of friends have differences." Shungu tried to sound sensible and philosophical.

"Anyway, let's move on." Ruva was relieved that she had aired her concerns. "The last time we talked, the boys weren't doing well. Have things changed?"

"Bill has at least three more years in prison. Joel promised to go back to school come January. Are you still going to school?"

"I'm now in university. Have you thought of going back to school yourself?"

Shungu laughed out loudly and heartily, which reminded Ruva of their better times together back in Highfield. She had almost forgotten about her friend's hearty laughter.

"Do you have to keep on going to school now that you have everything — a husband, a farm, money and children who are doing well?"

"It's about me," Ruva said, beating her chest. "I don't want to depend on other people for the rest of my life."

"I have some good news of my own. I secured a stall at the market. Thank you for sending me money. I saved it and used it to pay for the stall."

"Wonderful! How's it going?"

"Some days are better than others."

Shungu still had a healthy appetite. She kept piling food on her plate as they were talking. There was more than enough food for two people, and Shungu happily devoured it all.

"It's almost time for me to pick up the kids from school. Is it okay if I take you into town, and then you can catch a bus from there? I'm sorry to interrupt the visit but I appreciate you coming to see me."

"I have a small wedding gift for you," said Shungu, who looked much calmer than when she had arrived. She took it out of her handbag and gave it to Ruva. It was wrapped up in a newspaper that had the story of the farm burning while they were on their honeymoon.

"You can't do that. I didn't invite you to the wedding. You even have the newspaper," screamed Ruva.

"It doesn't matter. Did you see the article, since you were not here?"

"Friends saved it for us." Ruva took the gift and carefully unwrapped it.

"A silver jewellery box! This is beautiful. Thank you. Thank you." Ruva had polished enough silver at Beth's house to recognize its value. She kept the newspaper and was polite enough to nicely fold it and place it back in the basket.

"Promise me that it won't collect dust in some corner. If you decide to sell it, keep your little fortune," Shungu laughed again.

"It's the only jewellery box I own. It will be used," Ruva assured her.

"I'm glad you like it." Shungu did not explain how she found the treasure.

While driving into town, Shungu continued to update Ruva on what was happening in Highfield. Shungu never missed the local gossip.

"I miss you, our church and ongoing activities in the township. It shaped my character. For we all know every journey has a destination, and I'm happy with where I'm now. I wouldn't want to change anything. At times I pinch myself, for I never envisioned the path my life has taken."

Shungu listened attentively and replied without her usual anger. "I'm happy for you. As for me, I'll keep on working hard until I get there too."

Ruva saw this visit as a turning point for the better in their friendship.

"Drop me off here. There's the passport office." Shungu pointed at the office as she oriented herself with that part of town.

"Hold on. It's too dangerous to stop here. I'll turn on the next street." Ruva quickly changed lanes. "Are you thinking of travelling?"

"I want to go to South Africa and import products for my stall."

"Come again and visit when we're done rebuilding." Ruva stopped the car.

"Send me an official invitation." Shungu jumped out of the car.

"You don't need one." Shungu did not hear because the words were drowned by the traffic noise. She weaved in between traffic as she made her way across the busy road to the other side.

She left Ruva with something to think about. Ruva wondered if Shungu had used the wedding gift as a way to see where Ruva lived. What had changed to make Shungu a totally different person? Was it the money she had given her? Ruva drove away with her mind whirling with all these questions, and she could not overlook the high-priced gift.

The house was completed, and both Brian and Ruva were happy with the final result. Brian had sought the help of an interior designer who was his business partner's wife. Ruva was not happy with that arrangement because she had wanted to put her own stamp on the final touches.

"I hope your designer will take my input into account."

"Of course she'll work with you. Stop being over-sensitive and insecure. You're creative, but we should hire people with expertise."

"Suppressing my creativity is exactly what you're doing."

"Nonsense!"

The bickering ended when the boys interrupted them. This was the first time that they had argued.

When everything was done, the house looked spectacular, with a big kitchen, spacious rooms and an attractive layout. Modern furnishings completed the décor. This was to be her palace. Ruva liked the end result despite her resistance to outside help.

They took no chances and added extra security around all the buildings. They installed a new fence around the farm.

Chapter Sixteen

After Hilda completed her post-graduate degree in psychology, Brian and Ruva threw her a big party at their house. Hilda invited her university contemporaries to celebrate the achievement.

At the party an interesting guy approached Hilda. "Excuse me? Aren't you Tilda? I'm Julius. We met in New York."

She quickly brushed him off. "I'm sorry. It's a case of mistaken identity."

Julius blocked her as she was walking away. "I'm confused now, because I heard people calling you Hilda. When we chatted in New York, you said you were Tilda and came from Malawi."

"Hilda is my true name. I've never been to New York."

"It's truly bizarre." Julius went into detail describing the party at which he had met Matie and Fred. "I'm not making this up."

"I bet you there's somebody out there who looks like me. How coincidental can that be?"

"You and I need to talk. Here's my temporary number." Julius pulled out an old receipt from his wallet and scribbled a number before handing it to her.

"I'll be in touch." Hilda examined the receipt and put it into her pocket.

A few days later, Hilda contacted him. "Julius, I should have told you that I've a twin sister studying medicine in England whose real name is Matilda, but we always called her Matie. I don't know if she has been to New York. We're identical twins. Does that help?"

"Somebody gave me that information already," he quickly interjected.

"The last time Matie was home, she didn't even mention that she had been to New York. I can't put that past my sister. Our communication has been mediocre at best."

"Would you like me to put out feelers to friends in case she has been seen around New York lately? I'll keep you posted if anything crops up?"

"There's no need."

"You're upset, aren't you? I'm sorry to have raised unnecessary flags," said Julius.

"I'm more worried than upset."

It crossed Hilda's mind to tell her mother about Matie. After carefully thinking about it, she decided it was not worthwhile to sound the alarm over nothing. If Matie had been seen in New York, it was all right. She was an adult who had the right to go places whenever she pleased. Hilda concentrated on her personal life and continued to look forward to a bright future through education.

A few days later, Hilda received a letter from the University of Cape Town and told her mother, who was tending to her vegetable garden.

"I've been accepted into a Ph.D. program in clinical psychology at the University of Cape Town! I might be the first Dr. Ganda in the house, since we haven't heard about Matie's graduation." Hilda was happy that there was no longer any doubt she was going to get the highest honour in that field. "Thanks to Beth, who introduced me to Dr. Blyton, who has been a special mentor." She pumped her fist with joy.

Ruva rested her gloved hands on Hilda's shoulders before embracing her daughter tightly. She looked her in the eye and said, "I have a confession to make, due to my past ignorance. When you were young, I didn't know anything about doctorates and believed that Matie would be the only doctor in the family with a medical degree. She must be almost there now. I can't wait for the day when there will be two doctors in this family. What more can a woman like myself, who struggled all her life to bring a change to her children's lives, ask for?" Her eyes shone with happiness.

Ruva could not contain herself. She had to share this good news with somebody. She went into the house and phoned Beth, for she did not want to disturb Brian in case he had a client or was in court.

"I've exciting news to share with you."

"Spill it, I can't wait."

"Hilda has been accepted for her doctorate at the University of Cape Town. Please pass this piece of news on to your dad."

"Fantastic! That girl has proven herself beyond our expectations. She deserves personal congratulations. I'll talk to her soon." Beth ended the conversation but rang back immediately.

"How's your friend Shungu doing? What a woman!"

"She *is* a character, that one," Ruva agreed. "She paid me a surprise visit a few months ago. There's a remarkable change in her attitude, believe me."

"Oh, really?" Beth was skeptical. "I thought about her

because we've a new member in our church who reminds me of her. These women are two of a kind."

"I truly sympathize with Shungu. Life has dealt harshly with her. But I won't be asking her to join us for lunch soon, because one can never know what triggers her anger."

"Talk of being unpredictable. She's like a bomb waiting to explode."

Ruva put down the phone and it rang again. This time it was Brian.

"You must have been chatting on the phone. Can we go riding together this evening? You see what happens if people are working too hard, they overlook the important things in life."

"I was talking to Beth. Girl talk."

"See you later. Love you."

Brian got home earlier than usual. Ruva was not in the house. "Where is my dear wife?" he asked Sphiwe.

"She's waiting at the stables."

He joined Ruva and they rode their horses at a trot, enjoying the coolness of the evening and watching the sun disappearing into the darkness.

"I've some good news to tell you. Hilda told me this morning that she'll be starting her Ph.D. program in clinical psychology at the University of Cape Town in February."

"She is amazingly focused, that girl. You should go with her to Cape Town and help her settle down. You two need a bonding trip."

"She's an independent woman. She won't need my help in that regard. It's Matie we need to check on. We should go and see for ourselves where she's at in her studies. What do you think?"

"Great idea," Brian agreed. "When would you like us to go?"

"Next month is good."

"There shouldn't be any problem. Be warned that it'll be hellishly cold, since it's the height of winter there."

"Looking forward to seeing my girl and watching snow falling from the sky," said Ruva, visualizing that small wonder.

"Afterward, we can travel around England. I haven't been there in a while. Prepare yourself for surprises," said Brian, flashing a fake smile.

"Pleasant surprises will be easier to deal with, for sure."

❧

A month later, Brian and Ruva jetted to England. As they got off the plane, there were a few flurries of snow falling, and it was a treat for Ruva. It was so different from Zimbabwe, and she was engrossed.

During their month in England, she never saw the sun shining. The days were dreary with an occasional blanket of snow on the ground that made everything look fresh and clean. That was the first time her imagination captured the Zimbabwean sun that shines from dawn to dusk, except when a dark cloud passes by and gives warning signs of thunderous rain.

They didn't waste time in London. Ruva was dying to give Matie the surprise of her life. They took the train to Southampton to visit the Auburns first and were hoping to see Matie shortly after. Ruva had kept the Auburns' address.

By the time they got there, it was no longer snowing but it was chilly and drizzling. They got off the taxi. Brian knocked on the door and Mr. Auburn answered. He was a nice man, but his demeanour told a different story.

"Are you sure you're at the right place?" he asked.

That surprised Brian, who had to think of something pleasant to counteract that ungentlemanly approach. Mr. Auburn was ready to close the door when Ruva quickly said, "Are you Mr. Auburn? The man straightened up and his facial muscles relaxed. "I'm Matie's mother."

"Did I hear correctly that it's Matie's mother at the door?" Mrs. Auburn called out from inside the house.

"You're right, dear," Mr. Auburn replied.

She struggled to get to the door, since arthritis in her knees had flared up, and with one good look, she said, "Oh my goodness, there's no doubt that you're Matie's mother. She inherited those good looks from you. Come in, it's freezing out there. The English weather has no mercy at times."

Mr. Auburn pulled their suitcase inside. He went straight to the fireplace and threw two logs into the dying fire before sitting on his old rocking chair. Mrs. Auburn circled around, picking things up from the floor and brushing the cat's hair off the sofa with her hand before she sat them down.

"First, let me put on the kettle for tea, and we can get acquainted." She went into the kitchen and from there she shouted again, "Did you pass through London?"

Ruva and Brian did not respond loudly enough, and her husband repeated it back to her. "They said yes, dear."

"Did you see Matie?"

Brian and Ruva looked at each other again and instantly knew that there were more unpleasant surprises to come. Mr.

Auburn quickly caught on to their surprise. "Dear, you've got to be careful," he warned his wife.

Mrs. Auburn brought a big tray back into the living room. Brian stood up and took the tray from her. He took the opportunity to ask, "When did Matie move to London?"

"Don't ask old people questions regarding time, because we can never remember," Mr. Auburn said.

"Please have a cup of tea. It will warm you up, and enjoy the shortbread. It's fresh out of the oven. I enjoyed baking when Allison was younger, but now it's a chore."

"They believe you. The aroma is still lingering, dear."

"When you get old like us, pain is a constant companion. Hopefully, they will find a cure for arthritis in our lifetime," said Mrs. Auburn as she threw herself onto a sofa and tried to find a comfortable position.

"When they do, you'll have gone to purgatory," Mr. Auburn added with dry humour. "With all the money they get from donations and the chimpanzees they have poisoned, one would think they are almost there."

"Never mind him. The best thing is, I'll have a friend in purgatory." She looked at Brian, who was all smiles and warming up to their humour. "Matie has taken a few wrong turns along the way, which you'll find disappointing," Mrs. Auburn said.

Mr. Auburn cut in. "We should let Matie tell them herself. I don't think these folks know what has happened in the last five years."

"Has it been that long? Where has time gone? I can still remember a young, shy and innocent girl. Now she's a beautiful and confident woman who knows what she wants," Mrs. Auburn added.

Ruva had to listen attentively, for she had difficulty

understanding their English dialect, and she was falling behind in the conversation.

"How is your daughter doing?" Brian enquired politely.

"Allison is doing extremely well. Still going to university here, and she'll be finishing medical school this year, but she's grappling with choosing a specialty. I assumed it would be a no-brainer for her since she's an intelligent and decisive girl."

Mr. Auburn was proud of his only daughter, who they had adopted in their early fifties. Allison was born to a teenage French mother who gave her up for adoption. The young parents that initially adopted Allison died instantly in a car crash when she was six months old. The Auburns were babysitting that fatal night and by chance ended up adopting her, since they were related to the young couple.

"Good to hear that somebody stuck with it," said Brian, who had grasped all the hints that Matie was floating somewhere in London. "Ruva, we're in for a surprise, as I forewarned you," he said in a whisper.

"Ask them if she's still going to school, amongst the many things she has done."

"Come on, go ahead and ask them," Brian encouraged her.

Mr. Auburn, who was not as deaf as his wife, replied, "We're better off leaving that to Matie. Allison knows where she lives. They have remained good friends. I'll phone her and get Matie's address in London."

The Auburns asked them to spend the night at their house, but Ruva and Brian were eager to see Matie. Ruva thanked the Auburns for looking after Matie when she first arrived in Southampton, as well as the support they continued to give her.

Brian and Ruva had no problem finding the place in

Mill Hill. When they saw the house, they were in awe. Ruva immediately had a negative mental picture of her daughter living a life of shady deals. She concluded that was the reason Matie had kept quiet. She shared her thoughts with Brian, who was more open-minded.

"Give her time to explain. At some point, the truth will come out and we'll fit the puzzle together."

"I'm glad you're here with me. You go ahead and knock this door down," Ruva said humorously, standing behind Brian. She felt the cold wind blowing into her bones.

"Do we have a hammer to do that?"

Matie opened the door. Her two little boys were beside her, tugging at her jammies and vying to see who was there.

"Step in, it's frigid. Didn't anybody advise you on the best months to visit? This is the worst time to visit England." Matie's voice was subdued and unwelcoming.

Ruva went round Brian and hugged her daughter. She was unable to hide her emotions, but Matie's face was expressionless. Brian moved aside to give them space. Matie turned towards Brian, who was leaning on the door with both arms crossed on his chest and his legs crossed over each other. She extended her hand to him.

Matie invited them into her lounge off the hallway. There was an eerie silence for the longest time. Even the rambunctious boys sat quietly on the floor, sizing up their visitors.

"These must be your boys?" asked Ruva, who stooped down to hug them.

"He's Mukai," Matie said, rubbing his kinky and uncombed hair. "And this one is Atsu. He's named after my husband's brother who died in a car accident. Both family members died horrible deaths, and we wanted to honour them. That was weird, but we wanted them to live on. They should not be forgotten."

Ruva felt like she had been stabbed in the back. She never thought she would be calling that name again. Matie, seeing her mother's discomfort, quickly excused herself and ran upstairs to groom herself. The children disappeared into their playroom. Brian and Ruva remained sitting in the lounge, admiring the splendour. Then they followed the children and sat on the floor with them, putting together some toys.

"We should hold back on questioning her, for she is the guilty party," Brian advised.

"That would be hard." Ruva sneezed. "Oh dear! Am I catching a cold already?"

"Hope not. You let her do the talking. The truth might be somewhere in the middle, but she will come round."

"She talks about her husband. We weren't on the wedding invitation list. Hard to believe," Ruva remarked.

"I wouldn't make an issue of it."

"How's everybody at home?" Matie asked when she had come back down.

"They are all well, and how are you?" Ruva replied.

"I'm good but tired from running after these boys. They never stop. They have amazing energy."

"That's how normal growing children should be." Ruva was trying hard to follow Brian's advice but could not take it any longer and asked, "Did you forget to invite us to your graduation too?"

"You are going to be disappointed, but the truth is I never stepped into a medical school." Matie was forceful in her approach. "I took a job with a cruise line, and I thought it would be a temporary summer job, but I enjoyed it so much. I wanted to see the world while working before settling down to any serious profession. I couldn't pass on the opportunity."

"That's not what you came here to do." Ruva stared at her daughter, open-mouthed in disbelief.

"I learned things that I'll never learn anywhere else. That's where I met my husband, Fred. He's away on business in U.S. and Canada. He left yesterday and won't be back home for another two weeks." She paused. "Will you still be here to meet him?"

"We intend to see some interesting sites and travel north to Scotland." Ruva gave their short itinerary, but her tone was non-committal.

Now that Matie was talking, Brian also broke the rule and asked, "What does your husband do?"

"He owns an architectural design company."

"Impressive!"

Her mother pressed on. "When you came home, you misled us all to believe that you were in school. You even brought medical books to deliberately deceive us."

"Lying was the easiest thing to do to get over that hump of deciding what I wanted to do with my life. You were busy with the wedding, and the atmosphere at home was electric. I'm sorry, I didn't keep my side of the bargain of going to medical school, and I hope you'll understand. Isn't happiness what every parent wishes for their children?"

"I agree with that adage, but in this day and age, education remains important. You had choices, and hopefully you will never live to regret it," said Ruva.

"Regret is owning up to your mistakes. I won't do that. I made the choices willingly, and my conscience is clear. We won't be discussing this topic again soon. I've answered your few questions truthfully. It's not something I'm proud of, but I'm relieved that you know where I'm at this time in my life. Look at you, Mother, still pursuing your education. If the need arises for me to go back to school, I'll revisit my options. I haven't closed any doors."

Brian and Ruva were put in an awkward situation. Brian was filled with indignation because they were not allowed to ask any more questions.

"Come, I'll take you around the house," Matie said.

"Ruva, you go." Brian did not try to hide his disappointment. He went outside to literally cool down.

When they went into the kitchen, Matie asked, "Why is Brian pouting sullenly like a little boy?"

"It's not fair at all. He is not enthused by your secrecy."

"Well, if he wants to know anything outside of what I have said, I'll be open to discussion. But some things you just have to accept," Matie said firmly. "Let's go upstairs, and I'll show you your room. Remember how I loved Beth's house? I felt the same way when I stepped into this house. I hired an interior designer to help me with decorating. I love everything about it."

"Lovely place," Ruva murmured.

A few days into their stay, after a long day of visiting all the tourist attractions in London, Matie spoke of her late father. She boldly asked, "Why didn't you tell us the truth about what happened to our father?"

Ruva kept quiet.

Then Matie threw in an insulting jab. "Are you waiting for advice from your lawyer?"

Ruva glanced at Brian, who Matie had ignored most of the time. "I thought I had put all that to rest. What's the motive behind all this?" It was obvious that she was taken aback.

"When our father died, we were old enough to know the truth, and you decided to hide it from us. I know this was not your own doing." Matie was implying that somebody else was giving her wrong advice. "His way of life was not honourable, but you had the obligation to give us the full picture of what happened, for our own closure."

"Obviously you know what happened, but you're still enraged. Where is the closure? Do you know what I went through when I went for the trial? I didn't want to relive all that pain. There was no point in hurting you and Hilda more than you had endured already. Did you consider the betrayal of trust on his part?" Ruva looked her daughter in the eye and choked up. "Did you share this with Hilda?"

"It would ring better in her ears coming from the horse's mouth," Matie said rudely.

"Ruva, you have explained yourself clearly. There is no need to go any further. This is it for me. We should pack our things and leave. You can stay if you like, but I'm out of here," Brian said.

"I did what any reasonable mother would have done with kids of your age, and that was to shield you from those sins of the world." Ruva was still talking when the chair she was sitting on screeched under her as Brian pulled her by the arm. He threw their clothes back into the suitcase, and soon they were heading for the door.

While Brian was busy flagging down a taxi, Ruva ran back into the house. "Matie, will you be taking Ira any time soon, since you seem settled?" Ruva noticed that Matie hadn't moved and that her head was bowed.

"You have looked after him from day one. He's all yours."

"That's all I wanted to hear." Ruva walked back outside in slow motion, like a robot being remotely controlled.

Brian did not ask why Ruva went back, but he opened the door of the waiting taxi to let her in. "This is part of the trip I want to quickly forget," Ruva said.

"It's impossible because you love her so much."

Ruva never thought that she would ever be in the position of choosing between her daughters and her loving husband. The way she had parted company with Matie was not what she had expected, and as hurtful as it was, she felt that Matie needed space to work through the process of relieving her own pain and anger.

Matie remained frozen at the dinner table, sitting pondering and second-guessing her actions. She was not surprised by Brian's reaction, but what threw her off was that her mother did not try to stop him from leaving. The phone rang, and she made no effort to answer. She stared at it until it stopped ringing. When it rang again for the second time, she reached out, pulled off the receiver, and violently smashed it onto the floor.

Brian and Ruva rented a car and proceeded north through the English countryside to the rugged and rolling hills of Scotland. They stayed in small, quiet hotels along the jagged coastline. The beauty took Ruva's breath away. Wherever she looked out to sea, there were crashing waves. It gave her some inner peace, but Matie was an invisible companion who followed her throughout their journey.

After a month, they went back home without contacting her, although Ruva would have liked to have met Fred in person. There were pictures of him mounted in an album on the bookshelf. Ruva had an impression of a fun-loving guy who loved her daughter. In spite of what had happened, she was thankful for meeting her grandchildren and knowing that Matie was happy, besides the anger she felt towards her mother.

Ruva accepted that her high expectations of Matie were not going to be fulfilled. They agreed that their experience with Matie was a letdown, but what transpired would be etched into their memory.

Upon their return, Beth and Larry invited them for dinner. Ruva always looked forward to Beth's company. Besides being a cherished friend and a sister-in-law, she had become a confidante.

"How was your trip?" Beth excitedly asked them as they were walking in. "You both look relaxed, which is a good sign."

"Super! Thanks for watching over the boys," said Brian before sitting down in a comfortable chair.

"It's Sphiwe who deserves a pat on the back. I'm anxious to hear about Matie. How is she doing?"

"Disappointing," Ruva said softly.

Beth probed further. "And where's she at with her studies?"

"She didn't go to school. She's married with twin boys."

"Wasted brains!" Beth exclaimed then realized she was being too abrasive. "It's obviously not what you were expecting?" She was trying hard to find the right words.

"Of course not. Let's forget about Matie for now." Brian scowled. "And how are you guys?"

"Back to Matie. When we were working on the wedding preparations, I had my suspicions that she was not in school. I didn't want to make a hasty judgment about something I wasn't sure of," Beth confessed. "Whenever I asked her about school, she was vague or abruptly changed the subject. There was something different about her."

"Why didn't you warn them? Anyway, we all know the truth now. As for us, we're leaving for South Africa, for conditions are no longer favourable to stay and work here. One has to be living in a cave not to know what's going on," said Larry, who was mixing his brother's favourite cocktail with different liqueurs.

"I'm not surprised." Brian had seen this coming. But the news seemed to put a damper on his spirit.

"Our decision to leave has been made easier because of a job offer from another mining company. It would be a missed opportunity if I didn't grab the chance now," continued Larry.

"Each time we go away, there is distressing news awaiting us. Am I the only one who has noticed that?" Ruva asked.

"It seems so, my friend," Beth said. "There would never have been the right time to disclose our plans. We've been thinking about it for some time. It wasn't a rushed decision. We're ready for whatever change comes our way. There are many wonderful people like you, some members of our church, fraternities, friends and colleagues that have become like extended family. We'll definitely miss you all."

"When exactly are you moving?" Ruva asked.

"As soon as possible. Have you also thought of moving?" Beth directed her gaze at Brian.

"It hasn't even crossed my mind. I'll be here for the long haul," Brian promised.

"Good luck, buddy. When you finally get it, follow suit," Larry laughed, but beneath that chuckle was sorrow.

"We will make the best of it and we will survive."

"Don't wait for desperation to dictate before you take that leap of faith," Larry warned. "Whites are leaving in droves for political reasons, and we're jumping on the same bandwagon."

Larry was not only a big brother but also Brian's best friend. Brian counted on him to be there all the time. Larry felt as though he was betraying his brother, but his choices were limited.

However, Brian knew the situation was volatile and wanted his brother to be where he would be happy. His conscience would not allow him to uproot Ruva and his children, for Zimbabwe was their home.

Dr. Blyton had finally retired and moved in with Beth, since his health was failing. It meant he had to move too, although he was ambivalent. The change was going to be drastic, but there were not many options for him.

Despite their different backgrounds, Ruva and Beth had managed to bridge the gap and start a friendship that grew in leaps and bounds. Ruva could not have found a better friend and advocate. Beth did not judge her like Shungu did. These were two people on two ends of the social spectrum, and fate had brought them together. Beth and Ruva had openhearted respect for each other.

Chapter Seventeen

Ruva's part-time studies at the university were going well but slowly. She enrolled as a full-time student for the remaining year to hasten the process. She chose sociology as a discipline because she understood the hardships related to absolute poverty, and she had lived an underprivileged life herself. She was determined to improve the lives of many other impoverished people. With Auntie Sphiwe at the helm at home, Ruva could afford to devote more time to her studies and manage the farm.

After graduating in 1987, Ruva did not see the need to celebrate her own success. She believed that her accomplishments were measured by what she did for other people.

She had gone through several miscarriages and was aware of the lasting physical and mental effects. The affliction had been to her heart ever since she experienced her last miscarriage. She decided to found a support group for women who had suffered a number of miscarriages or could not conceive due to blocked Fallopian tubes.

She finally opened up to Brian about her past miscarriages.

"Why did it take you so long to tell me? You broke rule number one of our marriage contract: 'Thou shall not keep any secrets.'"

"My past marriage wasn't under discussion after the trial and inquest."

"I didn't realize there was a clause with exceptions, but I understand. So are you ready to draw the guns for battle?"

"I'm as ready as I can be."

Brian knew that for her to come to terms with her own problem, she had to follow what she believed in. He supported her both financially and legally in starting her foundation, Babies in Tubes. He cleared a small office space for her in his building to launch the foundation. Her main objective was to identify the affected women in hospitals and primary care clinics and help them join a support group where they could share their stories with other women who were in the same predicament. The primary aim of the project was to gather enough data to support the cause then raise money to educate women on methods of protecting themselves from diseases, to make them aware of gynaecological signs and symptoms, and to seek medical health services as they see fit.

She put together a volunteer committee with the help of an old doctor, consisting of nurses, doctors, social workers and community health workers. Its purpose was to advise the foundation.

In the beginning it was a slow process, but with word of mouth and pamphlets appealing to affected women to come forward, women trickled in. Ruva and her team of volunteers were mindful of the sensitivity of the issue and intended to treat the women who came forward with privacy.

When she started, the movement was focused in the big cities. Unfortunately, the problem was not regional, and this was happening all over the country and beyond. She travelled throughout the country, seeking volunteers and opening centres for the women to meet.

Ruva was bold enough to go into women's wards in hospitals during visiting hours to interview women who gave her all the information she needed, since they could talk when they were at their height of despair. Women loved her because she was giving them the tools to survive and equip themselves with the knowledge they required to make informed decisions, which was the opposite of when she was young.

During one of her visits at a small hospital she exposed herself to unnecessary attention by taking her time moving away when a doctor wanted to examine a patient. She regretted it and apologized, but she was reported to the police.

"Mrs. Sanderson, who gave you permission to come into this hospital and interview patients?" asked a policeman.

"Do I need permission to talk to people?" she asked.

She was accused of interfering with staff duties and working with patients without hospital permission. The police took her in.

Meanwhile, when she did not return home, Brian was very worried. He paced up and down the whole night. Early in the morning he went to the police station to enquire if she had been taken in. The records did not show that she was in police custody. He was sick with worry. He tried to get information from her office of where she had headed to that day, and he traced her to the hospital. He met obstacles there so he went back again to the police station.

Two, then three days went by, and there was still no word from Ruva. Brian phoned Larry and Beth to tell them what was going on.

Beth answered the phone. "Brian, I don't even know what to say. I didn't think it would come to this. I fear for the worst now that you say she has been gone for that long."

"I'll let you know if there are any new developments," said Brian, who was sitting in his study.

After that, when he was dialling Hilda's number, he heard Sphiwe talking to someone. "Welcome home. What happened to you? You look awful!"

"It's a long story," Ruva replied.

Brian quickly put down the phone and ran to the kitchen. "Ruva, you're home! We were all worried about you."

She looked worn out as she stood leaning on the kitchen counter. He gently pulled her by the hand, leading her to their bedroom.

"I need a good rest before telling you what happened," she said wearily.

"Do you know how worried I've been? I can't wait to hear what happened."

"I was thinking about you too, while sitting in jail."

"In jail! I went to the police and they did not have any record of you."

"That's strange, because I asked a policewoman who was sympathetic to the cause to call you. She even came back to tell me that she had left a message with somebody. She must have been lying. I'm sorry for all the trouble. I'm home now."

"Do you think I would not have come to get you? What was the charge?"

"It was trespassing and interviewing patients without hospital permission. They arrested me right there in the hospital. Being in the cells was an eye-opening experience. One could not sleep due to the continual clicking of the steel doors, rattling noises from the chains and drunkards making all sorts of noises. Thankfully, I managed to bail myself out, since I had some money on me. They told me that I'd be appearing in court."

"I'll find somebody to represent you. You've got to pull

back, or it won't be your last arrest. They are going to keep a close watch on you," advised Brian.

"That's the prize one pays to bring about intended results." Ruva was adamant.

"You think seriously about what I said. I'm glad to have you back home."

Ruva saw it as a small setback, and to her surprise the case fizzled out and never made it to court.

She continued to hand out surveys outside the hospital gates and at clinics. Some women sought input from their husbands, and this infuriated them and perpetuated their rage. They felt Ruva was accusing them of causing miscarriages and that she was interfering with their sexual lives. Community leaders who were greatly concerned signed a petition and protested at hospitals and clinics with placards to try to halt Ruva's quest and to have her arrested. Subsequently, that became their rallying cry. At one point even the police could not control the crowds. There were people who supported Ruva, especially women, but they were scared to make their case in the public arena.

Ruva had become a public figure through her social activism. Papers were full of unflattering coverage about her. She had not anticipated any of this, but she was relentless and fearless.

Brian was worried about her security because she was receiving death threats. He understood the dangers, but Ruva was not intimidated.

"You should lie low and change course. It's becoming very dangerous and violent out there. You need to be more vigilant now," he warned.

"Those men are doing what they have to do and I'm not backing down. This is a health issue, and for some women it's a matter of life and death. Do you understand where I'm coming from?"

"I don't even know where you are deriving all this strength from. Please, I want you to stop. You're going to be hurt or killed by these people," Brian begged.

Even the people who had supported her, including her committee, were forced to go underground and lie low, which made them ineffective.

Ruva stayed at home for a little while, waiting for emotions to calm down. One day she stepped out to go check on her mail at the office and she met her enemies. She had parked her car in a parkade and saw two men following her. She did not look back, though she sensed something was going to happen. She increased her pace but before she knew it, she was walking between them and they had put on masks. She didn't even have the chance to fight them off or scream.

One of the men said, "You'll pay for turning our wives against us." He slapped her on the face and quickly tied a scarf around her neck, ready to tighten it if she screamed. They blindfolded her before forcing her back into her own car. Inside the car they bound her arms behind her and drove her out of town to a deserted farm.

Her abductors kept her for ten days in solitary confinement in a small, thatched house with neither food nor water. During her captivity nobody went into the room to see her. She had a lot of time to think about Brian and her children. She wondered if there was a way to escape and if, given a second chance, if she could do it again. Her thoughts were all mixed and hopeless.

One early morning, when Ruva had lost all sense of time, four masked men opened the door and a ray of light beamed into the room, blinding her. Her captors waited that long to ensure that she would be at her weakest point and would reveal more information.

They dragged her out to an adjacent room which they

called "The Truth Room." The first time they let her tell them her story. After that they subjected her to long and torturous interrogations. At the beginning, whenever she was strapped, if she screamed she would get more beatings, accompanied by verbal abuse. She was given few spoonfuls of food and a tiny amount of water, not enough to quench her thirst.

After a little more than a month of captivity, Ruva became very ill and confused. In the end her captors felt they had achieved what they set out to do. They released her on condition that she would never be seen anywhere promoting her cause again. By then she was too far gone to comprehend.

Brian had not known where to turn. He went back to the police several times, but there was nothing on record. He filed a missing persons report again and hired a private investigator, who came up with nothing. After four days, he thought hard about telling Hilda; instead he decided to phone Larry and Beth first.

"We haven't seen Ruva for four days. It has been a trying time. I'm holding on to hope that she is safe and alive somewhere out there," he told Beth.

"I don't know what to say. We can only hope for the best. Would it help if I come and help you with the children?" Anopa and Ira were still at home and Tawaka was in South Africa studying business.

"It's difficult to shield them. Please stay away. I'll let you know if I hear anything."

"Larry wants to say something," said Beth.

Larry was blunt. "Brother, it's you I'm worried about now. You might be next. You better leave while you're still alive."

"That's ridiculous! Do you think I'd pack my bags and leave not knowing what happened to my wife? For your peace of mind, I've hired armed guards to patrol the farm at all times."

Brian banged down the phone. He had intended to call Hilda, but he could not because he was too upset. Minutes later, she phoned.

"Pop, it's Hilda." She had never addressed him by that name and Brian was taken aback. He sensed something good was happening in her life, which lifted his spirits.

"You have good news, I can tell from your voice."

"I successfully defended my doctorate, and I'm officially Dr. Hilda Ganda. I can't wait to tell Mama. Is she home?"

"Congratulations, Dr. Ganda! When is the show-off day?"

"If show-off day is graduation, then it'll be mid-December."

"Give us the actual date. Knowing your mother, she'd like to be there. I wouldn't miss it for anything either."

"You deserve a big thank-you for your support," Hilda said.

"It was my pleasure and I did it out of love. I'm sorry to spoil your celebration, but I've got to tell you that your mother has been missing for the past four days. I didn't tell you sooner because I kept hoping that she would walk in through the door, just like she did last time."

"I knew this would happen again sooner or later." Hilda started sobbing. "We talked about it after the hospital incident and I begged her to stop."

"Nothing was ever going to make her stop. On the day of her disappearance, she told Sphiwe that she was going to her office and we haven't seen her since. All that we know is her car was seen on the security monitor leaving the parking garage shortly after she drove it in. Nobody has an inkling of what's going on. It looks dire."

"I'm coming home."

"I'd rather you stay there. I don't want to put you in danger."

❧

Six weeks to the day after Ruva's abduction, she was released and driven back to Harare under cover of darkness. The police found her at a storefront in the middle of the city, lying with her face down and half naked. She showed no sign of life and was taken to hospital. Police identified her by the name written on her forehead in white chalk.

Brian received news from the police that Ruva was in Pari hospital. The message was not clear and he asked for clarification.

"Is she dead or alive, sir? I'm confused."

"Barely alive, according to the report."

Brian was stunned and prepared himself for the worst. In intensive care, Ruva lay motionless, connected to life support machines. The little he saw at a glance shocked him and he walked out to regain his composure. Brian did not even remember when he had last wept. After a while, he went back in again. Ruva was grossly emaciated, her hair was knotted and had been falling off, leaving bald patches, she had oozing pustules, her face was badly bruised, her eyes were tightly closed and puffy, and her hands and feet were swollen. He agreed with the officer that her survival was hanging by a thread. He deduced that she had been horribly tortured, and the situation was clearly hopeless.

"What are the chances of her making it?" he asked one of the doctors attending her.

"I never tell relatives things like that because I've seen gravely ill patients make it. On the other hand, a patient could be showing signs of getting better, and just like that you lose them. If we can control the infection, we'll have won half the battle. There could also be emotional issues that are likely to hinder progress," the doctor said.

Brian stayed at her bedside and over time he saw a finger twitch, an eyelid flicker and a hand jerking. He took each movement as a positive sign.

A week later Ruva regained consciousness and was transferred to a private hospital. She periodically screamed, since her whole body was painful to the touch. The stress and tension took a toll on Brian as well. He didn't know how Ruva was going to cope and the long-term effects it would have on the whole family.

Ruva's medical condition gradually improved and she continued to show signs of recovery. With her faculties improving, Brian hesitantly asked her a few questions, and the memories became vivid.

"Do you have any idea of who did this to you?"

"I was blindfolded most of the time and I couldn't even point them out in a lineup."

"What do you remember about the ordeal? If you're not ready, it's okay."

"Where would I start? When these men abducted me there were people who saw everything in the parkade. Did they report it to the police?"

"I don't know. The police didn't say anything to that effect."

"I don't blame them, because it was quick. Either they didn't know what was taking place or they didn't want to be involved. I was physically, verbally and mentally tortured in every way you can think of. They kept me starved in a dark room. There was a separate room where they interrogated and strapped me. I also remember them debating whether to kill me. 'Let's finish her off.' Those were their words. It was scary, but by then I had resigned myself to my own demise. There were other horrible things they did to me. Thinking of it makes me sick."

"You might as well say it. I want to know."

"As if the beatings and all that verbal abuse were not enough, they took turns raping me." Ruva fought back tears. "I believe in forgiveness, but it would be hard to show it for those four evil men who treated me like a dog." She fell silent for a while and kept on looking at Brian, then picked up her narration again. "The pain, the shame and powerlessness I felt, it's hard to talk about it. There was a special friend. We were both trapped in there and he was my sole companion. Occasionally he would interrupt the silence in the room. My little friend must have died, because all of a sudden he went quiet."

"Was he tortured as well, and why was he there?" asked Brian.

"It was a rat."

"That's interesting." Brian was short of words. It was funny, but he wondered whether it was a joke or if she was losing her mind.

"How did I get here?" Ruva yawned. She closed her eyes and fell asleep with Brian holding her hand.

When Ruva was getting better, Brian took Ira and Anopa to see her in hospital. They asked questions but Brian was careful not to reveal too much.

After two months in the hospital, Ruva was discharged.

She remained emotionally incapacitated by panic and anxiety attacks. The nights were the hardest, because she was scared of the dark, and falling asleep was difficult. If she did, she would wake up hallucinating and imagining the abductors breaking into her house and taking her away again. She had frequent flashbacks of the beatings, verbal abuse and rape, which made her powerless and fearful.

While Ruva was in hospital, Hilda graduated with a Ph.D. in clinical psychology. Beth was at the graduation and Hilda was happy to see her and know that she would be among the sea of people cheering for their graduates. But her happiness was not the same without her mother. After the graduation, Hilda went home to be by her mother's side and to see her through her struggles.

Brian and Ruva were sitting at the river, which had become their favourite place since the wedding. Ruva told Brian that she was not persuaded to bring her abductors to justice, because she believed that if there was a trial, the same people who wanted her arrested would make it unbearable. Also, she could not handle another painful experience of having to give evidence. They both came to the same conclusion. Brian went on to suggest something else.

"I've been thinking." He paused.

"What now?"

"It's time we adopted Ira. What do you think?"

"It's something I had given some thought. I didn't know whether it was the right thing to do. Matie is alive and well. I expected his father to come one day knocking on the door in search of his son. The two of them were children when Ira was born."

"You even gave a thought to that good-for-nothing boy? How many years has it been now? Matie gave you that child and all we need to do is to make the custody official."

"I agree, let's do it." Ruva perked up.

"Perfect! We'll get the ball rolling."

Brian gripped her by the arm as they slowly walked back to the house. Her legs were still weak and unsteady.

Chapter Eighteen

Matie and Fred had been married for five years when the strain on their relationship started to show. They grew apart and finally the marriage crumbled. The divorce was rushed through since Fred wanted to move on and Matie had had enough of solely shouldering all the responsibilities. In 1989 they went their separate ways. Fred relocated back to New York where his business was going through a remarkable growth spurt. Matie remained in England and took full custody of the children.

After the divorce, things were not easy for her, for she did not have the resources to continue with her glitzy lifestyle. The circle of friends slipped away, and she become estranged from her family. She hadn't communicated with her mother since the day they walked out on her. Although Matie wrote once to Hilda, she did not talk about the divorce. Instead she hinted that she would be going back to school.

Matie seriously considered going back to school. She vigorously pursued it and fulfilled all the requirements for medical school. She phoned Allison early one morning, since she had not been in touch with her friend for a while either.

"Guess what — you're the first one to know. I was accepted to the medical school at Southampton University. I'll be starting in the autumn. You have waited patiently for this call and there's your wish, girl."

"I can't believe that you've finally set your mind to building a career. What pushed you to do it?" asked Allison.

"My dear, when everything is taken away, you think of a way to survive."

"What are you talking about?"

"Fred and I grew apart and we mutually decided to call it quits. I was hurting and I needed to come to terms with the separation and the divorce before talking about it."

"I thought you two were glued together for life."

"That was my belief, too, but it's a closed chapter now."

"You've made the right decision—not the divorce but going to school. It's a lot of work, there's no doubt about it. Call me, and I'll help if I can."

In autumn of 1989, Matie started school. She knew right from the beginning that it would be a challenge juggling study and caring for the boys. She was determined to find a way to make it work. At one point she had to leave the boys with the Auburns, who were getting on in years. There were times when she wanted to give up, but around her was a great support system that gave her all the encouragement she needed. Those five or so years of hopping from lecture rooms to libraries to wards dragged on, but she persevered in spite of the hardships. Throughout those years in school, she was focused and painstakingly organized. Due to her strong willpower plus her wit, she had all the elements to succeed. She always had that competitive streak, and she maintained that in university as well. With her undergraduate degree under her belt, she focused on specializing in gynaecology.

In five years, Ruva's life on the farm had returned to near normal. After her ordeal, she gave up entirely her involvement with the Babies in Tubes foundation, but she managed to tirelessly put together the groundwork for the cause in a written paper, which she presented at the Southern African Symposium for Disadvantaged Women in Kampala. She agreed to speak only if there would be no media, because she was scared of retribution. Most of the speakers worked as advocates for women's rights, and they were emotionally charged as they talked about problems they encountered in their work and communities.

Ruva was the second speaker of the day, and when her name was called, she was ready, but she had the butterflies. She focused on Brian, and that calmed her down. She talked about the reasons why women were disadvantaged, such as family expectations, sexual diseases and the long-term effects of a miscarriage. She emphasized that women had been crying for help, and society needed to take heed of the problem. She concluded with an emphasis on sexual education that was lacking in poorer communities.

At the end of her speech, she sat down and broke out in a sweat. It was the last time she spoke publicly.

It was not long after they had returned from Kampala, on a Saturday afternoon after finishing her errands, when Ruva saw Mr. Georges in the rear view mirror of her car following her in his pick-up truck up the driveway. She had been scared of him ever since their last encounter. She nervously got out of her car and asked, "What brings you here today, Mr. Georges?"

"I didn't expect you to remember my name," he remarked politely.

"It's always good to know your neighbours by name, and you never know when you might need them. We are isolated here. We need each other."

"That's why I'm here. I don't think you're aware yet of what happened to your husband late this morning?"

"I hope it's nothing too serious, sir?"

"Sadly, I was called by one of your workers to take your husband to the hospital after he was shot at the main gate. Doctors worked on him unsuccessfully before pronouncing him dead."

"This can't be happening to me again."

"The farmer's association will be giving assistance, although Mr. Sanderson was not an active member. We don't forsake our own."

For a while she felt as if she was stuck in heavy mud and could not move her legs. Her mind could not interpret anything. She looked blankly at Mr. Georges, who helped her walk into the house.

"Ruva!" Sphiwe noticed the strain on her face, and she asked Mr. Georges, "Did you tell her?"

"Yes. I had come to tell her what happened at the hospital. I'll be in touch." He left.

Sphiwe told Ruva the story according to what she was told by the farm hands. "A stranger came by when they were mending a fence and started telling them that you stole his money, which was left by his brother. He wanted to see you, and according to those who saw him, he was very angry. The farm hands begged him to leave but he refused. Brian was riding his horse and happened to pass by. Brian recognized him and an argument ensued. The man got more agitated when they refused him to see you. Brian asked him to leave the property and that was when the man pulled a gun from his jacket and shot Brian in the head. The farm hands tackled him and pinned him down, and Charlie ran to Mr. Georges for help."

Ruva knew instantly that it was Batsirai, Mukai's brother, from whom she had not heard in a long time. Because of the time that had lapsed, she thought he had come to terms with the resolution.

She sat there with a blank look and overwhelmed with guilt. Sphiwe expected some wailing, but there was none of that. "Go ahead and cry, it's okay."

Larry and Beth flew in the following day, and they observed that Ruva was in distress, withdrawn and detached. Larry took charge and made all the funeral arrangements.

Hilda flew home as soon as she heard the news, together with Tawaka, who was also working in South Africa.

The placement of an announcement of Brian's sudden death in the obituaries sent shock waves throughout legal circles, since Brian was one of the best criminal lawyers in the country and was well respected by his peers. At one point he was touted as a High Court judge, but he was not interested. He did not want to lose the free rein he had in his own practice.

The funeral service was held at the Baptist church Larry and Beth used to attend. The church overflowed with people from all walks of life, the Law Society, the farmers' association, the horse racing association, University of Rhodesia white alumni, corporate boards that Brian had chaired and many people who knew Ruva through her philanthropic work, her church and the social clubs.

When Larry took to the pulpit, he spoke with great intensity about Brian's versatility in the way he managed his life and his love for his children and wife. He talked about how Dark Ash, Brian's horse, had a feistiness that matched Brian's fearlessness when they were together in open fields, and the joy he got out of it. Then Larry was overcome with grief and could not go on. He folded his prepared notes, put them back in his pocket and walked down from the pulpit. Beth took his hand and guided him back to his seat between Ruva and herself. He put his hands tightly together, bent his upper body, let it rest between his legs and broke down for the first time. The presiding pastor asked the choir to sing a hymn to mask the sobs and gasps of grief.

The floor was open to anyone who wanted to speak. A handful of close friends who knew Brian well spoke glowingly about his career and his devotion to those he loved. Unexpectedly, Tawaka stood up and gave an endearing message of thanks. Brian was laid to rest near his predeceased parents.

After the funeral, Ruva asked Hilda to write Matie a letter.

"It's a waste of time. She wrote me once, though, and there was nothing to talk about," Hilda said.

"We'll continue to do what is right," Ruva said.

Matie,

This is a short note to let you know that Brian passed away. When our father died, Mama quickly bounced back. This time around is different. She is not coping at all, and it might be a long time before she is able to come to terms with Brian's death. I will be around for a while to assist with some things that need her immediate attention. Wish you were here!

Hilda

Larry retained a lawyer to oversee everything, and he stopped consulting Ruva in important matters due to her condition.

A fortnight after the funeral, Ruva received a letter confirming Ira's adoption. She told Beth because she wanted to ensure that Ira would be included in the settling of the estate.

Larry and Beth went back to South Africa, aware of the insurmountable problems that were going to arise on the farm if Ruva's condition did not improve.

Matie had been thinking about her mother, and after passing her final exams, she had a change of heart and sent her mother a graduation invitation. Along with the invitation was a short apology scribbled on a piece of paper.

Mama

I'm sorry for the pain I caused you. I'll redeem myself, and I promise to rebuild my trust. I finally did it. Dr. Matilda Ganda.

When Ruva saw the invitation and the apology, she sank down in a chair and sobbed. All was forgiven at that moment. It had been eight years since Ruva left Matie's house in a huff, and she had never heard from her again, but there was still great love between mother and daughter. She could hardly put the invitation down.

She told Sphiwe, "Matie sent me an invitation for her graduation, and I have to go."

"You're not strong enough to travel," said Sphiwe with concern.

"Nothing is going to stop me. I can't miss the two most important graduations of my girls."

That was the first time Sphiwe heard her say something so emphatically since Brian passed away.

Chapter Nineteen

Hilda made all the plans for Ruva's travels and they flew together to England. It was a pleasure to see Matie and her boys waiting at the airport. She had rented a house to accommodate everyone, since her flat was too small. Ruva thought they were going to her house in Mill Hill until she saw signs taking them to Southampton. As soon as they got to the house, Matie directed her mother and Hilda into the small study.

"People, relax," Matie urged them, since there was an uncomfortable silence. "Graduation is still on. What has changed is that Fred and I divorced over six years ago. Don't expect him to barge through the door. That was the best thing that ever happened to me, because I began to examine my conscience and regretted what I had lost in life, and that was my own independence and my family." She made a sweeping movement that included the two of them. "I would be remiss not to thank you, Mama and Brian for your concern over the years. Mama, I'm sorry for my selfishness, and I hope you'll forgive me. Hilda, what can I say except to thank you for being the best sister? I have a surprise for you. I ask that we make the best of this reunion."

"We have all made mistakes, and the lesson is to learn from them," Ruva proclaimed.

"Is this a confessional forum?" asked Hilda.

"Hilda, your questions are always thought-provoking. We're here to see Matie start her new journey. Therefore, let's give her a chance to start with a clear conscience," said Ruva.

"We've a lot to chew over in the weeks to come," warned Hilda. "It will be for our own good."

"Nobody doubts that. Can we adjourn this meeting for a well-deserved English breakfast?" said Ruva, who was feeling claustrophobic in the little study and was still waiting for Matie to comment on Brian's death.

Later that day, Matie and Hilda shared a bed. They both longed for the closeness they felt as children when they could talk until the wee hours of the morning.

"Remember this morning, when I said I have a surprise for you?" Matie reminded her sister. "There's this guy who tracked me here from New York. This is a small world. His name never rang a bell, but he said we attended a few parties together. Those were my wild days when I was young and madly in love with Fred. Do you know who I'm talking about?"

"Is that Julius?"

"Yes!"

"What did he want?"

"He thinks highly of you. He wanted to know if there's somebody in your life."

"What did you say, because we haven't discussed my love life? And why didn't he contact me, if that's how he felt about me?"

"I wish I could answer that, but he sounded like a nice guy. I told him you were coming over for my graduation. He's not as crazy as Fred, who followed me around the world. Your career is intact, but now you need a male companion. Go along and see what happens."

"I would like to stay closer to Mama. I'm not going to America."

"Hilda, you should be flexible. It's not as if she's alone. She has Brian. It's time for you to have a serious relationship."

"Didn't you see my letter about Brian?"

"What are you talking about? Did he leave her?"

"Brian was shot dead at the farm."

"What?" Matie cried out. "I didn't see the letter. Honestly, I thought he didn't come because he was still holding an old grudge against me. When did this happen? It explains why Mother is looking dreary. I attributed it to jetlag."

"I gather the postal service is quite efficient here. How come you are the only one in the whole of England who does not receive her letters?"

Matie ran into the bedroom where Ruva was sleeping. "Mama, Mama!" She shook her lightly. "I'm sorry about Brian. Hilda just told me that she wrote a letter which must have disappeared en route."

"It has been hard to talk about it. Hilda can narrate it better," Ruva said with her head under the covers.

Matie tiptoed back to her bedroom. "Hilda, what happened?

"You won't believe it. Uncle Batsirai shot him in the head at close range."

"You mean that weird uncle of ours?"

"Yes, and Mama was the target. She's still in the grip of a psychological shock. Three brave farm workers wrestled him down until they got help. He's in jail where he belongs."

"That was terrible! At least she's taken care of," Matie said.

"Money is one thing," Hilda said. "She misses Brian."

"He was good to her. It feels good to have you both here

for the graduation. I never thought Mama especially would forgive me for my stupidity," Matie confessed. "I envy her work ethic. Look at the work she's doing at home. I thought she was carving her own niche in the world."

"You know about that too?" Hilda was surprised.

"I read the article she presented in Kampala. I might look into some of these organizations here for funding or for speaking engagements for her. That's a lucrative business. I would go to great lengths to help her now that I'm not under pressure to accomplish anything. She needs to get back on her feet."

"I would rather she take it easy for a while. She has gone through a lot, especially in the last five years. Beth moved to South Africa, Mama was arrested and was in jail for three to four days, abducted and tortured for almost six weeks and nearly died, struggled with depression, then Brian's death and she was devastated, and not to mention being estranged from her daughter."

"Wow, wow! I can't believe that she has gone through all that. I don't even know what to say to her. Mama and I have a lot to discuss." Matie left the bed and went to lie down on the couch, where she cried the whole night.

The anticipation of finally seeing Matie graduate as a medical doctor had been building up for a couple of months. Even Allison would not miss the day for anything. She attended with her mother, who was now in a wheelchair.

Ruva was bursting with pride when Matie's name was called out. Matie was smiling from ear to ear. She received her degree with deserving honour.

As they were exiting the hall, Fred introduced himself to

Ruva and Hilda. "My name is Fred. I'm Matilda's ex-husband. I'm glad to finally meet you two. At last she got her identity right. I will not hold you up. There must be celebrations to go to." It was a warm day and Fred was fanning himself with *The Daily Telegraph* newspaper. Then, in a flash, he was gone.

"What was that all about?" asked Ruva.

"He wants to spoil Matie's day. I wonder if Matie knows he's here. Remember, from that little conversation in the study, he was not supposed to be anywhere near here."

Matie had seen Fred talking to them and stopped for a moment before quickly weaving her way through the crowds to catch up with him. She pulled him from behind by his belt. He was startled and stopped suddenly.

"What are you doing here?" Matie asked angrily.

"Matilda, I would like to extend my congratulations."

"You don't mean it. Please, leave immediately!"

Fred caught a glimpse of the family watching them, so he walked away. Matie turned and put a spring into her step as she walked toward her mother and sister. It was obvious she was upset.

"Forget about him, let's go." Hilda took her sister by the hand.

Larry devised a plan with the lawyer to sell the farm. He did not tell Beth of his intentions, for he knew that she would try to block his action. Instead, he lied to her and said he was going to Zimbabwe on business for two weeks. When he got there, the farm was already for sale. He arranged for the sale of the horses to a well-known breeder in Nelspruit, South Africa.

"Beth, we have to talk," he said when he got back home.

"You might be disappointed, but I did the right thing under the circumstances. Ruva will never be able to run that farm, so I put it up for sale. We might have a buyer. I managed to sell all the horses except the Sphinx. Knowing what's happening, she might never ride again, but it's there anyway."

Beth felt as if she had been stabbed in the back. "Why on earth would you do that? That farm is hers, and she has the right to be there." She was furious.

Larry defended his position. "We don't know when she'll be well enough to run the farm. If we waited too long, things could be run down, the place vandalized and profits eroded."

Four months later, Ruva went back home, and her condition had greatly improved. She was anxious to settle Brian's estate and go through another criminal trial, but what she discovered was devastating.

The girls had phoned Sphiwe, who told them what had happened. Wanting to help with her recovery, they decided to keep her in the dark. She went to the farm and found a "For Sale" sign at the main entrance.

The house doors were locked and bolted, and when she peeped in, she saw that it was empty. All the horses were gone, except the Sphinx, who looked lethargic. Ruva was baffled.

Finally, she went to the servants' quarters and saw one of the gardeners basking in the morning sun.

"Hello! The place looks deserted. What happened here?"

"Your brother-in-law sold the farm, and for us who are here, it has been very difficult, because we haven't been paid since you left. Most of the farm hands were let go."

"I was assured that somebody would be paying your wages. Do you know where Sphiwe and my children are staying?"

"I don't know. Maybe people at Mr. Sanderson's office would know."

Everything had been decided for her, and she did not know what to do. She even contemplated the idea of fighting Larry in court.

After Larry and Beth immigrated to South Africa, she remembered Brian saying, "If I'm not here and you need something, go and see my partner, Matt Andrews. He knows me better than I know myself."

"Welcome back, Ruva." Matt Andrews gave her a hug. "How're you doing?"

"Slowly getting there. I went to the farm, and I'm not sure if it's either on sale or sold. Do you know what's happening?"

"The farm hasn't been sold. I understand Larry had a buyer, but the sale fell through. I couldn't believe that he sank so low and lost his conscience. He also came here wanting Brian's business shares. I tried to talk him out of it and instead to give you the shares, since he had taken possession of the farm. He would not hear any of it, but he hasn't filed any papers yet. Technically, Larry is within the law. I don't know why Brian didn't change his will. That was out of character for him. He was one of the most organized fellows I knew," Matt said. "I know a good lawyer who can help you out. I can't do it for you, because it would be a conflict of interest."

"I don't have the stamina to go through a legal battle again over money," Ruva confessed. "I didn't marry Brian for money."

"Think about it and let me know."

"Let's go through the murder trial first, then I might revise my strategy."

"I'll work with you. Please don't hesitate to contact me. By the way, Larry rented a flat for the children and the maid."

"It's sad indeed that things have come to this," Ruva said.

On the first day of the trial, the courtroom was packed with people who wanted to see the man who shot Brian Sanderson. Larry was there without Beth and he sat on the opposite side from Ruva and Matt Andrews. Larry kept on glancing over at Ruva, who kept her head down the whole time. There was a long delay before the court clerk announced that the defendant had committed suicide by hanging early in the morning and the proceedings would be abandoned. People went silent then quietly filed out of the courtroom. Disheartened, Ruva felt robbed of justice.

When Ruva picked up her mail from the letterbox, there was a letter, which was not stamped. She recognized Beth's handwriting on the front. She put it down and debated whether to throw it away unread or to rip open the envelope. She went with the latter option.

Dear Ruva,

As it is Brian's first anniversary, I felt it appropriate for me to tell you that I'm sorry about the problems surrounding Brian's estate. I know you will not believe me if I tell you that it all happened behind my back. I couldn't contact you before because I knew you were hurting, and I'm still ashamed to even look you in the eye.

I cannot imagine the pain this has caused you. I can only pray that you will forgive me for leaving you to fight this battle alone. I'll understand if you have some ill feelings towards me.

I'll always love you and fondly cherish you in my heart.

Beth

Ruva finished reading the letter then muttered to herself, "Beth, what do you know about pain? You need to walk in my shoes." She shredded the letter into small pieces before throwing them into the wastebasket.

She picked up the big bouquet of flowers she had bought the day before and headed to the old whites-only cemetery. It was quiet and peaceful. There was nothing moving except Ruva and her shadow. The only sound was from the crackling of the wrapping paper that covered the flowers. Ruva went down on her knees and placed her bouquet at the foot of the grave. She looked over the writing on the Italian marble headstone.

Rest in Peace
Brian Clayton Sanderson
Called by the Lord on 26 March 1995.

They hadn't given her any input when the headstone was installed. Although it was different, she liked what was written on it. However, she decided to add words from her own heart. She pulled a red marker from her purse and wrote below the inscription.

'Ruva loved you in life and will love you in death.'

She sat down and had a good cry. She had shed enough tears for Brian, but this time the tears were for the injustice done to her by Larry. Suddenly she heard people murmuring. She lifted her gaze and saw Beth, Larry, their pastor from their old church and two friends walking towards the gravesite.

Ruva quickly stood up and went in the opposite direction toward her car. She weaved her way through the graves and even jumped a little fence before reaching the path leading to the car park.

"Ruva, stop! Please stop!" Beth yelled, but Ruva quickened her pace. She sat in her car for a while, catching her breath and trying to figure out why Beth and Larry had turned against her. She remembered when Shungu warned her that when these people wanted to get rid of her, they would not feel a pang of shame.

"This is exactly what she meant, but I trusted these people, and they became my family."

Her thoughts took her way back in a mental run-through of what she could have done differently to avoid Brian's death, but her thoughts were all muddled up. She started the car, not knowing where she was going, but instinctively she drove off straight to Highfield to see Shungu.

"Hello, Shungu. You're looking well and healthy." Ruva could see that all the anger that used to consume Shungu had dissipated. She was relaxed and calmer.

"You look drained. That glow on your face has vanished," said Shungu, who assessed her well.

"Brian died a year ago today. You must not have heard. His death affected me so much that I ended up with a mental breakdown. It was awful. I'll never be the same again, but life goes on. I'm sharing this with you as a friend."

"I heard about it and came to offer my condolences. You

had just left for England two days before. You've been through this before, and you managed to ride out the storm. I hate to welcome you back to reality. Life without ups and downs doesn't exist, my friend. All the same, I wish I was there with you through all this tragedy."

"You came to the farm?" asked Ruva, touched by Shungu's loyalty. "I appreciate that you tell me as it is. Being widowed for the second time was harder." Ruva sighed.

"You'll get over it. Can you believe that Joel straightened out? He's studying carpentry at a technical school. Billy is out of jail. Your tenant helped him get a job at Coca-Cola. They call him by some fancy name. He moved out on his own. My boys were brought back from hell. I'll keep my fingers crossed that they'll stay on track," said Shungu with enthusiasm and hope. "And tell me about your girls?"

"Both are doctors and have their own lives. Hilda is getting married to a nice fellow in December, and Matie is coming home with her twin boys to the wedding. I'll have a special invitation just for you. Note that the wedding will not go on without you," Ruva said with a grin.

"Matie has two more boys?" Shungu asked.

"Yes! Lovely boys and one of them is called Mukai."

"That's wonderful that she named him after her father. I hope you are keeping tabs on your many blessings. Give me a hug, girl." Shungu finally felt important and loved, and it brought on a few sniffles. They held each other tightly in a warm embrace then stood there in silence for a moment.

"At last I'm welcome back into your life." Shungu rubbed her eyes as tears streamed down her cheeks. "It feels good to know that I mean something to you."

"It's wonderful to be standing where it all began," said

Ruva, loosening the hug. "From now on, nothing will come between us, and we shall remain bosom buddies forever."

When she went back home there was a message from Matt Andrews: "Ruva, call me, I've some encouraging news."

Ruva immediately phoned back. "What do you have for me?"

"Larry might be reconsidering his position. He's in town and wants to strike a deal with you. Therefore, I encourage you to hire Jason Humphrey to represent you. He said he would like to meet up with you here in the office on Friday."

"Thanks, Matt, I'll contact him as soon as possible. I'd rather do that than fight him in court over property."

Ruva thought about it then decided to take whatever offer Larry would put on the table. She decided not to hire a lawyer. She was ready to close that chapter without a fight. Upon entering the office, the first person she saw was Matt.

"Jason never got a call from you. Why?"

"I might call him. For now it depends on what they've got to say."

"Ruva, you can't do that. You've a legal-minded opponent in Larry Sanderson. Don't be stubborn."

Larry and Beth were seated in the boardroom without any legal representation, and they were equally surprised to see Ruva walking in by herself. Ruva shook their hands confidently in a business-like manner and sat across from them, reading their faces.

"How are you doing?" asked Beth, who looked uncomfortable.

"I'm okay, considering all that has happened in the last few years. Please, forgive me for the way I behaved the other day. My emotions were running high on Brian's first anniversary. How's everybody in your world?"

"We're all doing well," Beth answered.

"Are you expecting someone?" asked Larry.

"Not at all. I haven't talked to you since Brian died and I thought this would be a family discussion. That's if I'm still family — and then go from there."

Ruva's demeanour did not show any bitterness toward them.

Beth quickly jumped in before Larry could say anything. She wanted to make amends for the discord that ensued after Brian's death.

"We are here to apologize for the way we handled this matter. After Brian's death, we made some blunders and hasty decisions that turned out to be detrimental to our relationship as a family. We had no right to literally push you out of the farm and from the home you had shared with Brian. He might not have left a will, but everything considered, it's all yours. I speak for Larry, too. We're truly sorry."

"What's the way forward?" Ruva immedaitely sensed that she had the upper hand.

"We're going to rectify the mistake. You'll get the farm back, the business shares are all yours, I'll reactivate the business account and …" Larry paused.

"And you'll keep all the proceeds from the sale of the horses." Ruva unexpectedly finished his train of thought.

"We can't. That was a big chunk of the business capital," Larry responded.

"It doesn't matter. What's important is we've come to an amicable resolution," Ruva said.

"If you say so." Larry chuckled.

"Please, promise that you'll come and visit us soon," said Beth.

"Since there's a standing invitation, I'll be there before you know. I'd like you to know that I don't harbour any hostile feelings against you. Hopefully our relationship will remain as strong as ever." Ruva beamed her usual smile and bid them farewell.

In amazement, Ruva walked out of the boardroom still digesting the unpredictable turn of events. She stopped at the coffee shop next door to ponder why Larry had a change of heart. Eventually, she convinced herself that she would never know and did not want to dwell on it.

However, thoughts ran through her mind of what Brian would do if he were to start all over again at the farm. Those thoughts gave her ideas of a new beginning. She quickly pulled a pen and paper from her purse and jotted them down. She knew that there would be endless possibilities, but it was too soon for her to have a plan.